Danny was born in Manchester and graduated in law from the London School of Economics and in theatre studies from the University of Strasbourg, France. While at university he was introduced to the Hindu epic *The Mahabharata* by a friend and thus began a lifetime obsession with storytelling. After a brief foray into journalism, he set up a company specialising in storytelling theatre and travelled all over the world from Sarajevo to Siberia. This led to work in more conventional theatre, TV and film and saw him perform at the Royal National Theatre, with Alan Ayckbourn in Scarborough, and all over the UK. For nearly two years he was part of the David Glass Ensemble's Lost Child project, which involved creating theatre with street children in Manila, Bogotá and Phnom Penh. Danny co-wrote and starred in the indie movie *The West Wittering Affair* with his wife Sarah Sutcliffe, and in 2014 he won the Pears Short Film Award for his screenplay *The Divorce*, which he co-directed with his brother, David. Danny lives with his wife and three children in North London.

His debut novel, *Random Acts of Heroic Love*, was a bestseller in the UK and subsequently translated into 21 languages.

The Half Life of
Joshua Jones

Danny Scheinmann

With illustrations by Hannah Cutts

unbound

This edition first published in 2016

Unbound
6th Floor, Mutual House, 70 Conduit Street, London W1S 2GF

www.unbound.co.uk

Text Design by PDQ

Illustrations by Hannah Cutts

A CIP record for this book is available from the British Library

ISBN 978-1-78352-118-0 (trade hbk)
ISBN 978-1-78352-120-3 (ebook)
ISBN 978-1-78352-119-7 (limited edition)

Printed in Great Britain by Clays Ltd, St Ives Plc

1 2 3 4 5 6 7 8 9

In memory of John and Maggie and
a love that knew no boundaries.

Dear Reader,

The book you are holding came about in a rather different way to most others. It was funded directly by readers through a new website: Unbound.

Unbound is the creation of three writers. We started the company because we believed there had to be a better deal for both writers and readers. On the Unbound website, authors share the ideas for the books they want to write directly with readers. If enough of you support the book by pledging for it in advance, we produce a beautifully bound special subscribers' edition and distribute a regular edition and e-book wherever books are sold, in shops and online.

This new way of publishing is actually a very old idea (Samuel Johnson funded his dictionary this way). We're just using the internet to build each writer a network of patrons. Here, at the back of this book, you'll find the names of all the people who made it happen.

Publishing in this way means readers are no longer just passive consumers of the books they buy, and authors are free to write the books they really want. They get a much fairer return too – half the profits their books generate, rather than a tiny percentage of the cover price.

If you're not yet a subscriber, we hope that you'll want to join our publishing revolution and have your name listed in one of our books in the future. To get you started, here is a £5 discount on your first pledge. Just visit unbound.com, make your pledge and type halflife in the promo code box when you check out.

Thank you for your support,

Dan, Justin and John
Founders, Unbound

The Half Life of Joshua Jones

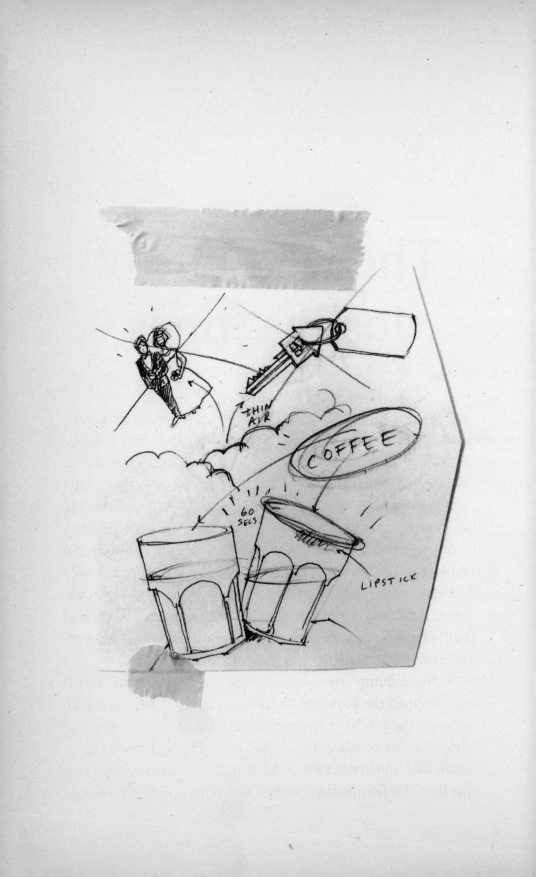

CHAPTER 1

My life was unravelling in multiples of seven. It had been exactly fourteen weeks since I had lost my job, seven weeks since Sheryl had left me for a woman and now I was facing eviction from my flat. I call it my flat but was it ever really mine? Of course, Sheryl and I had persuaded ourselves, like so many homeowners, that it belonged to us, but in truth it belonged to the National Bank of Scotland and now the bank was taking it back. For five years we had paid only interest on the debt, and recently I had paid nothing at all, which was why a plump, balding man in a cheap suit and scuffed shoes was waiting impatiently in the corridor with his hand outstretched.

It was a dump anyway, or at least that's what I told myself as I dropped the keys into his sweaty palm. Icy draughts stole through the cracks in the window frames in winter. The fuse tripped every time we boiled the kettle. The bathroom was so small that our knees rubbed against the bath when we sat on the loo. The floorboards creaked and bowed. The low ceilings

1

hung over the rooms like a threat and the walls were so thin we could hear the neighbours farting and fornicating.

The door closed for the last time and a chapter in my life was over. I carried my case down the steps onto the street and sighed heavily. The bailiff said that a locksmith would be coming shortly to change the locks, so there was no point me trying to get back in. Then he put his hand on my shoulder and said he was sorry. I wanted to smack him but I smiled thinly and said thank you.

He walked over to a blue Astra and squeezed into the driving seat. I noticed that another man, burly and unshaven, was sitting in the passenger seat like a Rottweiler in a cage. He was probably the back-up when things got heavy. The car jumped into life and disappeared down the street. For a long while I stood on the pavement and then, slowly, I set off down the road. My mother was expecting me for lunch. She said she had something very important to tell me, and I suppose I had something very important to tell her too, because I hadn't yet found the courage to inform her that I was being repossessed. In fact, I hadn't told a soul.

As I rounded the corner onto Juniper Street I saw the bailiffs again. They were rapping on the door of a white Georgian house. I heard a woman's voice shout, 'Fuck off'.

'We have a possession warrant, please open up. We don't want to use force but we will if we have to,' the plump, bald man said.

There was no response. The unshaven man went back to the car and returned with a tool kit. He took out a jemmy and a hammer and began to force open the door. I stopped on the pavement to watch. I was not the only one; neighbours peered through their windows and passers-by gawped as the door frame split with a piercing crack and the bailiffs shoulder-charged the door until it gave way and they tumbled into the property. The woman's voice was louder now as she hurled abuse at the men. There was a scuffle and then the woman emerged with the two men holding her by the arms.

'Let go, you wankers,' she screamed. The men dumped her on the pavement.

'We're just doing our jobs, miss. It's not our fault,' the plump man said.

'Don't give me that shit. No one's making you do this job, you fuckers. Get me my bag.'

The unshaven man scuttled back into the house and emerged with a black case.

'Go fuck yourself,' she said to him as he put it down beside her. For the first time that morning I smiled. If only I were endowed with such fighting spirit. The woman pulled up the handle from her case, straightened her shirt and, with a final 'you people are scum', walked off towards the main road. I trundled after her with my bag, which whined like a spoilt child on its broken wheels.

'Hey,' I called as I caught up with her. 'Are you OK? The bastards did me too.'

She looked at me, at my noisy case, at my disgruntled face and she let out a bitter, ironic laugh. 'The repo men must be doing Finsbury Park today.'

Her name was Angela. Ten minutes later we were having coffee. She was slim with wavy, shoulder-length, coal black hair. A few stray tendrils dangled provocatively over bright blue eyes. Her skin was milky and smooth as if it had never seen sunlight. There was something other-worldly about her, almost gothic. I found her hypnotically beautiful and it would be dishonest if I didn't admit that one of the very first thoughts that crossed my mind, as she tucked into a doughnut, the

3

sugar sticking to her cheeks, the jam oozing over her fingers, was that I wanted to make love to her immediately and recklessly so that I might escape from everything I despised about myself.

It was a day for extreme thinking. Only an hour previously I had envisioned my own death in a half-hearted morning fantasy, which saw me as a Japanese samurai committing hara-kiri, in the most honourable fashion, with a kitchen knife in the living room, the bailiffs stumbling into a gory blood fest, a suicide note daubed on the walls reading, 'You have ruined my life.' (I had wavered over the wording, considering 'the banks have ruined my life' or 'the government has ruined my life' or 'Sheryl has ruined my life,' all of which felt ridiculous, and in the end I wasn't sure who was most to blame for my misery, so I settled on the all-encompassing 'you' because whoever it was that ruined my life, it certainly wasn't me and I wanted as many people as possible to feel guilty.) But I couldn't find a pen or a kitchen knife worthy of the task, for I had already packed everything and put it in storage. And even if I had a hundred swords I doubt I would have killed myself in that way, because although I am prone to such extreme thoughts, I never act on them.

Angela seemed more interested in her doughnut than me. Some women know how to take out their anger on a pastry. She devoured it in less than a minute. The cake massacre seemed to lift her spirits – at least temporarily – because she smiled and asked me what I planned to do.

'I'm going to have lunch with my mother. Beyond that I have no plans until the end of time.' Which reminded me, I needed to call my mum. 'Please excuse me.'

I pulled out my mobile and dialled her number.

'Hello Mum, it's me ... No, it's me, Josh ... no, Josh ... Josh, Mum ... JOSH.' The café patrons turned to stare. I covered the phone with my hand. 'Sorry,' I whispered to Angela, 'she's a bit deaf.' I noticed a man wearing a hearing aid on the table next to me. I threw him an awkward smile, unsure if I had been in any way offensive.

'Mum ... turn off the TV ... THE TV, TURN IT OFF ... that's better. God, you have that thing on so loud ...No, I've never watched it ... No, I don't watch daytime television ... Yes, I'm sure it is very interesting. Mum, I'm going to be late. OK? ... I don't know how long ... I'll see you later ... What? No, Sheryl isn't coming back ... I don't know, Mum ... you'd have to ask her ... She's decided that she doesn't love me any more. Look, I don't want to talk about it now ... I'm upset too. Is that what you wanted to talk to me about? Sheryl? ... No, well, what was it then? Why can't you just tell me on the phone if it's so urgent? Alright ... I'm sorry ... put it in the fridge ... I'll eat it later ... OK. Bye, Mum ... oh, and Mum ... you still there? ... I meant to tell you, I ... I, erm ... this morning I was ... oh, it doesn't matter. I'll tell you later ... I know. Love you too. Bye.' I hung up.

'God, she drives me nuts sometimes.'

'Who's Sheryl?' Angela asked.

'No one ... my wife ... my ex-wife.'

There was a silence. Perhaps she was waiting for me to say more.

'So tell me, what do you do, Angela?' I asked, irritated with myself for using the question of last resort, the one I use if I am introduced to someone I have nothing in common with and can't think of anything to say.

She looked around furtively and dropped her voice, 'I'm a part-time terrorist.'

I admired the cute way she had sidestepped the question and turned it into a game.

'Sounds like a fun job, what kind of terrorist?' I said, playing along.

'An eco-terrorist – but keep it quiet. I have to be careful, I get followed all the time.'

'By who?'

'The authorities. I don't normally tell people but today I don't care about anything.'

'What does an eco-terrorist do?' I asked.

'We blow up airline offices, send death threats to oil executives, embarrass unscrupulous banks – that kind of thing.'

'Oh,' I said, 'is the pay good?'

She laughed. 'And you ... what do you do?'

I hesitated.

'I am a biscuit designer.'

It was the first thing that came to mind. I have never been good at making things up.

'Really,' she said dubiously.

There was another silence. We had run out of lies to tell each other. Angela began to fiddle absent-mindedly with the salt and pepper pots.

'It's days like this that make you wonder what life is all about,' she said forlornly. 'I feel like I've achieved absolutely nothing of any value and the chances are that I never will. Today is the day when every dream I ever had fell out of the sky and landed like a dead bird on the pavement in front of me. I can't make sense of it all. Do you know what I mean?'

I knew exactly what she meant. I understood what it was to lie helpless under the juggernaut of life, when one event after another conspires against you. In the past my strategy was to keep myself busy so I wouldn't have to ask myself any challenging questions, rather like a human ostrich. Although since I had become unemployed I had done nothing but ask myself challenging questions.

'I don't know how we get ourselves into these situations,' I answered. 'It's like suddenly you're an adult and you're doing a job you don't care about and you're living in a place you don't care about and you're with a woman who doesn't really love you and you're up to your neck in debt so you can't escape from it and nothing seems to excite you any more, or at least not like it used to, and it feels like you're under a huge blanket. And you think back to when you were a kid, when everything seemed possible and you had dreams and you thought you would never get stuck in the quagmire of responsibility that has squashed your parents, or in my case, my mother. And all you can think is: I've failed, I'm watching it fail and I can't seem to get off this conveyor belt that's leading me precisely nowhere. Fuck it all ... I don't know how it began and where it will end. Over the past couple of months I've been thinking things I've never thought before. I can't carry on like I have been. Something has to change.'

'I'm with you on that,' she mused.

'Have you got somewhere to live?' I asked.

'I can go to my friend's house for a few weeks until I sort myself out but ... '

'But what?'

'But this morning, as I drank a cup of tea for the last time in my kitchen, I decided this was the moment to do something truly radical.'

'Like what?'

'Like ... I don't know ... I mean what are my options? I go to this friend, look for work, save some money, put down a deposit on a place, join the rat race. The same pointless bullshit all over again. I've had it with all that.'

'So what are you going to do?'

She stared at me strangely, then stood up abruptly and came over to my side of the table. Without even pausing for permission, she sat on my knee, wrapped her arms around my neck and kissed me. I was taken aback and not a little embarrassed. The café's eyes fell upon us. Flagging conversations descended into smutty whispers. I shut them out and melted into Angela's unexpected embrace.

For weeks I had been starved, not only of affection but also of attention. I was no longer a husband, a worker or a homeowner. I was nothing. My existence was systematically being struck off files and registers. I was being stripped of my obligations and responsibilities. I was slowly disappearing, though I had not fully acknowledged my fall, for I still had hope. Not hope in anything concrete but the kind of hope that lags behind reality – like an echo. The kind of hopeless hope that the relatives of those lost in a tsunami might cling on to that one day their loved ones will emerge alive from the sea. The kind of hope that drops slowly but inexorably like a parachute into a pit of total darkness where no hope can possibly survive.

For one endless minute I was somebody again. In the simplicity of human touch, the joining of flesh, I soared once more and everything was possible. A thousand neural pathways, recently dormant, sparked back into life and I saw all that I had lost and all that could be built. I didn't care that she was behaving erratically. I didn't care that she was a stranger to me. I existed only in her kiss.

Her arms tightened around me as if she were trying to squeeze the last drops of life from me. Then, as abruptly as all this kissing had begun, she released her grip, stood up and without another word walked purposefully out of the café.

She stopped at the kerb, then turned and smiled at me sadly, before quite deliberately stepping out into the middle of the busy road. The number 7 bus had not yet entered the frame of the café window. She took two more steps before I saw it bearing down on her.

CHAPTER 2

There was a terrible screech of brakes. The bus slid into her and she was launched in a spray of blood into the air before landing out of view behind a parked car.

For a moment I couldn't move. The imprint of her lips was still warm on my mouth, then I was on my feet and running. I tumbled over a chair, picked myself up and pelted out of the café. There was a commotion in the street, people were charging from all sides towards her, I was aware of shouting, the traffic had come to a halt, car doors were opening, drivers jumping from their vehicles. The bus driver had stumbled from his cab, his head in his hands. The passengers on the bus were up and rushing forward to see what had happened. Angela looked as if she had been broken in two, her arms and legs arrayed at impossible angles on the tarmac. There must have been twenty people around her and more were joining every second. 'Is she dead?' someone said. No one dared to touch her, they were just staring. I pushed through. 'Angela, oh God, Angela.'

I didn't know what to do. I put my head on her chest. I couldn't hear a thing. An Asian man pulled me back.

'Don't move her,' he said. 'I'm a doctor.' He got to his knees and felt for her pulse.

'Is she alive?' The question echoed around the crowd.

The doctor didn't reply. He removed his jacket, leaned over her and put his mouth where, a minute earlier, mine had been. He pinched her nose and breathed deeply into her lungs. Blood was leaking on to the tarmac, it began to dribble towards the gutter. I could hear the faint sound of a siren in the distance. The whole street seemed to focus on Angela. Even the red-brick terraces, the lamp posts and the road signs were leaning in to get a better view. The doctor pressed down on her chest over and over. I turned away.

I remembered that our cases were inside the café, so I went to retrieve them. I don't know why I did this. I guess I didn't want them to get stolen and there was nothing I could do at that moment to help. Perhaps I didn't want to hear the doctor say she was dead. As I grabbed the cases, I saw that there was a small wooden box, a little larger than a ring box, on the table, which was odd because I hadn't noticed it before. Angela must have left it there and, in all the commotion, it had escaped my attention. I hurriedly slipped it into my pocket and made my way out.

By the time I had emerged the police and ambulance services had arrived. A policeman was urging the crowd to get back onto the pavement while the paramedics carefully manoeuvered Angela onto a stretcher. One of the policemen was asking if anyone knew who she was and I stepped forward with her suitcase. I told him that she was called Angela and that she lived at 14 Juniper Street. He asked me how I knew her and I said that I didn't really know her at all.

Then I heard a voice behind me say, 'He was kissing her in the café.'

It was the waiter.

'Is that true?' asked the officer.

'Well, yes ... I hardly know her but she's sort of ... my girlfriend.' I hadn't intended to use the word, it just seemed to fall out of my mouth, but it elevated me immediately to the centre of the tragedy. The onlookers gazed at me with sympathetic eyes and the policeman put a comforting arm on my shoulder.

'She's just lost her flat,' I said. 'I guess she was depressed.'

The policeman nodded. He asked me a few questions about what had happened, took my name and phone number and then suggested I accompany Angela to hospital in the ambulance.

Angela was already on a drip with an oxygen mask over her face by the time I climbed into the ambulance. Up until that moment I hadn't been sure that she was alive and I was relieved. Her head was bandaged and her eyes were closed.

When we arrived at the hospital, Angela was rushed down a corridor towards an operating theatre. We tore into an ante-room where three nurses were waiting, one pulled out a large pair of scissors and began to cut away her clothes. At first I felt embarrassed and wondered if I shouldn't look away. I hadn't earned the right to this intimacy but – and I am ashamed to admit this given the circumstances – I couldn't take my eyes away. The fact that she was hovering between life and death made her unbearably precious.

I don't know if it is possible to fall in love for a brief instant of time but at that moment I felt as if I was in love. This is not unusual for me; I am the kind of man who imagines himself in love with many women at many moments. These love affairs of the imagination are deliciously short-lived but nevertheless have an intensity about them that is as pure as any consummated love. I once fell in love with a stranger in the park on a warm afternoon in autumn. I was taking a leisurely lunch break. She was sitting a few yards away on the grass engrossed in a magazine. She must have been reading something amusing because at one moment she chuckled to herself and a few locks of hair fell in front of her eyes. I had hardly noticed her until then but this insignificant event made her seem so lovely that I spent the rest of my break quietly observing her. I didn't speak to her because I didn't want to break the spell.

On another occasion I was in the library doing some research on potholing. I was sitting opposite a woman dressed in a red cashmere sweater, a knee-length grey woollen skirt and opaque black tights. I remember the clothes vividly because, along with her waist-length blonde ringlets, everything about her was soft and velvety. She was like a cat that needed to be stroked. I understood, by glancing at the titles of the books on her desk, that she was studying melancholy in art, which in itself was weirdly attractive. Her gaze never once fell upon me and yet I was filled with longing. I am not talking of a base sexual longing but of something far more profound – a deep yearning of the soul. Is it genuinely possible to fall in love with women in such circumstances? Or am I uniquely blessed with the ability to project my fantasies onto them because I have never truly been in love myself? Perhaps many men have these thoughts but I wouldn't know, because I have never spoken to another man about it for fear of appearing foolish. My discussions about women with other men rarely extend beyond the physical. I might say such and such is attractive or that I would like to sleep with a certain acquaintance but I would never say that I felt a deep connection with a girl who had not even looked at me; this kind of conversation I cannot have with other men.

The only thing all these women had in common was that I had been able to observe them in an intimate moment whilst I myself had remained unobserved. To my eye, there is something unspeakably beautiful about anybody that behaves unselfconsciously. Perhaps this is why I felt most affection for my wife when I watched her sleep. There was only one occasion when I actually spoke to one of these women and that was on a train, long before I met Sheryl. Her name was Miranda Wilks but that is a story so tinged with regret I find it hard to think about.

The nurse carefully but quickly cut along the sides of Angela's blood-stained jeans, from the ankles up to the waistband, and peeled away the denim. The gruesome sight that greeted me made my stomach lurch and my mouth fill with vomit: Angela's right tibia had broken clean in two and the lower half had lacerated through her skin and was protruding vertically upwards. I turned away and managed to swallow down the acidic liquid that had flooded into my mouth.

I didn't know what else was broken and what could be fixed; I didn't know whether she could be saved or whether she would walk again. I looked at her naked body for what I presumed would be the first and last time. I looked at it for what it was: a creation of magnificent complexity and loveliness destroyed in a second. A fourth nurse appeared with a doctor. The nurses stationed themselves, one at Angela's head, and the others at her shoulders, waist and legs. Carefully and in a coordinated manner they rolled her over onto her side so the doctor could examine her spine. I withdrew a few paces, not wishing to get in their way. They log rolled her back to her original position, placed some head blocks on either side of her, covered her in a hospital sheet and wheeled her away into the operating theatre. All this had taken place within a few minutes of our arrival.

I found myself in the hospital waiting room. Realising that I was going to be very late for my mother, I reached for my phone.

'Hello Mum, it's me, Josh ... JOSH, yes ... Good idea, turn it off, yes ... I'm going to be later than I thought ... I know. I'm sorry ... I don't know, I don't think I'll be there until this afternoon ... this afternoon ... yes ... I got caught up in some business ... I can't explain now ... No, not that kind of business ... No, Mum, I don't think I'll ever get that job back, the company's about to go under ... I told you, put it in the fridge, I'll eat it later ... I don't mind ... It's OK, I'll eat it cold ... Of course it'll be fine ... What? ... Yes, of course I knew Hilary from down the road was a lesbian ... Well, because she's been living with Maureen for twenty years ... Everyone knew ... What do you mean the newsagent told you? Why were you talking about lesbians at the newsagents? Oh, please, Mum don't tell everyone about it ... because I don't want to have to talk about it with everyone ... No, I don't know why she married me ... perhaps she didn't know at the time ... look, can we stop talking about lesbians, God, I wish I'd never told you ... What? ... Christ, Mum, what's Martina Navratilova got to do with it? Listen, I've got to go. Bye ... Yes, love you too.'

I hung up and put the phone on silent.

There was nothing to do and for the first time since I met Angela my attention turned back on myself. I became aware of how stiff my shoulders and back were. I felt a terrible anxiety in my stomach. Could I have done anything to prevent this? What was I going to do now? Maybe I should stay at least until someone else came along to look after her – a mother, a father, a sibling – someone was bound to show up sooner or later. A wave of resentment swept over me; I didn't know this woman, she wasn't my responsibility, yet for some reason she had sucked me into her suicide attempt – as if my day wasn't going badly enough before I met her. Now all I could see was the image of the bus bearing down on her. And the worst part of it was that I cared. She had made me care, I was worried for her, I wanted her to live and I wanted her to kiss me again with all the passion that had been missing from my life. I wanted to be there when she awoke and I wanted to show her life was worth living. It was not as if there was anything else for me to do. I could sit in that hospital for a week and no one would care. I could sit there for a month, a year. At least while I was in the hospital I had something to concentrate on and it would keep my mind off the huge gaping emptiness that was the rest of my life.

Remembering the box I had found on the table, I took it out from my jacket pocket and inspected it. A faint scent of sandalwood wafted over me like a half-remembered dream. I turned it over in my hand; there was a tiny labyrinth carved on the top. On the bottom, printed in one corner, was a website address: 'yoursoul.com'. There was a small keyhole on the front side and the lid was firmly held shut. I was trying to force it open when I felt a strange heat coming from inside. It took me so much by surprise that I jumped up from my chair. What on earth could it be? I looked around the waiting room to see if anyone was watching, almost as if I were looking for witnesses to tell me I wasn't going mad, but no one seemed in the slightest bit interested in me and my box. I placed it carefully back in my pocket and switched my attention to Angela's suitcase. Maybe it contained some clues to her life and why she had wanted to end it. For a long while I stared at the bag, knowing that I had no right to open it. My eyelids began to feel heavy. I yawned, the hum of the hospital began to fade and I drifted into sleep.

I dreamt that I was tenpin bowling with Sheryl. Sheryl was scoring strike after strike but I couldn't seem to lift the bowling ball out of the tray. Even with two hands. I went to complain that the balls were too heavy but the man behind the counter was a frog who only spoke Serbo-Croat. He didn't seem remotely interested in my ball problem despite my best attempts at mime and gesticulation. I came to realise that this man-frog was a war criminal in disguise and that he was responsible for the deaths of hundreds of Bosnians. I ran off to tell Sheryl but when I got back to our lane Sheryl was making love to the bald bailiff in the middle of the alley. Strangely, I didn't seem to care and then, when I looked around, there were scores of couples making love, on banquettes, on the ball return boxes, in the lanes, in fact everywhere I looked. The women were naked but all the men wore dark suits and for some reason I knew they were all repo bailiffs. Then I saw Angela's face smiling at me just before she was hit by the bus, except the bus wasn't there. I called out to her and told her to be careful because I knew what was about to happen but she laughed, and I saw that she was surrounded by doughnuts and other sticky pastries and that she was drowning. I heard a noise behind me, I turned round and saw the bus thundering down on me.

I woke myself up with a scream. I looked around and wondered if anyone had heard me. My attention was drawn once more to her suitcase, it was staring at me begging to be opened so I unzipped it. Everything was mostly green; green nightie, green dress, green jumper but there was also a pair of jeans, a wash bag and a piece of folded paper. I wondered if this could be a suicide note, so I rushed to unfold it. It read, '36 Tudor Row, EC4, Thursday 2.00pm.'

It was written in the middle of the page in what I assumed was her own hand. I looked at my watch. It was 12.30pm and it was Thursday. A cheerless nurse in a blue check uniform stared at a computer screen across the room.

'How long will the operation take?' I asked.

'You were with the girl that was hit by a bus?'

I nodded.

'I don't know.'

She looked back at her screen and continued her work.

A minute or so passed.

'Can you find out?'

'No,' she said without shifting her gaze from the screen.

There was another silence.

'Well ... how long do these things normally take?' I asked.

She looked up in exasperation. 'It depends what they find – she could be in there for four or five hours but she may not come round until tomorrow. I'd go home if I were you and phone in later.'

I stood up and sat down again and looked at the note. Perhaps I should go to Tudor Row myself and tell whoever she was supposed to meet there what had happened. I didn't know if the police would contact the next of kin or whether as the putative boyfriend I was expected to do it. Tudor Row could not be the home of a family member or a friend for why would she need to write it down, but maybe the person who lived there knew something about Angela and could point me in the right direction.

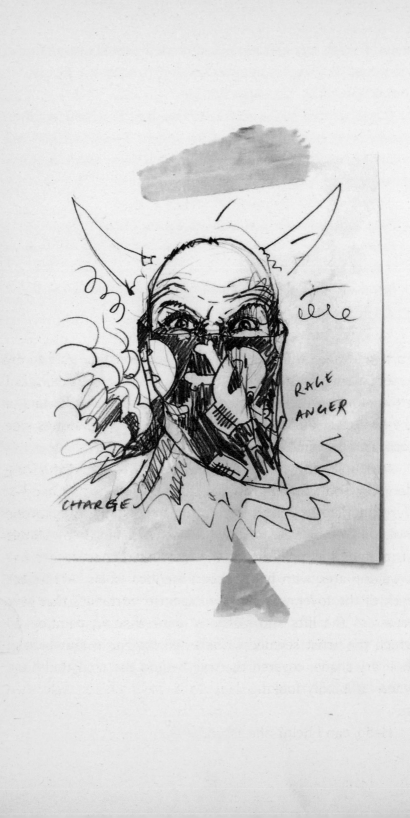

CHAPTER 3

I arrived fifteen minutes early and discovered, contrary to my
expectation, that 36 Tudor Row was not a private dwelling but
a five-storey office building that housed the headquarters of
the National Bank of Scotland Invest. It stood in a quiet side
road off Cheapside alongside similar offices.

A couple of women were smoking in a neighbouring
doorway and a small group of incongruous looking hoodies
were huddled in conversation across the street, but no one
looked like they were waiting to meet Angela. After a couple
of minutes I stepped inside the building. In one corner was
a waiting area with half a dozen identical sofas. Across the
back of the foyer was a row of security turnstiles that gave
access to the lifts and stairs. A giant abstract painting, in
which the artist seemed to be exploring the colour blue in
its every shade, covered the wall behind the reception desk,
where a kindly-looking lady in a navy blazer welcomed
me.

'Hello, can I help?' she asked.

'Erm yes, maybe', I said uncertainly. 'I've come on behalf of a lady called Angela, I think she may have an appointment at 2pm with someone.'

'Oh right, do you know who she was meeting?'

'Well that's the thing you see, I don't know who she was meeting. It's probably something to do with ... money ... it's just that she has been in an accident and she won't be able to make it.'

'Oh, I'm sorry to hear that ... let me see if I have anything here.' She scanned her computer screen. 'Do you know her surname, sir?'

'No, I'm sorry – oh, it doesn't matter – it's not important', I said apologetically, wishing I had never come.

'Hang on. I've got a Miss A. Knowles coming into see Jacob Freeman at 2.15pm. Could it be her?'

'Yes, yes it could be her, yes, why not?'

'Would you like me to put you through to Mr Freeman?'

'Yes, that's very kind.'

The receptionist dialled a number and handed me the phone. I heard shouts from across the street. I looked out and saw that there were now twenty or so people gathered there and they were yelling about something.

'Hello', a tired voice said in my ear.

'Ah hello, Mr Freeman, you don't know me, I'm a friend of Angela Knowles ... she's supposed to be meeting you later but she has had a terrible accident and she won't make it.'

'Oh no! What ... what happened to her?' his voice cracked.

'She was hit by a bus this morning in Finsbury Park.'

'Oh God, is she OK?'

'I don't know, she's in hospital now, she hasn't come round since it happened. When I left they were operating – she had severe internal bleeding', I explained.

'But what was Amanda doing in Finsbury Park? She normally stays at the Royal Lancaster on Haverstock Hill when she's in Lon ... '

'Angela.'

'Sorry?'

'Angela. She's called Angela, not Amanda.'

There was a pause and immediately I understood that I had made a terrible mistake.

'Er ... ' the voice said, 'you're talking about Miss Knowles ... it's definitely Amanda. But what did the doctors say? Is she ... '

'Excuse me ... sorry to interrupt, Mr Freeman. I don't think I am talking about Miss Knowles. I'm talking about Angela.'

The noise from outside was growing louder. I turned and saw that the gathering had swollen further and was now blocking the street. A panelled door behind the reception swung open and a security guard came bounding out.

'Angela who?' Mr Freeman asked.

'Let me explain, you see, I didn't really know this lady but I found a piece of paper in her handbag and it had an address on it ... of this office ... and it just said 2pm on it and ... well, it's 2pm now so I thought ... '

I stopped mid-sentence and looked at the mob outside. Some were holding placards and chanting angrily but I couldn't make out what they were saying. Many wore scarves and balaclavas over their faces. Others carried buckets and jerry cans. A few of them carried sticks and clubs.

'What? You thought what?' the voice said. 'You thought you'd scare the living daylights out of me?'

The receptionist was talking to the police on another line and the security guard was hurriedly locking the doors.

'Sorry,' I said in a daze, 'there's a riot going on outside and ... so that's who she ... Jesus ... she wasn't lying.'

I put the phone down. I could hear them clearly now, they were chanting about fat cats and greedy bankers. I walked towards the door, I wanted to get out but the security guard ordered me back.

'Sorry sir, I can't let you out right now. The police will be here in a minute.'

Someone in the crowd hurled a brick in our direction, the window cracked but didn't shatter. The mob rushed towards us, venom in their eyes. They pressed up against the glass only a few feet away. I was terrified. Their anger was directed at the three of us in the atrium as if we were personally responsible for the financial crash. One of them pulled out a club and started hammering at the cracked window. Then another, hidden behind a skull and crossbones bandanna that was stretched across his face, charged the door, rattling the locks. The receptionist scrambled to a red alarm box on the wall behind her desk and smashed the front; a siren sounded through the building. She flicked on the tannoy and announced that the building was under attack and that all employees should remain in high alert in their offices until the police arrived. Then she fled up the stairs, leaving me alone with the security guard, who now had his back up against the door while the protestors bombarded it with their shoulders and sticks. The guard shuddered with each hit, the vibrations growing steadily bigger until the door plate began to bend and the lock give way.

'It's going to break,' I shouted.

The guard abandoned his post and ran back towards me, grabbed me by the arm and pulled me towards the room from which I had seen him emerge. The entrance burst open behind us and the protestors came charging in.

We dived inside the room. It was a small office with a desk and a bank of security TV screens. There was no other exit.

The guard pulled out a chain of keys, there must have been twenty of them, and fumbled around looking for the right one. On the screens I could see the protestors swarming into the building. The man with the skull and crossbones bandanna leapt over the desk, sending the computer crashing to the floor. Two others were heading determinedly to our door. The guard had found the key, but before he could turn it in the lock, the door pushed open. I threw myself at the door and between us we managed to ram it closed again and turn the key.

There was a thudding on the door.

'Where are the fucking police?' the guard yelled.

I looked at the screens. The protesters were emptying their buckets and cans. It looked like they were spreading shit and oil and grease all over the sofas, turnstiles and reception desk. A woman protester was scrawling something on the wall with spray paint and all the while the thudding against our door grew stronger. Somebody was up a ladder trying to break one of the cameras, his bloodshot face filled the screen. Then suddenly the screen covering reception went blank. I could hear glass breaking. The chanting had dissipated into random shouts. I stepped back from the door and pressed my back against the furthest wall and watched events unfold on the outside camera. There were still protestors on the street, some of them seemed uncomfortable with the violence. One man was arguing with another protestor and holding him back.

Suddenly our door smashed open and a blind fear gripped my bowels. Two men burst into the room and fell on top of the security guard. I picked up a chair and tried to fend them off with it. Behind them came the cry 'Run! Police,' and for the second time that day I heard sirens. The two men pulled themselves to their feet and beat a hasty retreat. The protestors charged out of the building just as two police vans were pulling up. One van seemed to drive off in pursuit but the other stopped and six policemen entered the building. The security guard got to his feet and brushed himself down. We stepped out into the carnage that was the reception area. There was broken glass and overturned furniture everywhere and the terrible odour of human excrement filled the air. A policeman approached us.

'Are you all right?' he asked.

'I need the toilet,' I said and rushed across the lobby to the gents.

Thankfully the loos had not been damaged in the protest. I suppose there would have been no point in smearing shit in a toilet. I ran to a cubicle, sat down and let out a gasp of relief as I emptied the runny contents of my stomach down the pan.

I sat there for some time until I felt my heart return to a regular beat. So Angela hadn't been joking in the café, this really was how she spent her time. I couldn't equate her with the mindless violence I had just witnessed.

I washed my hands and emerged into a sea of panicky bankers, policemen and a TV crew who pushed their camera in my face and bombarded me with questions. I batted them away and tried to leave the building but I was stopped by a policeman who asked me to make a witness statement. I told him what I had seen and gave my mother's address. Of course, I didn't tell him about Angela and why I had really come. She was in enough trouble as it was.

CHAPTER 4

As I entered the hospital the smell of bleach bruised my nostrils. All municipal buildings smell in varying degrees of the same cheap disinfectant. The degree of odour depends on the frequency of application. Top of the list are hospitals closely followed by schools. Armies of cleaners patrol the corridors at night with buckets and mops, removing germs and replacing them with low grade poison that is slowly ingested by the workforce, patients and pupils, giving them eczemas, asthmas and cancers.

Angela was now in a ward on the third floor, attached to a drip and a heart monitor. Still unconscious. She looked like a broken toy, this girl who had entered my life in such dramatic fashion. A bandage covered her left eye. Her right leg was in plaster and had been carefully propped up on pillows. A red graze stained her cheek like a squashed strawberry. The room contained eight other beds with curtains between them, some open, some closed. A frail African woman who looked as old as the moon was snoring opposite and a pallid looking teenager with a slash from ear to mouth was chatting to her mother to my right.

A fly sat listlessly on the window behind the bed. The distant hum of traffic blended with the gentle throb of monitors and the indistinct hubbub of hospital life. I felt indescribably lost. My attention fell upon my silent audience of one. I examined her delicate features, her fine brown eyelashes, the soft downy skin on her ear lobe, the quizzical half smile on her pale lips.

'What am I doing here, Angela? Since you kissed me everything's gone haywire ... no one's ever kissed me like that before ... I didn't understand what you were doing ... I thought we'd found a connection, I didn't know you were about to ... Maybe you were saying goodbye to life ... maybe it was an act of charity or the last bounce on the diving board before the big leap. Whatever it was, I don't suppose you even stopped to think what that kiss would do to me. There's so much I want to talk to you about, Angela. Please wake up.'

I took her hand in mine and rubbed it. I felt the weal of a scar on her wrist. I rolled her arm over and saw a ladder of knife cuts, long since healed, rising up to her bicep.

'Oh, Angela,' I whispered, 'so many cuts, what have you done to yourself? I don't even know who you are. Where are your parents? Where are your friends? Why is there no one here but me?'

I became aware of a presence behind me. I swivelled round to see a man staring at me from across the ward. He was an elegant, slender man in his forties with a brush of brown hair. In his hand was a notebook and a pen. He seemed to be weighing my turbulent soul in his eyes. He smiled sympathetically as if he had heard my lament, although I don't think he could have done from where he was standing, then he began to scribble something in his pad. He wore no identification badge and did not appear to be a doctor, nor did he seem attached to any particular patient. He could have been making an entry in the book of life: a tiny observation on the fragility of hope, but I took him to be no more than a hospital administrator checking up on the availability of beds or some such duty.

I felt the middle finger of Angela's left hand twitch as if she wanted my attention. I turned back to her.

'You can move that finger? Maybe you can hear me. If you can hear me move it again.'

I waited. After a moment it twitched again.

'Ooh, you can hear me ... or was that just random? Can you move anything else? Go on, try.'

I watched her intently.

'Come on, you can do it.'

Her chest rose and fell and I thought I noticed a subtle acceleration in the rhythm of her breath.

'You're trying, aren't you? You want to tell me something? OK, let's go again. Move your finger for me.'

Nothing came. I focused all my attention on the middle finger of her left hand and then after a minute or so it twitched again.

'I'm going to take that as a sign. So now we can talk, Angela. That's good. I'm going to ask you a question and you answer with your finger, OK?'

It took me a moment to think of something to ask.

'Er ... can you ... '

There was a twitch before I had even asked the question. 'Oh, am I being silly? You're just twitching around, aren't you? It's got nothing to do with me, has it?'

She twitched again.

'Angela, you're driving me crazy here. Can you hear me, yes or no?'

She did a double twitch.

'What does that mean? Oh I know, how about you do one twitch for yes, two for no, OK? Or is that too difficult?'

I waited patiently for a sign but nothing came. It did not occur to me that I might have been asking too many questions at once.

'Maybe we'll try again later. So what shall we do now huh? How about I tell you a story, that way you won't need to answer any questions. When I was a kid I hated being asked questions. Especially about my dad. I didn't like talking about what happened to him. The only person I could speak to was one of my primary school teachers. He was called Oliver Feldenberg. He was the only Jew in the school and he worked on the weekend at a liberal synagogue as a part-time Rabbi. He was my favourite teacher because he had a way of turning everything into a story; even multiplication tables had a narrative ... like four blind men wearing eight mittens bought twelve eggs for their sixteen grandchildren who would play twenty questions twenty-four hours a day during the twenty-eight days of February and so on. He would do mysterious things like disappear early on a Friday in winter because he wasn't allowed to do any work after the first star appeared in the sky, and he wore a round skullcap which he said was like a manhole cover so that God could always find a way into his brain.

'Now there was a little boy in my class called Clive who nobody liked. I think he came from a troubled home. He always came in sleepy, never listened and if you got in his way he would scream at you. One Monday morning he came to school with a black eye and the next day he didn't show up at all. Rabbi Feldenberg sat us on the carpet and told us that when Clive came back we had to make a special effort to be nice to him. He said Clive needed us more than we could ever know and then he told us a story. We all knew it was about Clive. I have never forgotten it. It's about two rabbits and a tree and … you know, maybe it's about me and you … anyway there were two rabbits. One was called Mr Rabbit and the other was called Mrs Rabbit and guess what? They were married. To each other. And of course they loved each other in the way that only rabbits can. You could hardly keep them apart. One day they were on their way home after a gruelling day's work. The sun was particularly strong that day and they were exhausted, ready to drop, when all of sudden, in the distance, they saw a giant plane tree. They had never seen this tree before, it was magnificent with its immense trunk and colossal branches. They couldn't help but be drawn towards it; almost as if the tree was beckoning them over. When they got to the foot of the tree the full force of their fatigue hit them and Mr Rabbit bowed his head and said, "Great Plane tree, you are so beautiful. We are humbled in your presence. We are hot and tired and in need of rest. Please may we sit in your shade a while?"

'And the tree replied in a deep sonorous voice, "You ask so politely, with all my heart I offer you shade."

'So Mr Rabbit and his wife gratefully slumped in the shade of the tree and rested their weary bones. After a while they realised how thirsty they were. So Mrs Rabbit said to the tree, "Magnificent tree, our throats are dry like straw, please may we drink a tiny mouthful of your sap and then we shall be on our way?"

'And the tree replied in a voice that sent vibrations deep into the earth, "You ask so sweetly, Mrs Rabbit. With all my heart, you may drink of my sap. Drink until you can drink no more."

'So they drank until their thirst was quenched and they

were filled with a light-headed joy. "Beautiful tree, we are so touched by your kindness," said Mr Rabbit, "may we see this heart of which you speak?"

'Without even a moment's hesitation the tree opened up its heart and invited the rabbits to enter. The heart of the great plane tree was magical beyond belief. There were bubbling springs of creamy sap, drops of warm dew fell like rain from above and everywhere, hanging from branches and spilling over from troughs and thickets, was treasure – glittering diamonds, nuggets of gold, silver rocks and all kinds of riches. And at the very heart of the tree was a hollow filled with the most beautiful, white luminescent pearls they had ever seen. So bright that it made their little red eyes hurt to look at them. Mr Rabbit imagined how pretty his wife would look with one of those pearls around her neck, but he was far too polite to ask if he might have one.

'Within an instant the rabbits found themselves once more outside the tree and around Mrs Rabbit's neck was a necklace containing a single white pearl, a gift from the heart of the Great Plane tree. The rabbits were overcome with gratitude and they fell to their knees. "Thank you, and a thousand times thank you," they said. "How can we ever repay you?"

'"Your happiness is payment enough," said the great tree. Mr Rabbit and his wife could not believe their luck and, full of excitement, they continued their journey home. Mrs Rabbit was so delighted with her necklace that she showed it to all her friends and in her pride she even showed it to her enemies. And when Mrs Wolf saw the pearl her eyes narrowed with jealousy. "Where did you get it?" she demanded and after Mrs Rabbit had told her the whole story Mrs Wolf ran to her husband. "I want a pearl from the heart of the Great Plane tree."

'Mr Wolf jumped to his feet and barked that he would get her one. So the two wolves ran to the tree. "Give us some shade," they growled.

'The tree welcomed them under its branches.

'"Now give us some sap," Mr Wolf snarled.

'"Please drink, until you can drink no more," said the tree.

'The wolves gorged on sap and when they were full Mrs Wolf bayed, "Open your heart."

'So the tree opened its heart and the greedy wolves stepped inside. It was just as Mrs Rabbit had described it. There were bubbling springs of creamy sap, drops of warm dew fell like rain from above and all around was treasure; diamonds, gold, silver, all manner of delights and there, at the very heart of the tree was the hollow filled with the beautiful white luminescent pearls that Mrs Wolf so coveted. The wolves could not believe their eyes. For a moment they simply ogled at the splendours around them and then Mr Wolf suddenly came to his senses. "Quickly," he shouted, "fill your pockets."

'The wolves began to grab at the treasure. The tree cried out in pain but the wolves paid no heed, snatching up everything as fast as they could, stuffing their pockets with gold and silver, filling their arms with diamonds and pearls until they were up to their necks in it and the tree could bear it no longer. With an almighty crash it slammed closed its heart, suffocating the wolves inside.

'Since that day the Great Plane tree hasn't opened its heart to anyone. Rabbi Feldenberg explained that a very long time ago we humans were like the Great Plane tree; all you needed to do was gently ask and we would open our hearts to anyone, but we have changed, bad things happen to us and ... well you know how it is. He said when people get hurt they close their hearts. He told us that if we ever met anyone like the

Great Plane tree we should be gentle with them and try to understand them and maybe they would open up their hearts once more.

'Clive's mum and dad were taken away and a fortnight later Clive came back to school. We only ever saw him with his grandma after that. I tried really hard to be nice to him, but some of the other kids started to call him Wolf Heart. Poor kid. I've no idea what became of him. So that's my story.

'I don't know much about you, Angela, but I figure something got to you, huh! Made you close down. Because why would you do it? Why did you do it?'

Her fingers began to twitch rapidly.

A baggy-eyed nurse whom I hadn't seen before was waddling down the ward.

'Excuse me,' I asked, 'is she going to be alright?'

'The operation went as well as could be expected. She had severe internal bleeding and she broke her leg. The scan picked up a tiny amount of subdural blood on the left side of her skull but it's hard to tell at this stage how serious that is. We will have to assess it when she comes round.'

'And when will that be?' I asked.

'She's heavily sedated now, we're not expecting her to wake up until the morning. If I were you I would go home. Visiting hours are over in a quarter of an hour anyway.'

'Has she had any visitors?'

'No.'

'Do you know if her parents have been informed?'

'I'm afraid I don't know. That's not my job. Ask the police.'

She bustled past and disappeared behind a curtain in the far corner.

I found myself delving into Angela's bag again; this time I found a man's black leather wallet in a side pocket. I rifled through it; there was £320 in cash, a couple of credit cards and a driving licence. So there it was – her name, Angela Morton, and an address for a place called Glenthorpe Hall in Norfolk.

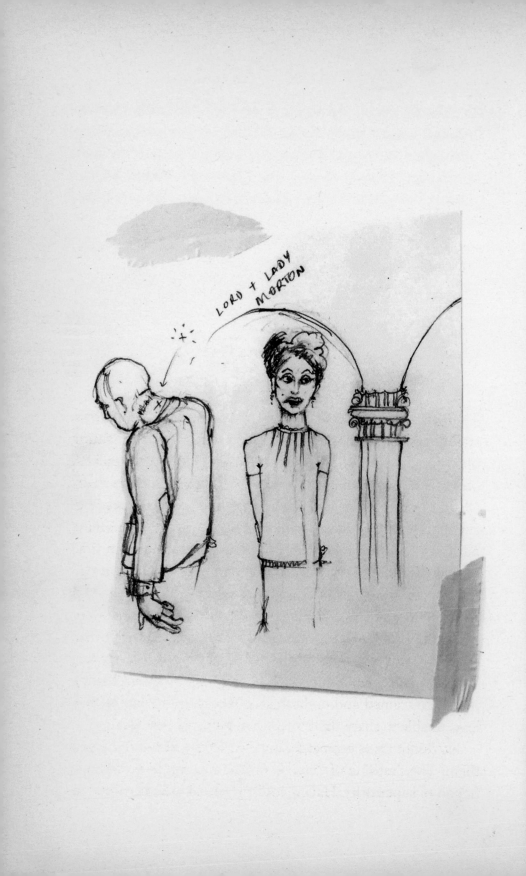

CHAPTER 5

The train to Norwich was packed full with commuters, standing between seats, leaning on luggage racks, sitting opposite the toilets, pressed against each other like pickled onions in a jar, their backs bowed from slumping in office chairs all day, their eyes brutalised by computer screens, beads of sweat glistening on their foreheads, wet patches mushrooming out from their armpits, their frowning faces pallid from time served in office blocks, their thoughts meandering through trivia, data, meetings. Their spirits crumpled like rubbish in the dustbins of their souls. Each man and woman a windswept island of solitude. Strangers with nothing to say to each other, speaking only on mobile phones, finalising deals, making appointments, giving information on arrival times or chatting in tiny restrained and embarrassed voices to the people they love, unable to share their feelings in public on the train.

No doubt I was projecting my own feeling of solitude upon them. The first line of defence for the insecure is to create a fiction of superiority. Having lost my job, I was in no mood to be charitable. Work may be an edifying activity but the dignity of labour is surely lost in the commute which daily reduces people to cattle. I was once one of them; freshly shaven, wearing a crisp white shirt under a grey suit, elbowing my way on to tubes and trains.

I looked at them with a mixture of envy and relief; envy because they had homes, food and security; relief because I had escaped the mindless commute to a job so laden with repetition that it had suppressed my thinking. I was a victim of my own lack of ambition, I had taken work far beneath my ability at a time when my mother needed money and only had me to rely on. My father died when I was six and though I was young, I was aware of the change it brought upon our circumstances. We moved from a leafy West Hampstead street to a council flat in Kilburn. My mother did not take work at first, preferring to dedicate her time to her only child, but actually it was I who looked after her. As the sole focus of all her attention and the only reason for her happiness, I felt an enormous responsibility to please her. It was as if her mental health was in my care. If ever I rebelled against her she would not so much tell me off as crumble before me. As I got a little older, she took some cash-in-hand cleaning jobs to supplement the benefits but I remember wanting to earn my own keep as soon as I possibly could. When I left school, I took a gap year to earn some money for college. I found a job in an auto parts firm in Essex. At first I was on the production line, then I started a mechanical engineering degree but continued to work there in the holidays, mainly covering for staff vacations, sometimes in the offices, sometimes on the shop floor. When I graduated they offered me a job and I never left. After ten years I had reached the dizzy heights of middle management: a kind of graveyard for conscientious, unimaginative people with marginally above average intelligence. And then of course the crash happened and no one bought any cars for a while and, like a useless bag of sand, I was the first one to be thrown out of the balloon. By the time I'd served my four week notice period the company was on the verge of bankruptcy.

Steadily the train emptied station by station, spitting out its passengers until it rumbled into Norwich. I picked up a discarded newspaper, headed out to the bus station and boarded a bus bound for Swaffham. The headlines were all about Sir Frank Godley, the ex-CEO of the National Bank of Scotland, the same bank that had repossessed Angela's flat and mine. Having been responsible for their near collapse, he was now walking away with a twenty-eight million pound pay off and pension deal. This after the government had bailed out NBS to the tune of twenty-four billion pounds. Perhaps this was the reason for the morning's demonstration. An hour or so into the journey, as darkness was beginning to descend on the fields, the driver signalled that I had reached my stop.

I got off the bus and tried to find my bearings. I was standing at a crossroads; there was no sign of any houses for miles around. Presumably the only reason for putting a bus stop here was the crossroads itself. There was a brick and flint wall that rounded one corner of the crossroads, extending west in the direction the bus had gone and north down a narrow lane. A sign on the wall read 'Berry Lane'. I knew from the address on the driving licence that Glenthorpe Hall was somewhere down Berry Lane. I set off at a swift pace, hoping to find the house before night robbed me of my eyes. A thin, pink lining traced the edges of the clouds to the west. I had at most twenty minutes before the last sliver of light would succumb to the relentless march of darkness. I followed the wall for several hundred metres until it began to grow in height and sweep inwards towards a huge archway over a driveway leading into some kind of estate. At the top of the archway were two stone lions on either side of a coat of arms. Beneath the archway was a formidable black wrought-iron gate that was locked shut. I presumed this was Glenthorpe Hall although there was no way of knowing for sure. A sign saying *Private* was staked in the ground to the left of the gate. There was no sign of life, no letter box, no bell; it was perhaps the rear entrance to the estate. I continued walking. As the lane curved round to the left, a chill breeze enveloped me, my muscles tightened, steeling themselves against the unexpected flurry of cold air. I pulled my jacket tighter around me.

The light was all but gone, only a memory of it clung tenaciously to the clouds ahead of me. I reached another break in the wall. Here there were two gatehouses on either side of another entrance. Beyond the gates a gravel road disappeared into the trees. On its verges, a spartan row of half-broken lamps produced an eerie tunnel of dim light under the arboreal canopy. In front of the gate to the right was a rusty chain that stretched up the wall to an old bell about the size of a man's head. I pulled down on the chain and the bell rang out across the estate. For a long time nothing happened, so I rang the bell again. I heard the whirring sound of an electric engine and a man in an old golf cart appeared on the gravel road from beyond the trees. The cart whirred and spluttered but made little progress. Like a child learning to swim, it expended enormous effort for little gain. As he drew close I could see in the lamplight that he was a rotund man in his fifties, dressed in a black three-piece suit. He had a bald pate which he tried unsuccessfully to hide under a few lank hairs which he had combed over from one side. He came to a halt in front of the gate, got out of the cart and looked at me curiously.

'We wasn't expecting visitors,' he said in a Norfolk brogue.

'I have some urgent news for Mr and Mrs Morton,' I explained. As soon as I spoke these words I realised how odd all this must have appeared. Who on earth delivered urgent messages in person these days? Who would show up on foot at night-time at a country estate in the middle of nowhere? It might have been acceptable in a Jane Austen novel; I could have been Darcy's manservant carrying word to Elizabeth.

'You want to see Lord and Lady Morton?'

'Lord and Lady? Erm, yes.'

'At this hour?'

'It's urgent.'

The man, whom I presumed was a butler, tutted and shook his head. 'I'm afraid I can't just let any Tom, Dick and 'Arry come in. If you've got somethin' to say you can tell me and I'll pass on the message.'

'It's about Angela. She's in hospital.'

The man's demeanour changed instantly as a look of anguish swept across his ruddy features. 'You'd better come in.'

He put a hand in his pocket and pulled out a remote control. The gate creaked slowly open. He gestured for me to climb into his cart and we rolled off down the driveway at a little less than walking speed. The man didn't say a word on this brief journey but stared fixedly ahead of him, like a racing car driver who might crash if he lost concentration even for a second. Everything moved as if through syrup. Eventually we came out into a vast open lawn and there ahead of us was a magnificent Palladian hall built in white stone. The driveway looped round a fountain in front of the main entrance, where eight steps led up to an Italianate portico supported by four pillars. Once upon a time, ladies and gentlemen would have drawn up in magnificent horse-drawn carriages. I was arriving in a golf cart.

The butler took me into the hallway and I ogled the gilt framed portraits of big-eared lords with riding crops and hats, which hung from floor to ceiling around the staircase. I was ushered under the antlers of a roe deer into a formal drawing room and left to my own devices. The chairs, with their upholstered straight backs and carved legs, looked like museum pieces. Above the fireplace was a warped mirror that made my legs look short and my head look big. It was incredible that people still lived like this and I couldn't quite fathom how Angela, with her anarchist tendencies, could have grown up here.

Time dribbled along interminably before the butler returned and asked me to follow him. We passed back through the hallway and took a door that led into the back of the house. The austere marble tiles gave way to carpet and we entered a high ceilinged sitting room supported by ancient oak beams from which spiders spun their webs undisturbed. A set of brown curtains hung limply over the window. To one side a couple of saggy sofas were languishing in the jaws of an empty fire-place. On the walls, between paintings of the hunt, were a series of individual portraits of Angela and two boys trussed up in their Sunday best. And at the far end of the room was a photograph of all five of them, probably taken in the late eighties from the look of the children's hairstyles and clothing. The background was hazy and the photographer had used the kind of whimsical soft focus that makes one think of pink candyfloss, coiffured poodles and fairies. They were all smiling dutifully for the camera, except Angela who stared inscrutably into the distance with her large sad eyes. She must have been five or six years old but already she looked like she did not belong.

A door behind the piano swung open and a tall elderly man with a hideous stoop entered the room. He was tall even with the stoop; he would have been a giant without it. He looked as though he had bowed his head to avoid banging it on a low door and had never been able to straighten it again. It hung at right angles to the rest of his spine such that his chin appeared to rest on his chest and his eyes were looking at his slippers. From this position I saw he had no bald patches. His straight grey hair drooped down over his brow like a flag on a still day and I couldn't make out his features beyond the bridge of his nose. There was no sign of this stoop in the photographs, so it was reasonable to assume that this was part of a progressive condition or the result of an accident.

Lord Morton was closely followed by Lady Morton, who was a sprightly greyhound of a woman. There wasn't an ounce of fat on her, nor was there any suggestion in her tiny hips that she had once pushed out three babies. Her bust was as flat as her stomach and didn't create so much as a wrinkle in the white short-sleeved shirt which she wore above a grey tweed skirt. Her arms were tanned, tightly wrinkled but well-toned and her neck was as elongated as her husband's was curved. She looked like a cartoon character that had been flattened by a steamroller. I was half expecting her to pop out back into her body at any moment. The room seemed to wilt in their joyless presence; the walls slumped, the wallpaper groaned and the carpet turned a shade more yellow.

'Please sit down,' Lady Morton said with the calm and authority befitting someone who was probably 103rd in line to the throne. She gestured to the sofa.

'Thank you.'

I sat down facing the window.

They parked themselves opposite me, Lord Morton's hunched shape making a perfect question mark. He peered at me through his hair and said in a strangled voice, 'I believe you have news about Angela?'

'Yes sir, I do.'

I don't know why I called him sir. I've never called anyone sir in my life but in the circumstances it felt right. Lord Morton nodded at the butler, who discreetly left the room. Lady Morton picked up an ivory letter opener that was lying on the table and began to fiddle aimlessly with it. I have an issue with letter openers. I think they have to be among the most pointless objects on the planet, along with back scratchers, bidets, crocheted toilet roll covers, holy water and penis enhancement cream. That someone would kill an elephant to make such a thing was beyond my comprehension. I imagine Angela would have felt the same. I remember getting a wooden one for Christmas when I was 17; it came in an office set that my mother bought me along with a paperweight and a desk toy with seven swinging ball bearings. All bloody useless. It had upset me that she should have spent her hard earned money on such expensive junk. It was a decade before I dared to throw them away and I swear I never used them once. Actually that's not strictly true – I must have swung those balls a couple of times a year in boredom and on one occasion I used the paperweight to knock a nail into the wall, but the letter opener never. It was Sheryl that made me throw them away soon after we moved in together. She couldn't bear clutter. The very next day Mum came round and noticed that they were gone from my desk. I'd kept them on display out of respect. I don't think she ever trusted Sheryl after that. It came up a few years later in an argument when she asked me how I could have let Sheryl

46

persuade me to throw them away; like I had thrown away a piece of her heart. Then she said, 'I lost you the day the letter opener disappeared.' Can you believe it!

'What is your name, young man?' Lord Morton asked.

'Joshua Jones.'

'Well, Joshua,' Lady Morton said, 'what has she done this time?'

'She tried to kill herself. She threw herself in front of a bus.'

Lady Morton nodded impassively – at least I think she was impassive – it's hard to read the expression of a woman who has had three quarters of her face pinned behind her ears; certainly there were no gasps of horror. Lord Morton leant back in the sofa and sighed, a pained look in his eyes.

'Is she all right?' he asked.

'She's still unconscious, sir, I wanted to let you know as soon as possible.'

'When did this happen?'

'This morning – they operated on her. She has a broken leg, I think there was some internal bleeding. She's lucky to be alive. It was horrible. I saw it happen.'

There was an interminable silence as Lady Morton tightened her fist around the letter opener. She seemed to be sucking all the energy out of the room like a black hole. Time was on its knees.

At length she said, 'She's gone too far. This is another attention-seeking exercise.'

'Mary!' Lord Morton rebuked her.

'Well, it's true. Are we supposed to feel sorry for her? Well, are we, Tom?'

'We don't know the circumstances.' Lord Morton gazed at me sideways. 'Do you know why she did it? Did she tell you?'

'No, sir. She had just been repossessed. It could have had something to do with that. Did you know about that?'

'No, we haven't spoken to her for nearly two years. But I can't say it surprises me. We secured a mortgage under her name and acted as guarantors. The idea was that she would get a job, behave like an adult and pay her own bills. This is what she said she would do. She didn't keep her part of the bargain so I stopped the payments. What do you know about Angela, Joshua?'

'Nothing really. It upset me that someone so lovely should want to kill herself. I want to help her.'

Had I been honest, I might have added that in so doing I might help myself, for I recognised that there was something about her that chimed with my highest aspirations. She made me want to be romantic, optimistic, amusing and courageous, all qualities which have eluded me for much of my life but which, since meeting her, were beginning to grow inside me. I would never have claimed I was Angela's boyfriend, jumped into the ambulance, sat at her bedside telling stories or trekked up to Norfolk if she hadn't had this effect on me. People who knew me well would have said I was behaving out of character.

'Be careful. She's a very wilful woman, Joshua,' said her mother. 'She's been nothing but trouble since she was born. You seem like a nice chap but you have no idea what you are dealing with. You are not the first man to fall in love with her and you won't be the last. They say she is wild and free, uninhibited, passionate. I understand why they fall for her. They see what they want to see, only later do they get burnt. She will destroy you. It pains me to say these things of my own daughter but believe me, Joshua, we have learnt from experience. We've given her everything a child could want and she's thrown it back in our face. Every time we tried to start again she rejected us. All we want is for her to have a normal life.'

I learnt a lot about Angela that evening. As a baby she had not been a good sleeper. She would howl all night and sleep all day. Her mother could not bear the screaming so she hired a night nurse and moved her into the opposite wing of the house. Nannyed by day, nursed by night, the tiny Angela became an outsider in her own home. She was tutored by the brightest graduates until her brain fizzed with facts and figures and, from the age of eight, was sent off to a top class boarding school in Kent, where she spent a desperately unhappy three years during which she tried to escape on numerous occasions. In the end it was not only Angela who was begging to leave but the school itself was making quiet representations to have her removed. Lord and Lady Morton relented to the pressure and packed her off to a less academic but stricter boarder on the east coast of Scotland, not far from Edinburgh, which they hoped would knock some sense into her. For a couple of years all appeared to go well. She had good friends and rarely complained but then, when she reached fourteen, things began to go wrong again. She was caught smoking cannabis and was nearly expelled. Then there was an incident when some boys from the town were found running around the grounds at night. Used condoms were found in the bushes and, though no one could prove which girls had been involved, suspicion fell on Angela, because someone had cut a hole in the fence with garden shears and she had been on gardening duty that day.

Then along with two other girls she had got into this 'dreadful cutting thing'. It happened the first time when she was seventeen. She had been cutting herself periodically ever since. She did her best to hide it but they knew the signs. They had tried to take her to a therapist but she refused to cooperate. She would spend each session with her fingers in her ears and then afterwards scream at her parents and tell them that they were the ones that needed therapy. If Lord Morton hadn't made a hefty donation, she would have been expelled from her school, following an incident when eight girls had to have their stomachs pumped after a drunken pyjama party that she had initiated by smuggling alcohol into the school.

Inevitably she failed to get into Oxford or Cambridge and instead went to that 'hotbed of socialism' the London School of Economics to study geography and development. She dropped out after the first year. While at the LSE she had joined the Revolutionary Communist Party purely to annoy her parents (as they saw it) and had extorted as much money as possible from them to put in the party coffers. Her affiliation to the communist party did not last long but it led seamlessly into an association with a climate action group to whom she was more genuinely attached. During this period she had been living off a hefty trust fund that had matured when she was twenty-one years old. But Lord and Lady Morton had sought to change the terms of the trust to prevent her from using the money freely. They felt that she needed to find a job and could not be trusted with the money, so from then on she had to write to them whenever she needed money, saying exactly what she wanted to use it for and they in turn would attach conditions. They had thought this sensible although Angela had accused them of holding her to ransom. She said it was humiliating and that they had never truly given her a single thing in her life that wasn't attached to conditions. This outraged them. Lady Morton then recited to me a well-rehearsed list of things she had given Angela, all of which had been hurled back at her. The only thing missing from her list was love.

In the midst of all this I learned about Lord Morton's neck. Angela had taken exception to her father's hunting and shooting. She had begged him not to shoot for sport but he was not going to break a family tradition that went back two centuries. One day when the hunters were scattered around the wood stalking deer, she had tried to sabotage the hunt by throwing herself in front of their guns. Her father was so furious that he charged after her, forgetting that the rifle he was carrying was loaded and cocked. As he ran he let the gun swing on its strap and it finished pointing upwards. He managed to grab hold of her and in the ensuing struggle the gun went off into his neck. He showed me the neat hole where the bullet had entered, severed a muscle and emerged the other side, missing his spinal cord by less than a centimetre. He could have been killed or at least paralysed, but he had to be grateful that the only lasting injury was that he could no longer lift his head. Of course he had never been able to hunt again. She had come to his bedside in hospital and said she was sorry; she hadn't meant for him to get hurt. It was the only time she had shown any remorse. She had said she loved him, but he was too angry to hear it and told her he never wanted to see her again.

'I regret saying that now, but you must understand I was livid at the time,' Lord Morton said.

There followed a couple of years in which they only communicated by mail and even then only to discuss the payment of bills. Then one day they received news that she had been held in custody overnight for a protest that had got out of hand at the site of a new bypass in Shropshire. They hired a private investigator to snoop on her. They learnt that she was donating large sums of money to what they believed was an extreme breakaway group of anti-capitalist climate campaigners. Over one two-month period £30,000 had been transferred from her bank to a Swiss account. This was the last straw. Lord and Lady Morton had cut her off completely, refusing to pay a single penny towards her upkeep. That was nearly two years ago and there had been no contact between them ever since.

'What are we to think? The minute she has to fend for herself she throws herself in front of a bus to make us feel sorry for her. It is deeply distressing. If we come running now and give her more money then she will think that this kind of over-dramatic behaviour pays', Lady Morton said firmly.

'What are you proposing, Mary?' Lord Morton asked.

'We have to see this through. We decided to break her financial dependency on us and we can't give in at the first hurdle. She has to find her own way. Otherwise she'll never grow up.'

'Is this really about money?' I heard myself say with new-found courage. 'Is that what she needs right now? I respect your desire for her to be independent and I'm sure, in time, she will too, but I have one question for you. Are you cutting her off emotionally as well as financially? Because that's how it looks.'

'I'm not here to be lectured, young man. You have no idea what we have been through.' A faint ripple of anger forced itself through the botox.

'No, I don't, but I do know that in the course of this whole conversation, you haven't said one nice thing about your daughter and frankly, I'm shocked. I understand that there is a pattern of behaviour that you don't approve of and that it is reasonable to assume that she will continue to despise you but what if you surprised her? What if you broke the pattern and did something she didn't expect?'

'Like what?' she said angrily.

'You could come and see her and bring some flowers and tell her that you love her. Surely that would cheer her up?'

'I'm afraid our presence would have the opposite effect,' Lord Morton tried to assure me.

'Well, you know best. If you think ignoring her is good for her then I have nothing more to say. I'm sorry to have bothered you,' I said bitterly.

'I will not be spoken to like this in my own home,' said Lady Morton as she rose to her feet and stormed to the door. 'Come on Tom, this meeting is over.'

Lord Morton watched his wife leave and then slowly stood up.

'I'm afraid there are no more buses back to Norwich at this hour, or trains to London for that matter. Harvey will take you into town. You'll have to find a hotel.'

He plodded to the mantelpiece with his head lolling on to his chest and rang a bell. Then, somewhat formally, he held out his hand. I accepted it politely, though his skin was as cold as a frozen paving stone.

'Good night,' he said and made his way to the rear door. Then he turned back to me, and tried to lift his head to meet my eyes. 'Thank you for coming to tell us. I appreciate that you want to smooth things over but it's not your business and you are going about it the wrong way. Angela has always been out of control. There is nothing we can do for her. It's in her own hands.' He sighed heavily and then, almost as an afterthought, he said, 'Sometimes I think we're under a curse.'

He rolled his head heavily from side to side like it was on a ball and chain and wearily left the room. I was alone. I noticed the tension in my shoulders. Everything about the Mortons oppressed me. No wonder Angela had been so miserable.

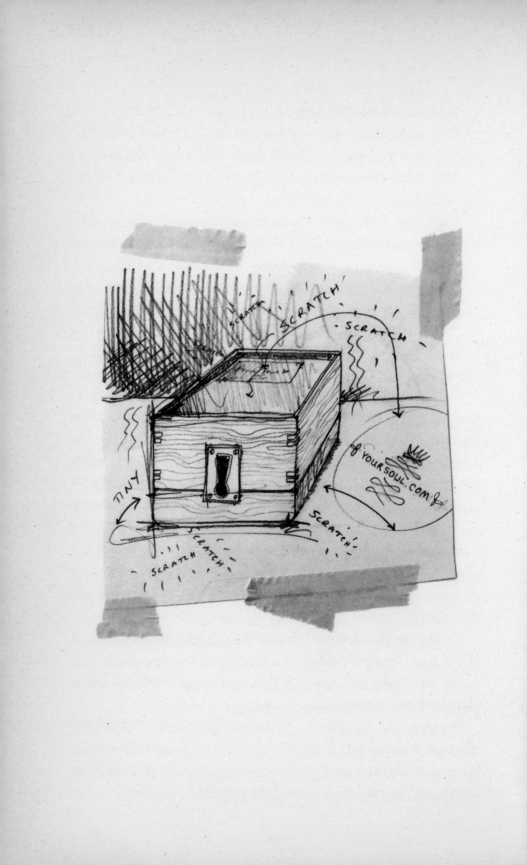

CHAPTER 6

Harvey slowly led me back through the house; it was as if he were walking the wrong way along a conveyor belt, so slow was our progress. We lumbered down corridors lined with faded paintings of the house in its former days; plodded through a giant kitchen with two Aga ovens, four sinks and a wasteland of pamment floor tiles; trudged through a wide arched door into a cobbled yard where he got momentarily waylaid in the eddies of an invisible cross-wind before finally we reached a garage.

'Sorry to make you come out here, sir, I'd put her away for the night.'

Inside the garage was a gleaming black Daimler that looked as if it had been polished until it hurt.

As we drove through the moonless countryside I asked Harvey if he enjoyed working for the Mortons.

Harvey stared at me keenly through the mirror and for a moment I wondered if perhaps I shouldn't have put him on the spot. Then in a quiet voice he said, 'No, sir,' and, somewhat unexpectedly, his face cracked into a broad smile.

'Why's that?' I asked.

'Because they are horrible people. Mean, arrogant, pompous. Specially lady. She is worse than a pack of hyenas, that one.'

The stuffy butler was dissolving before my eyes.

'Should you be saying this in front of me?'

'Well, you asked, didn't you?'

'Yes I suppose I did.'

'Besides, everyone knows in these parts what they're like. There isn't any one that'll say different.'

'Did you know Angela?' I asked.

He nodded and his eyes twinkled fondly. 'I did, sir, she was ...'

'Please don't call me sir. My name is Josh.'

'Oh right ... Josh ... well, I knew Angela very well. She was the only one that would talk to me normally, like I wasn't a servant. I don't mind being a servant, that's my job, isn't it, but they have a way of talking to you, like you don't have a heart. You know what I'm saying?'

I nodded.

'I was happy when she came back from school in the holidays. She'd help me round the house and we'd have a right laugh. Lord and Lady weren't best pleased about it but she'd sneak off and find me. Sometimes, when she was angry with them, she'd come to my cottage in the grounds and hide from them. One time she was at my place for three days. They were going spare looking for her. They sent me all round the county and I didn't say a word. All the while she was eating their food and living on their grounds. It was me and her against the rest of them. And she's as beautiful as they come, isn't she, Josh? I mean you don't come across many girls as lovely as her. I used to tell her that all the time, that she was lovely and I think she liked that, you know. I could see her spirits lift when I said it. When she was here I'd do everything I could to cheer her up. I got two daughters now and I loved her like my own.'

'What about her brothers?' I asked.

'Masters of the Universe, those two. One's a Tory MP and the other is a diplomat in South America. They were alright, said please and thank you. I did most everything for those boys. Washed their shoes, cleaned their pants, drove them around, and they were OK. They had their friends and they got on with it – never really bothered with me. I don't think they ever got to know me, not like Angela. Me and her, we'd go fishing together, play cards, she'd sit down with me and my wife at our dinner table and eat with us. I used to say she was a pearl amongst swine. I don't want to pry, but would you mind telling me how she is and what happened to her?'

When I told him that she had tried to commit suicide, he was distraught. His eyes overflowed. For a full five minutes he blubbered uncontrollably, before he was able to master himself and say he wasn't surprised it had turned out this way. He wanted to know in every detail about the moments immediately preceding her stepping out in front of the bus, the exact nature of her injuries and when she would come round. I told him as much as I could including how I felt about her. I explained what her parents had told me and that they had decided against seeing her. Harvey shook his head in anger.

'It's not right, is it?' he muttered. 'She gave their money away on principle – not because she was irresponsible. Besides, a good chunk of it came to me.'

'What do you mean?' I asked.

'A few years ago, one of my daughters, Lily, fell seriously ill. She'd been having difficulty breathing, kept getting bronchitis and it was getting worse and worse. She were nine. Doctors didn't know what it was. They did loads of tests and eventually they said she had a rare lung disease and there weren't nothing they could do. They said one day the tubes might close up and she could die. Well, that was when we discovered that there was this doctor in Switzerland that had pioneered some new surgery and cured a couple of people that had had this condition. But it would've cost us an arm and a leg. Lord and Lady knew about it but they weren't going to pay, were they – in fairness, I didn't ask them for the money but they didn't offer it neither. When Angela found out, she offered to pay all the fees from her own money. The whole lot. It were a lot of money but it did the trick, Lily is right as rain now. Angela never asked for it back, but I been saving up 'cos I wanted to give it back. I tried already last year but she wouldn't have none of it.'

'How much was it?'

'The hospital bill was £30,000. I've saved up 4k so far. So I haven't even touched the edges of what I owe her.'

I almost choked when I heard this number. Their private investigator had been wrong about her funding an environmental group.

'Did Lord and Lady Morton ever know about it?'

'No, she told me not to tell them. And don't you, neither.'

I shook my head, I would never say a word.

We drifted into the outskirts of Norwich, crossing the outer ring road and turning on to the inner towards the train station.

'Lord Morton said they were under a curse. What do you think, Harvey?'

He thought long and hard about this. 'Well, I'm not sure what you mean by curse but I would say that they probably deserve some bad luck. Going back to Lady's father – he was the lord of the manor before her – I heard he was a piece of work. There were lots of stories about him.'

'Like what?' I asked.

'Like his little peccadilloes. With the girls. They said he got a taste for it when he was with the army out in India. He was a general and the story was he was sent home after he raped some girls out there. Young'uns. He was never tried for it, the army kept it hush. In those days the officers did what they wanted, but it got out of hand, he was like a bear what's got a taste for killing, and it was better to bring him back where there were less temptations and they could keep an eye on him. All this is hearsay, mind. I don't know how many girls he did that to out there nor what he did to them but I do know what he's done here. Apart from the prostitutes that he was bringing in, there was one serving girl that he took a shine to, he was messing with her for a couple of years. In the end he paid a huge amount of money to keep her quiet. Maybe he did get cursed out in India – who knows – maybe the female line is destined to be miserable. Misery has many colours. Lady and Angela are miserable in very different ways but they are both miserable.'

'What happened to the general?' I asked.

'He died of syphilis in the fifties. He could have been cured. They had penicillin but the story goes that the doctor misdiagnosed him on purpose. He wanted to see him die a horrible slow death. And he did. The old man had lumps and boils all over his body. They say he died in agony.'

'Why did the doctor do that?'

'Revenge. Rumour had it that the old general had touched up the doc's daughter. Some say he attacked her but she fought him off. Back then it was hard to do a man for attempted rape. It would have been his word against hers and she were only twelve. Who was going to believe her? Besides the old fellow played golf with the Lord Chief Justice. It was a lost cause and the doc didn't want to put his girl through the whole court thing. So he kept his mouth shut and bided his time. Then when the opportunity arose he did what he had to do. They said the general was howling and screaming by the end and every day the doctor came and gave him useless pills and potions until at last the bastard died. No one wept for him except Lady. She can't have been more than a few years old.'

I felt sorry for her. I'd never thought I might have something in common with Lady Morton. I too knew what it was to lose a father. There was a stuckness about the Mortons. They were like a pair of rusty old radiators that had never been topped up, the same stagnant water was swilling round and round at the bottom.

We had arrived at the station. I thanked Harvey and we exchanged numbers. He promised he would come up to London to visit Angela as soon as he had a couple of days off. I watched as the black Daimler left the car park and wondered what I was going to do. The next train was at 6am. I couldn't afford a hotel. I would have to wait at the station. I decided to kill time by wandering into town. It was 10.30pm; it wouldn't be too late to call my mother. I felt bad that she was still expecting me.

'Hi Mum, it's me Josh ... I know ... I'm sorry I didn't make it today. Maybe I'll catch up with you tomorrow ... No, I'm not at home ...'. I wondered when I would have the strength to tell her I no longer had a home. 'I'm in Norwich ... Don't ask ... No, it's not for a job ... I'm sure I'll find a job soon ... don't worry ... I know it's hard, you don't have to tell me that ... Jodie Foster? ... Yes ... interweb? What did you do that for? ... Oh God, I wish I'd never given you that computer ... Well, what did you think was going to happen if you googled lesbian? Well, don't click on the pictures if you don't like them ... Oh

God, Mum you're driving me nuts with this stuff, please just leave it alone ... No, I don't care, the point is she left me, that's what hurts, it makes no difference to me who she's with, she's not with me anymore and that's that and I've got to live with it ... You're not helping, Mum ... Listen, you know that thing you wanted to tell me? Why don't you just tell me ... What do you mean, it has to do with Dad? Just tell me ... OK, OK, we'll discuss it when I see you ... I don't know when that will be, I'm kind of busy right now. I'm helping a friend who's in hospital and I'm not sure when I'll be ... No, you don't know her. I'll be in touch soon ... I promise ... I'm with someone. I've got to go. Bye ... No, I can't come tomorrow ... I'll call. Love you, bye.'

I felt unsettled and slumped to the ground, wondering quite what my mother had to say so urgently about my dad after all these years. I was brought to my senses by a faint scratching sound. I looked around. The street was deserted. There it went again, the tiniest of sounds. It was coming from very close by. I brought my head towards it and realised that it was coming from my jacket pocket. In a frenzy I yanked it off and threw it to the ground. Then I remembered that I'd put the box I'd found in the café in that pocket. The scratching continued. My mind flapped for an explanation. Was it a toy with a random sound generator? The kind of thing that one might find in a joke shop that sneezes and farts unexpectedly. I inched towards the jacket and got down on all fours. Gingerly I pulled open the pocket and peered inside. The sound came a little louder now. Something was definitely inside that box. I pulled it out carefully and placed it on the palm of my hand. The scraping suddenly stopped as if whatever was in there was now aware of my presence. I examined the inscription on the base of the box: yoursoul.com. I took out my phone and googled it. A sky blue screen popped up with the words *Sorry, this site is currently under reconstruction* emblazoned across the middle. I didn't even have time to exit the page before my phone lost power.

With a sigh of resignation I put the phone and the box back in my pocket and wandered on. I found myself outside a cinema; the lights were still on. There was a late show on – some French film. I'd missed the first twenty minutes. I looked in through the door, there was no one in the box office. I sneaked in quietly. I could see a guy through an archway clearing tables in the café. I ghosted past and up the stairs. Better to kill an hour or two in the cinema than sit in the station. The film was a study on the solitude of childhood. It was about some kid who was shunted about from his school, to clubs, to piano lessons and from his grandparents to babysitters whilst his busy single mum tried to earn a crust and build a relationship with a new man. It had no beginning and no end. And, in the fashion that only a French filmmaker is allowed to get away with, it was relentlessly depressing, not because the child had a bad life but because the child had all the manifestations of a good life. He was a sweet kid, he always did his best to please the adults around him, but he spent all his life being told what to do, where to go and how to behave. He only saw his mum in hurried snatches in the frantic school run, or club drop off or at bed time. His life was full but emotionally barren. Occasionally a red balloon drifted playfully into shot and the kid would look up at it longingly, but it always remained tantalisingly out of reach.

I stayed until the end of the credit roll. It must have been some time after midnight. The film had got under my skin, thrown me back into the darker days of my childhood and left me feeling melancholic. I sunk into my seat and stared at the black screen, for a moment I was alone in the room.

I began to think about the day my father died. He was a man who liked to get to the top and bottom of things, a keen climber and caver. We spent all our holidays following him from hill to hole. I have an image of me and Mum walking with him along a valley to the entrance of a cave. He looked like an alien with his green wetsuit on, waddling down the road. We came to a fissure in the rock and there were three men, also dressed as aliens in yellow helmets, waiting for him. He picked me up and enveloped me in his colossal, neoprene-coated arms. I asked if I could go with them and he laughed and said one day when I was bigger. I switched his helmet light on and off a few times. He gave me a big kiss and set me down. There was a dark ominous rectangular cleft in the rock in front of which was a large hole. At the bottom of this hole was a metal grille like the cover on a wishing well. A metal ladder had been bolted to the sides of the hole to facilitate access. One of the men climbed down, opened the grille with a key and disappeared inside. The others followed him down until all I could see was the tiny lights on their helmets. My father was last down. He closed the grille over his head and looked up at us, smiling. 'See you at dinner time,' he said and descended into the shadows.

We went back to the cottage that we had rented and played in the garden. It began to rain. Just drizzle at first but it soon developed in to a proper downpour. Mum said it wasn't meant to rain until the evening. She went on about it all day. As the afternoon drew in, a black storm cloud billowed over the hill and descended into the valley. We had to turn the lights on in the cottage. The rain was thrumming on the roof, cascading over the edges of the drains and thumping on to the paving stones. Then, for a moment, everything lit up and before I could ask Mum if it was lightning, there was an ear-splitting crack of thunder and the pounding on the roof grew even stronger. The water seemed to be falling in slabs. My mum was growing agitated and I sensed that it wasn't the storm she was worrying about but my dad. I thought he would be fine because he once told me that when he was in a cave he had no idea what was happening above ground. I don't suppose he cared.

We had dinner on our own. That was when I began to understand that something might be wrong because he said he'd be back and he wasn't. Mum said she had to make a phone call; there was no phone in the cottage, so she went out in the rain to the phone box across the road. I watched her through the window. When she came back she said it was bedtime but I wasn't tired. I wanted to see Daddy. We had an argument about it and I started to cry. She wouldn't back down so I went to bed in tears and lay awake listening to the rain. I heard a knock at the door. I got up and came to the top of the stairs. I thought it was going to be Dad but a soggy policeman was standing there. He said something about informing the caving club and a rescue mission. None of the men had come home yet. I called down the stairs and asked Mum if Dad was alright. She turned round and there were tears streaming down her face. She told me to go back to bed and this time I didn't dare argue with her. I can't remember if I drifted off or not, but some time later there was another knock on the door. I snuck from my bed and edged my way to the top of the stairs again. It was the same policeman but this time he was with one of the men I had seen go down the cave with my dad. The caver looked bedraggled and exhausted. I couldn't understand why this man had come to the cottage without my dad. Had he left him underground? Why hadn't he brought him home? I decided to hate him.

The two men came in and Mum took them into the living room and shut the door. I could hear them talking but I couldn't hear what they were saying. Then suddenly there was a piercing yowl. I had never heard a sound quite like it before. It was barely human. It came from the living room. I hurried back to bed. In the morning Dad still wasn't home. Mum had shrivelled to half her size, like someone had removed her bones in the night. Her eyes were red and empty. She told me the others had all got out alive. There had been a sudden build-up of water in the cave and as they were navigating a narrow passage a terrific surge of water had gushed towards them, filling the entire cavity and sending rocks and debris crashing down towards them. One of the survivors said my father was hit by something and lost his grip. He was washed away along the subterranean riverbed. The other three had managed to pull themselves through the sump to an opening where they could breathe and they clambered up to a higher passage. They waited for my father to appear but, when he didn't show, used the last of their strength to haul themselves out of the cave and fetch help.

For the next couple of days we hung around waiting for him to return. Rescue parties with divers from the local caving club scoured the cave system but conditions were treacherous. There are over thirty miles of passageways in that network and there was only so much they could do. He had disappeared without trace, not a single thing was recovered. Eventually we gave up the search and we returned home without him. I went to school but I still expected him to come home one day. There was no funeral, no service to commemorate his life, nothing. One day I began to cry at school for no reason. The same the next day and the next and every day after that for a hundred days or more. I couldn't stop crying. I was learning to read at the time and every story I read had mums and dads in them, there were dads at the school gate, there were dads in breakfast cereal commercials there were dads everywhere. The world was full of dads. Everyone had a dad except me.

Then, as suddenly as I had begun crying, I stopped crying. I dried up like an African riverbed in a drought. I had cried every last tear and since that day I have hardly felt a thing.

I got up from my seat and headed towards the exit but when I got there the door was locked.

'Hello!' I shouted. 'Hello, I'm still in here!'

There was no response. I banged against the door but no one came. I was locked in.

CHAPTER 7

I sat down in one of the cinema seats. I was exhausted. I let my eyes close. My heart was heavy with the day's bizarre events. More had happened in this one day than had happened in my entire life and I still didn't know how everything was going to turn out. It was as if that single kiss with Angela had catapulted me into another universe. All I wanted was to save Angela from herself but perhaps this masked a much deeper want – to wake myself up to a new way of living, to start over with love and passion as my guiding lights. The encounter with her parents had made me aware that, just as they had tried to suppress Angela's spirit with the imposition of rules and norms, I had quietly been doing the same to myself for many years. Perhaps there is a Lord and Lady Morton lurking like the enemy inside all our heads, stopping us from being free, telling us we are not good enough, judging our every mistake, filling us with fear.

Even when Angela did come round, how could I help her? I had nowhere to take her. I didn't even know where I was going to spend my next night. I would have to come clean with my mother, tell her that I had been repossessed and then humiliate myself by asking if I could stay with her, but the thought of going back there filled me with dread. Everything was just how it had been on the day I left home in 1994. My mum hadn't changed a thing. The bed was always made, the poster of Pamela Anderson in *Baywatch* was still on the wall. There was the Arsenal scarf and the school desk with the old fashioned inkwell I had inherited from my father – nothing had moved. The minute I walked through the door, she would hold me in her arms and hug me as if I were little again, as if all it took was Mummy's cuddle to make me forget the hurt and then she would ask me about lesbians. No. The thought of going home was not attractive. Not at all.

I fell into a fitful sleep. I dreamt about Sir Frank Godley and his huge salary, his huge pension, his huge bonus, his huge number of shares and his many huge houses around the world. Because of him I had lost my job, my home and, arguably, my wife. He was standing pompously on a plinth in Trafalgar Square. His pose was one of self-importance and grandeur, his head raised up in haughty disdain, his eyes set on the horizon beyond concern, his lips clamped tightly shut like a miser's purse. He could have been Field Marshal Haig who, from the comfort of a chateau many miles behind the front line, needlessly sent millions to their deaths in the battles of Passchendaele and the Somme in the First World War and who was later immortalised by a statue in Whitehall. Godley was being similarly rewarded for his 'contribution' to society. Except unlike Haig, Godley's victims were not dead and a rabid mob surrounded the plinth baying for him to be brought down and lynched. I was there at the front, salivating in fury. Never in my waking moments had I displayed this kind of anger, but in the shadow of night my true feral self had been unleashed. Godley didn't move an inch from his adopted pose. The square was packed full of the dispossessed, the homeless, the unemployed, junkies and prostitutes in a seething mass that demanded to be heard. They bore clubs and knives and they pushed against each other, jostling to get closer. From nowhere, Pontius Pilate appeared on the balcony of the National Portrait Gallery and, hearing the clamour of the people, ostentatiously condemned Godley, to death with a downward gesture of his thumb. There was a hush and all eyes turned to me. Apparently I had been appointed to crucify him. I hadn't realised it until that moment but I was carrying a tool kit. I was hoisted onto the plinth by the crowd. Godley bristled with arrogance; he showed not an atom of remorse. I searched through my tool kit for the longest and rustiest spikes I could find. A cross magically appeared behind Godley, and with my trusty hammer – the same one I had used to hang pictures in my living room – I proceeded to bash the spikes through his wrists and ankles. The crowd screamed with satisfaction as I smashed through his bone into the wood and blood leaked onto his pinstripe suit and dripped on to the floor. Godley looked down on me as if none of this made the slightest bit of difference to him, and he laughed unrepentantly. 'You have immortalised me. Now I am Jesus.' This enraged me so I smacked my hammer into his cosmetically enhanced white teeth a few times, but it didn't stop him from laughing.

A great fire had been lit in the middle of the square. The crowd hauled Godley down from the cross and I saw that a far greater torture had been devised for him. From my tool box, I pulled out a six foot-long white hot poker. It was like my favourite moment from *Mary Poppins* when Julie Andrews pulls a very tall lamp from a very small bag. The universe was in that bag. The mob were pecking at Godley, pulling off his clothes like vultures. I brandished the poker in front of him. 'Will you apologise for what you have done?' Godley smiled at me again, his teeth had grown back and he pulled out a prepared statement: 'I have not broken the law. All pensions and bonuses were set by the NBS remunerations committee ... '

A voice from the crowd shouted, 'And who is on the remunerations committee, you bastard?'

Sir Frank ignored this question and continued with his statement. 'They are part of a legally binding contract and I am entitled to receive them. I too have lost my job as Chief Executive of the National Bank of Scotland and have received compensation for my dismissal. This is the norm in the banking world and I do not see why anyone should be surprised by it.'

'Where's my fucking compensation?' someone yelled.

'I didn't get ten million quid for losing my job, you cunt,' chimed in another.

Delay was pointless. It seemed nothing would make Sir Frank see the error of his ways and, in that way that dreams have of making extreme things appear normal, I realised that the time had come to eat him. I pushed the poker up his rectum, busting through his intestines and stomach wall up into his oesophagus and out of his mouth. We hoisted him on to the fire and watched with glee as his skin began to blister and bubble in the flames. We turned him over and over in the fire until he was burnt pink like a spit roast pig. The hordes surged forward. A group of men grabbed the poker and flung Godley on to the ground. The mob dived on top of him like a pack of starving wolves and hacked him to pieces with their knives and axes; some sunk their teeth into his thighs and stomach. Chunks of flesh flew up into the sky, to be caught and eaten by whoever could get to them first. The rabble tore through him in minutes until all that remained was a bloody carcass and a few pieces of gristle. And yet, somehow I knew he was still laughing at me because nothing we did to him was going to make our lives any better.

All night I tortured Frank Godley without success. He was like a mythical beast that can never be slain. Whenever I thought I had killed him he came back stronger. There was nothing I could do to bring him down. I awoke battle-weary and upset. I was shocked by the violence of the dream, but perhaps more shocking was the depth of my anger, somewhere at the very core of me was a well of emotion that never saw day.

I remembered that I had to get to the train station, and I didn't want to be found in the morning by some unsuspecting cleaner, so I went back to the exit door and tried without success to force it open. Then it occurred to me that in a room that size, there would have to be at least one other fire exit. Hugging up against the wall, I walked down the ramp towards the screen until I had reached the bottom step. There I found a fire door and pushed down on the bar to open it. I had hoped it would open on to the street but I found myself in total blackness. I stretched out my arms in front of me and I could ascertain by the proximity of the wall that I was in some kind of corridor. Suddenly the fire door crashed shut behind me. I wheeled round, found the handle and pulled it. The door was locked. I yanked on it harder but it wouldn't budge. I began to feel scared. I fumbled along the walls trying to find a light switch. I ventured further and further into the darkness, feeling my way. The corridor seemed to go on forever. At last I felt a doorframe. The door had to lead somewhere, but again it was locked. I found a key hole with my fingers, it was large like a Chubb lock. I had two Chubb keys on my key ring – perhaps one would fit. I thrust my hands into my pockets and only then did I remember that I had given them to the bailiff that morning. I cursed out loud and punched the door.

I carried on inching down the corridor, probing the walls with my fingers. Suddenly the floor disappeared beneath my feet and I found myself falling head first down a staircase. I bounced down the steps, my limbs flailing hopelessly like a crash dummy in an impact survey until I reached the bottom with a thud and my head smacked into a large metallic object that was leaning against the wall at the foot of the stairs. I felt shooting pains in my wrists and neck as if someone had pierced them with a needle. I lay there groaning a moment, rubbing the bruises on my back and thighs. In my dazed state I became aware of the nose-scrubbing stench of bleach emanating from the rubber floor. It was the odour of my youth.

My nose for bleach is as a dog's snout for urine. Just as a dog can tell how long it's been since the last bitch passed by from sniffing her urine on a tree, so I can tell how long ago bleach has been applied and in what concentration. I learnt this from my mother. She would return home in a haze of bleach that wafted from her clothes and percolated through the flat. Her hands were desiccated and cracked from constant exposure to abrasive materials. As a teenager this would embarrass me and I was forever asking her to hide them away in public. I guessed the bleach was fresh that evening, applied with a rotten mop because it stank like the plastic wrapping on a stale cheese.

Something trickled down my temple and into my eye. I was bleeding from the head. I got to my feet and tried to get my bearings. I felt a draught of cold air to my right. I put out my hands and found another fire door with a horizontal push bar on it. I pressed it down but the door met with some resistance. I heard a woman cry out in surprise, followed by a man's voice similarly shocked. A couple were having sex up against the door.

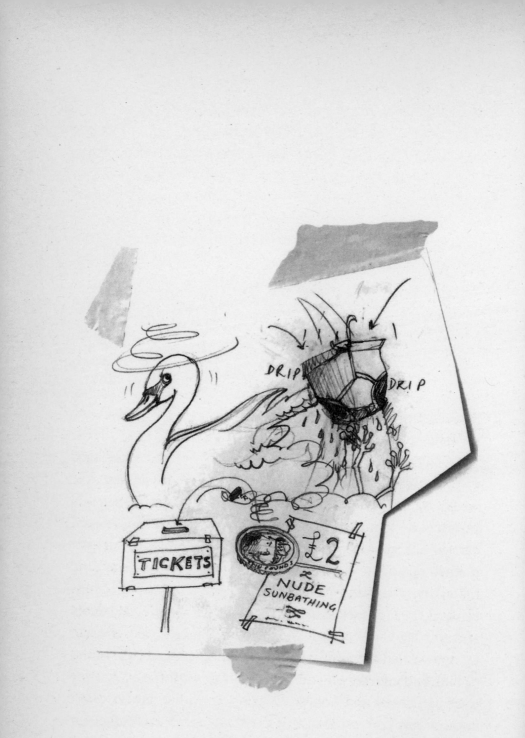

CHAPTER 8

'Excuse me,' I said, 'I need to get out.'

'Jesus,' the man grunted.

I could feel them shuffling along the door and I managed to poke my head through and slip out into an alleyway. The weight of their bodies closed the door behind me. They paid no attention to me at all but merely rearranged themselves and carried on. She was pressed up against the door with her skirt hitched up and he was piling into her with his trousers around his ankles. They were at a critical moment; if they stopped now all would be lost. I felt something soft underfoot. I looked down and saw that I had caught my foot in her knickers. I kicked them off and walked away, although I could not help but turn round to look at the lovers one more time before I left the alley. They were as natural and honest as two dogs in the park. I didn't know if they had just met or if they had known each other for years but these people desperately needed to make love and it couldn't wait. They didn't care who was watching or where they were; their desire was irresistible. They were magnificent.

I wanted to applaud them. I couldn't remember the last time I had made love like that. Sheryl had never abandoned herself to me in this way. Our love-making from the outset was tender and careful but never wild. It took place in bedrooms at the end of the evening or occasionally in the morning before work. We did not vary from the positions that came easily, neither of us ever risked a pulled muscle, a bruise or a graze during sex and yet I never felt dissatisfied with our love-making. In hindsight perhaps I should have recognised that she was never fully engaged. She rarely initiated sex but equally rarely did she spurn it. Despite her passivity I felt secure in our relationship. It may not have been dynamic but it was always comfortable. A wave of nostalgia washed over me. I was shattered. I wanted to go home – to *my* home, to *my* wife.

It was still early when I arrived at Liverpool Street station. The first waves of city workers were beginning to drift into their offices before the full onslaught of rush hour. Visiting hours at the hospital were still some time away. I was not in a good state; Angela's parents had left me with a bitter taste in my mouth and my head was throbbing with fatigue. Something had happened on the train that had left me shaken. The man I had seen in the hospital, the elegant man with the notebook who I thought must have been an administrator, was sitting a couple of seats behind me in the carriage; the same notepad open on the table, the same sympathetic half-smile on his lips. Halfway through the journey he passed me on the way to the toilet and on his return we nodded at each other in polite recognition. His eyes darted up to take in the cut on my forehead and he looked at me curiously before regaining his seat. I tried to persuade myself that it was one of those strange coincidences that happen all the time. Although in my fevered imagination I couldn't help but think that he was following me. It was not inconceivable, from the little I knew about Angela, that she had fallen foul of the law – what with her history of civil disobedience. She was involved with extremists. She had called herself a terrorist. Hadn't she even mentioned that she was sometimes followed? Perhaps this man was a police officer or worked for Special Branch. For the rest of the journey I imagined those eyes poring over my back and I studiously refused to turn round. Once on the platform, I began to run and managed to lose him in the crowd.

I jumped on the 214 bus. My body was aching from the fall. I felt like I was held together by bruises. I got off by Hampstead Heath and found myself on a park bench overlooking a pond. The morning sun shone gold over the water. It was unnaturally hot for the early hour and my skin prickled with sweat. My attention was drawn to a squawking above me. A green parakeet had emerged from a tiny hole in the trunk of a nearby beech tree and appeared to be communicating with another parakeet perched at the end of a branch. I marvelled at how these beautiful creatures had managed to escape their cages and find love in the park. They sidled up to each other and, in silent agreement, swooped down together over the pond to disappear into the arms of a towering oak.

A middle-aged woman in a beige jogging suit, beige trainers and a matching beige face devoid of make-up, walked by with two bouncy cocker spaniels. Her peroxide blonde hair, the only part of her that was not beige, was coiffed up into a beehive so it looked like a scoop of vanilla ice cream in a cone. One of the spaniels came bounding over to sniff me out. I put out my hand so it could lick me.

'Are you alright?' the lady asked.

'Fine yes, I've had a bit of a long night.'

'You should get that seen to.' She gestured to my forehead.

'Oh it's nothing,' I said, feeling for the gash on my temple, 'just a scratch. I fell down some stairs.'

She looked at me suspiciously. 'There's a lot of blood for a scratch.'

'It must look worse than it is.'

'It's all over your clothes,' she said.

'I know.' I looked down at where the top of my bomber jacket and shirt was stained with blood.

'I'd get that seen to,' she said again.

'Thank you, I will.'

The lady smiled weakly and trotted off in a vanilla beige haze with her dogs in tow. I remembered that I was close to the Men's Pond where male swimmers are allowed to plunge into the algae-filled water at their own risk. I had been there once many years ago. I don't much enjoy swimming but I wanted to wash before I saw Angela so I walked along the path towards the entrance. The pond was surrounded by trees and thick bushes on three sides and was all but hidden from the rest of the Heath. There was a ticket machine at the entrance asking for a voluntary two pounds to help with the upkeep of the pond. There was no one there so I ignored it and walked in. A sign which read 'Nude Sunbathing' pointed off left to a small rectangular paved area, bordered by a shoulder height wooden fence. I peered over it. Three young men lay naked on the concrete like oily seals catching the early morning rays. Given the natural beauty of the setting, this man-made slab looked grim and unappealing. The men were laughing at something. One of them sported a semi-erection with shaved genitals. He threw me an insouciant glance. I turned to the right where there was an open-air changing area with long wooden benches and hooks. I stripped down to my underpants and headed towards the pond, which was empty but for one muscular bald-headed man ploughing through the water with a powerful, sloping crawl. I walked down the wooden jetty to the diving board, took one bounce and plunged in. It was cold. A jolt akin to an electric charge snapped through me and my body tingled.

I was swept away in a shot of optimism. It was the first time in months that I had been able to rise above the domestic pressures of my demise. I trod water for a moment and took in the glory of my surroundings. A family of swans were paddling majestically through the middle of the cordoned-off swimming area and I watched as a heron glided over the trees to land on top of its finely constructed nest, which appeared to be floating a couple of metres in from the water's edge, but must have been built on a platform that was placed there for that very purpose. It had caught a frog for its young, and three tiny beaks appeared from nowhere and fought over the frog even as it hung from their mother's mouth.

I swam lazily towards the nest. Today was the birth of all possibility. My life was empty of clutter, I had no responsibilities, no obligations. It was as open as the sky. Could I ever be freer than I was at that moment, swimming towards a heron's nest in a pond on the Heath? Above me the whole universe was watching, marvelling at our little planet that had miraculously spawned life in all its variety. And there was I, a little piece of life bobbing on the surface of a pool of liquid in the middle of a green and bushy paradise and I could go wherever I wanted to go, do whatever I wanted to do, there was no end to it all. Today I could be someone new. I wanted to cry.

I swam suspended in this bubble of hope for an hour or so before I emerged as hungry as a hyena from the water. I made my way back to the changing area. There was only one shower and the bald swimmer was soaping off in it.

'Is it hot?' I asked.

'No,' he said, 'it's actually colder than the pond.'

I laughed. A sudden breeze caught me, and I shuddered. I went over to my clothes, took off my wet pants and began to dry myself off with the inside of my jacket. I felt a presence behind me. It was the bald man – he was wringing out his trunks into the drain.

'Do you need a towel?' he asked.

'No it's fine, I'll dry off.'

'Why don't you borrow mine?' he said.

'No, really, then you'd have a soggy towel.'

'It's already soggy, and I'm dry.' He pulled it from around his waist, and threw it towards me. 'Here, take it, I don't mind.'

'Thank you, but I couldn't.' I handed it back.

I noticed his eyes wander downwards, checking out the size of my penis. I was marginally better endowed than he was.

'Hey,' he said, 'do you fancy going into the trees with me?'

I looked at his well-toned body. Could I do this with a man? Is this what had happened to Sheryl? One day, in a moment of vulnerability, had a beautiful woman propositioned her? What had she seen that could turn her away from me and from men in general? What had changed?

She had told me that it had nothing to do with sexuality and that all she wanted was love. It didn't matter where it came from. She said that after seven years of marriage, she realised that I would never love her. I was bewildered. I thought that I did love her, but she told me I didn't know what love was and nor did she until then. Our relationship was nothing but a shadow of love, a pale imitation. Sure we got on well, we didn't argue, we had built a home, but it was passionless, it was a limp rag-doll of a relationship. It was bland and featureless like endless fenland. There were no contours, no soaring rock faces, no waterfalls, no plunging valleys, there was nowhere to go that wasn't like everywhere else. It was tedious, monotonous and unexciting. She couldn't bear the idea that she would live another fifty years and there wouldn't be a single surprise – not even on her birthday or at Christmas (I always asked her what she wanted and bought it). I was incapable of doing anything unconventional or unusual, I was a conservative with a small c, a conformist, a total bore. I asked her why she had married me and she said because I was nice. Nice! Can there be a more damning word? Nice, reliable, trustworthy. I was a safe pair of hands. Steady. An even keel. The marrying sort. But in the end she had discovered that I was dull, dull, dull.

She said all these things the day she left.

I looked at the bald man. Here was an opportunity to prove Sheryl wrong. I could go and experience something I had never experienced before, do something daring, outrageous, brave even. Supposing she was right and I was incapable of love, I still had physical needs. What difference does it make who we have sex with after love is removed from the equation? Once the act is reduced to the simple mechanics of the orgasm gender becomes irrelevant. Strangers – men and women in any combination – can meet in hotels or parks and wordlessly fornicate until their bodies are relieved of sexual tension, then disappear into the night never to meet again. I was dead to myself. Heart cleaved from body. I hadn't had sex for a very long time.

'Alright,' I said.

I got dressed quietly. My underpants were wet so I left

them on a hook. He led me towards a clump of dense trees in a quiet part of the heath. He seemed to know exactly where he was going. The sun was still a few hours from its zenith but it was already stifling, I felt a trickle of sweat roll down from my armpits as we ploughed a furrow through a sward of long grass, no words between us, only our heavy breathing and the swish of our feet. We passed into the shade of the trees and weaved our way into the undergrowth until we were alone. A solitary cricket chirruped enthusiastically. My heart was thumping against my ribs. The man loosened his belt and let his trousers drop to the ground. I looked dispiritedly at the bulge in his pants. My body began to shake involuntarily.

'I've changed my mind,' I said. 'I don't want to do this.'

The man smiled. 'First time?' he asked. 'Don't worry, I'll be gentle.'

'No. I can't. I'm only here because my wife did it.'

'Did what?'

'It doesn't matter. The point is I don't want to.'

He took hold of my arm and tugged me forcibly towards him.

'Come on,' he said, 'it will be OK. You've got this far.'

'Look, I'm not gay.'

'Nor am I,' he grinned. 'I've got a wife and baby. This is just a bit of fun.'

I tried to pull away. 'No, thank you.'

His grip strengthened.

It amazes me sometimes how I remain civil, even when I am being evicted from my home or a strange man is trying to bugger me in the woods. I am neither outraged, nor offended, I am nothing more than polite. Perhaps this is what frustrated Sheryl, I can't seem to get worked up about anything.

'I appreciate your interest, but I really have to go now.'

He let go and I set off at a swift pace away from the scene, leaving the man to deal with his bulge by himself. I was starving. I hadn't eaten since yesterday morning. I found a cheap workers café by Archway tube. The menu board boasted a full English breakfast with tea for £3.80. I sat down by the window and ordered. When it arrived it looked more like a crime against humanity than a breakfast. The sausage had the look of an over-barbecued dog's dick. The bacon was like the sweaty insole from a fat man's shoe. The beans, which had been microwaved to extinction, had crawled to the edge of the plate looking for an escape route. The mushrooms looked as if they had been picked in 1974 and left at the back of the fridge to shrivel and die a thousand deaths and the bread was starched as white as an albino rat. The tomato looked good though. So I ate it first and then ate the rest regardless.

It was 11am and I crossed the road and farted up the hill to the hospital.

The stench of fresh bleach was stronger than ever. The neon lights still buzzed wastefully even though the sun was streaming through the windows at the far end of the ward. The excess of light did little to brighten up the ward, rather it highlighted the drabness of the curtains, the dullness of the brown and white floor tiles and the cracks in the cream walls.

When I got to Angela's bedside she was still asleep, her broken leg on a pile of cushions. The only thing that had changed was that now there was a man at her bedside. The tattoo of a mottled green snake with a red tongue was crawling out of his shirt and up his neck. He had three ear piercings in his left ear and a nose stud. A strip of dyed blond hair was sleeping on his head like a Mohican taking a nap.

'Hello,' I said, 'I'm Josh. And you are?'

The man looked at me angrily. 'Angela's boyfriend. Who the fuck are you?'

CHAPTER 9

It hadn't even crossed my mind that Angela might have a boyfriend.

'I am nobody really,' I said meekly.

'They told me you brought her in – pretending to be her boyfriend.'

'I'm not pretending to be anyone. I just happened to be there when she tried to kill herself,' I stammered.

'Thanks for your help. Now clear off,' he snapped.

'Well, actually, I don't want to clear off. I'd like to be here when she wakes up.' I sat down in a plastic chair at the foot of the bed.

'I need to talk to her in private. I've got some business to settle with her,' he insisted.

'Oh, right, well, when she comes round I'll just … I'll just, you know … see if she's OK and then I'll leave you in peace.'

He shrugged his shoulders in irritation. There was a long silence.

'So,' I said at length, 'what's your name?'

He glowered at me, and puckered up his lips. 'Mikey.' He might as well have spat in my face.

'Oh. Mikey. Hmm.'

There was another brooding silence.

'And how long have you been with Angela?' I asked.

'Jesus, you're a fucking chatterbox, aren't you?'

He turned away. He must have had a lot on his mind. He was upset about his girlfriend. For this I could forgive him everything, even though I had invested my last flicker of hope in her and I felt jealous and forlorn.

I noticed the tail end of a skull and crossbones bandanna hanging from his pocket and a chill went down my spine.

'Weren't you at the NBS building yesterday?'

'I don't know what you're talking about,' he snarled.

'The demonstration ... I saw you.'

'How do you know about that?' he asked guardedly.

'I was there.'

'With us?'

'Er ... yes ... sort of.'

He glared at me suspiciously. 'I've not seen you around.'

'I came because of Angela.'

'A lot of people come because of her.'

'Do they? Why?'

'I guess they see something in her that they want for themselves. It's not the cause; it's her they're interested in. Anyway, how come you brought her in – who are you?' he barked.

'I was repossessed on the same day. I live round the corner. It was a chance meeting. We went for a coffee and we'd been there about ten minutes when she got up and walked into the road. It was strange because there was no indication of what she was about to do ... she ate a pastry and then she ... '

'And then she what?'

'Nothing ... ' I said, pulling back from the revelation that she had kissed me. 'She tried to kill herself. I don't know why she did it.'

'Angela needs to believe she can make a difference. I think she stopped believing. She began to feel useless. She's had crises of faith before – it's not the first time I've had to ring around the hospitals trying to track her down – but obviously nothing like this.'

'Did she talk to you about it?'

'No, she didn't. Christ. Look, if you really want to know, we had a fucking argument two days ago. A great big mother of a bust up, OK?'

'Oh, I'm sorry to hear that,' I said, and the tiny flame of hope burst back into life like a trick candle on a child's birthday cake. 'So is it over between you?'

'I don't know. It is now. I can't believe she did this to me.'

'Did what to you?'

'Tried to top herself to get at me.'

'You think she tried to kill herself because of you?'

'Look, do me a favour and fuck off. You've done your good deed, OK? Thank you for helping. Goodbye.'

I stood up, not sure what to do. I felt like a baby deer in the sights of a tiger. One wrong move and he would tear me in two.

'Maybe I'll come back later, shall I?'

'That really won't be necessary. Thank you. Goodbye, Josh.'

Frustrated by my cowardice, I backed out of the ward and unwittingly fell into the arms of the 'administrator' at the doorway. I almost jumped out of my skin.

'Hello,' he said in a serene voice.

'Oh hello,' I said nervously.

91

'Hello,' he said again. There was an awkward silence as we waited to see who would break it first. After a moment I realised he had no intention of saying anything more.

'Are you following me?' I joked.

He raised an eyebrow and grinned.

'You know the answer to that question.'

My throat went dry. There was something about this man that scared and attracted me in equal measure. His manner was gentle, almost fatherly, his dark eyes shone with compassion but his unwavering gaze, his self-confidence was profoundly unnerving and he smelt of something acrid which I couldn't place. Perhaps he wanted information about Angela but I wasn't going to wait around to find out. I barged past him and the next thing I knew I was running as fast as I could down the corridor to the stairs. I hurtled down them two at a time until I was through the foyer and out of the building.

When at last I had caught my breath on the street I tried to take stock of the situation. I was now convinced the administrator was following me because of my association with Angela. He must have mistaken me for Mikey or one of her violent colleagues for until that moment my life was utterly blameless. I had never broken the law or even received so much as a parking ticket. Perhaps he wanted the box. Could there be something in it that was of interest to the police? Some evidence of some crime or misdemeanour of which I was unaware? I reached inside my pocket and rolled it over in my fingers.

I wondered why the man wasn't more furtive in his pursuit; indeed, I think he wanted me to know he was there. He was waiting for me to come to him. Perhaps he wanted me to spy for him and pass on any information I could glean about the cell that Mikey and Angela were part of. Would this explain his apparent benevolent attitude towards me?

After long reflection, I resolved never to go back to the hospital. Not because I feared this enigmatic gentleman, but because I was wasting my time; deluding myself that Angela would love me when she came round. Ours was a fantasy relationship. It was based on nothing. I felt ridiculous for investing in her. I wandered the streets aimlessly, too tired to think any more. I was delirious with exhaustion.

I realised that I was only a few minutes away from the storage facility that housed all my furniture on Holloway Road; maybe I could sneak in and sleep there. I made my way towards it.

It was a purpose-built, four-storey, modern warehouse containing several hundred metal units of varying sizes. My lock-up was one of the smaller ones on the second floor. I opened it up and a wall of heat engulfed me. Everything was there, just as I had left it the week before. My marital bed, our two-seat sofa and armchair from Leatherland and a few cupboards and shelves from Ikea. Leaning against the wall was my old bike and on the bed there were some twenty boxes filled with kitchenware, books and CDs. I shifted the boxes on to the floor, pulled closed the squeaky metal door and lay down on the bed.

And so began a new phase in my descent. For a week I lived inside my tin. Every night at 11pm, I crossed the road to the local supermarket and rummaged through their rubbish, picking out sandwiches, fruit and vegetables that had passed their sell-by date. I had no means of charging my phone and although I was aware that it would be invisibly accumulating messages from my anxious mother, I could not face the thought of speaking to her. Each night I slept less than the night before, tossing and turning in the unnatural heat of the airless container, until I could not sleep at all. I thought obsessively about Angela. She was like a cracked vase that miraculously still held together. It would take only the slightest knock to break her once and for all. I worried about her more than it was my place to and yet I stuck doggedly to my resolve not to visit her. For comfort, I found some photos of my mum and I in happier times and put them around my bed. As my exhaustion deepened the pictures danced around my head and every morning I would find them somewhere different, absent-mindedly rearranged in the swelling madness of my fatigue.

Halfway through the week my days and nights switched over entirely. I began to spend the nights re-reading old books by torchlight or chatting with the Sudanese security guard who I had befriended and who very kindly turned a blind eye to my comings and goings. He had known hardship in his life, and did not have it in his heart to report me. During the day I would nap in one of the parks that surrounded the hospital but I was often awoken by dogs and children.

One day I scaled the railings at the bottom of Chester Road into Highgate Cemetery. The cemetery sees few visitors in the daytime. It is wild with trees and dense undergrowth. There are a couple of gravel paths that are lined with the tombs of the more famous occupants but most of the graves are hidden and inaccessible, swamped under sprawling bushes and creepers. I could lose myself in the overgrown pathways and thickets and find myself a resting place where I would not be disturbed by anyone. Here at last I might find some peace of mind.

There was no one around, I climbed hastily over the railings and jumped into the bushes and soon stumbled across the giant bust of Karl Marx. There was a bunch of freshly cut roses in a grey stone urn next to the inscription and all around were the graves of Eastern European communists who had used their ill-gotten gains to buy a berth near the great man. No doubt a heated discussion about the distribution of wealth was taking place at that very moment beneath my feet. I found a small grassy path beyond the noisy Bolshevik quarter and headed off into the cool calm shadows.

The deeper I ventured, the more the path became snagged in nettles and brambles. I veered off towards a small glade, which had selfishly stolen a pool of delicious sunlight for itself. A couple of bright yellow butterflies, enjoying their brief life, were flitting through the rays. Two lopsided gravestones with faded eulogies were leaning towards each other as in furtive conversation. A fine dressing of moss and ivy clung to their weathered stone. Between these graves was a narrow bed of thick grass. I stretched out on the green bed and joined the corpses in sleep.

I awoke to the click of a camera. A woman had crept into the glade and was taking pictures of me surreptitiously.

'I'm sorry,' she said when she saw that I had opened my eyes, 'I didn't mean to wake you.'

A trail of dribble had formed a tiny rivulet from the corner of my mouth to the top of my neck just below my left earlobe. I wiped it away and blinked hard as my eyes adapted to the light.

The woman was in her late forties and had short-cropped grey brown hair which revealed two sticky-out pixie-like ears. Her mouth slanted ever so slightly downwards like a painting that had not been hung straight, her eyes angled inwards as if staring at each other to see who would blink first and her nose seemed to arc left as if avoiding an invisible obstacle. She was a living Picasso, and despite her extraordinary lack of facial symmetry she wasn't remotely ugly, for she had the labyrinthine beauty of crazy-paving in a Japanese garden or the beguiling charm of an Almodóvar heroine.

'I hope you don't mind. I'm doing a photographic project,' she said.

I pulled myself to sitting and wiped away the memory of the dribble from my cheek.

'What on?' I asked.

'Famous London cemeteries.'

'Oh, can I see?' I said pointing to her camera.

'The ones of you?' she asked.

I nodded.

'OK, let me find you some good ones.' She scrolled through her pictures. 'Here, I like this one.'

At first glance I saw that I was nothing more than a fuzzy blob in the centre of the picture. The tombstones were in sharp focus but, like a tuning fork that has just been twanged, I looked as if I was in several places at once. I had two distinct heads and one of them was laughing and although I was bathed in an impossibly bright light there was an eerie darkness around me. One had the impression that the graves had opened and I was rising from the dead. There were two distinct Joshs in the picture and I didn't know which one had made it back into the real world.

'Wow. How did you do that?'

'It's two exposures superimposed,' she said, smiling a slanty smile.

'But my face is completely different. It's like I'm schizophrenic or something.'

'I know, you were laughing in your sleep.'

'Was I?'

She nodded. 'I don't think I would have found you if I hadn't heard you. What were you dreaming about?'

96

'I don't remember. Oh yes, wait a minute … my dad, I was dreaming about my dad. He was calling my name … I'm not sure why I was laughing. God, I haven't dreamt about him for ages. It's coming back; we were in an outdoor swimming pool, he was throwing me in the air. I was looking down at his outstretched arms, my knees were tucked up to my chest. Water was pouring on to him. I must have been four years old. We were both laughing. Then he was gone and I couldn't find him but he was calling my name over and over like I was lost but it was him who was lost. Wait a minute … '

I rooted around in my jacket and pulled out my wallet. 'Here's a picture of him.' I handed her the laminated picture of my dad that had been languishing in my wallet for years. She held it next to the image of me in the camera.

'You look just like him.'

I inspected the two pictures. 'Yes, don't I? It's funny, I've always thought of him as older than me, but now I've caught up with him.'

'What do you mean?' she asked.

'He died when I was six so in this picture he's probably 31 or 32. It's never occurred to me before but pretty soon I'll be older than him.'

'That's a strange thought. Maybe this dream was some kind of visitation. Do you think he was trying to tell you something?'

'I don't know. It could mean anything. Could you send me a copy of your photo?'

'Sure, give me your email address.'

I told her and she wrote it down on a piece of tissue and folded it into her pocket.

'So who is your project for?' I asked.

'It's not a commission. It's for me primarily. If it turns out well I'll try and get a gallery or a magazine to take it.'

'How did you get into photographing cemeteries?' I asked.

'One day I was sitting in a graveyard, and I had the strange feeling that the people wandering down the pathways and kneeling at the gravesides were not real people at all, but corpses who were tired of being cooped up underground. I realised that if I photographed them in a certain way I could capture this on camera. By focusing on the headstones and leaving the camera on long exposure I would capture the traces and blurred outlines of these people as they wandered around the graveyard. I don't normally put them at the centre of my pictures, leaving them at the peripherals like forgotten people, but I put you smack bang in the middle. I've seen people sleeping on benches before but not like this in the undergrowth – between two graves. I was completely spooked when I saw you. I still am if I'm honest, you could easily be a ghost.'

Her facial features appeared to undergo a tectonic shift, creating new angles and perspectives. She was staring at me intently.

'I wouldn't rule anything out,' I said equivocally. I had the uncomfortable impression that the me that had gone to sleep was not the me that had woken up. Sleep had washed away the detritus in my mind like the incoming tide swallows rubbish on a beach. All the imprints of human activity – the digging, the mounds, the moats and the footprints – had been smoothed over and I felt new. Different.

'Let's walk back up to the path?' I suggested.

'Sure,' she said, folding away her tripod. 'I think I'm done for the day anyway. By the way, I'm Laura.'

'And I'm Josh.'

We waded through some bushes back on to the path and headed to the exit.

'Why were you hanging around in graveyards in the first place?' I asked.

'My partner died.'

'Oh I'm sorry. Recently?

'Last year. He was only forty-eight. I had only been with him just over a year, but I had been in love with him for thirty years before we even had sex.'

'Really? That's a long time to wait for a shag.'

She laughed. 'It's a long story. Shall we go for a coffee? I owe you for the photographs.'

We wandered into Highgate and found a café in the village. When we were settled, Laura with a macchiato and me with an Earl Grey tea and lemon drizzle cake, she resumed her tale.

'When I was in my final year at school I was introduced to a guy at a friend's party. He was terribly handsome but, unlike so many good-looking men, he seemed to have no self-confidence. I was used to the odd guy hitting on me but there was nothing about his demeanour that showed he was the slightest bit interested in me. Strange though it may seem, I found this attractive. He was earnest and gentle and although he was undoubtedly intelligent, he spoke with a strong working class East End accent which in my narrow-minded teenage years I equated with poor education. My mum and dad were lawyers and I would have been punished for talking like him. Any prejudice was soon brushed aside and we began to see a lot of each other. His name was Roger Kerry and he was the loveliest person I ever met. His father was a refuse collector who had ruptured a disc in his spine and was on sickness benefit. His mother worked as a barmaid. They lived in a council flat in Hackney and the one time I went to meet them I was scared to walk down the street. He was always broke and hated going out because I would have to pay and he found it embarrassing. It didn't bother me at all but it pained him greatly that he couldn't pay his way. He was happier to meet in parks or wander around markets than hang out in bars so that's mostly what we did. One day we were mooching around Camden when he stopped in his tracks and said there was something he had wanted to tell me for months but had been too frightened. He couldn't bear it any longer. Then in the tiniest, most apologetic voice he told me he loved me. Of course I was delighted because I was so terribly in love with him. I flung my arms around him and I kissed him and, can you believe it, Josh, he actually burst into tears. All those pent-up feelings came pouring out of him. We did nothing but kiss for weeks. We had nowhere to go to take it further. Nowhere we were allowed to spend the night together. We built up a torrent of suppressed desire.

'I didn't talk much to my parents about boyfriends – not because I was scared to, more because I was immature and didn't think they would understand me, but they guessed I was seeing someone so I told them about Roger. My mum seemed genuinely excited and said I must invite him round, which I did. They did that typical middle class thing of cooking a lovely dinner. I was mortified because I knew where he was from and how intimidating it would seem. I was paranoid about appearing posh. The mainstays of our dining table – the crystal decanter of red wine, the Italian pepper grinder, the plaited beeswax candle, the stuffed olives screaming for attention in their hand-painted designer bowl – suddenly seemed vulgar and showy. There were two sets of knives and forks by each plate and he looked at them disconsolately, not knowing which ones to use first. My mother clocked his anxiety and explained that one always starts from the outside and moves in. I watched him shrink before my eyes. When he spoke, his cockney accent sounded dreadfully out of place. No one but repairmen and gardeners spoke like that in our home. The evening slipped into stilted formality. I was blushing with embarrassment. The conversation staggered along like a decrepit old dog and in the presence of my parents I forgot why I loved him and saw only that we were different.

'When Roger left, my dad put his hand on my shoulder and said he was a very nice boy but not for me.

'"You can do much better than that, darling," my mum added.

'Perhaps they were right. What did I know? I was eighteen. The evening had gone so badly and I was confused. I just wished Roger had a job and a bit of money, then things might have been different, but I had to admit, albeit reluctantly, that his prospects were poor. I had plenty of time – I would surely find someone more suitable. The next day I broke his heart and ended the relationship. I told him my parents didn't approve, which was cowardly of me, and he surprised me by declaring that they were right. He said I was wasting my time with him and that I would find someone much better who would love me and be my equal like he never could. His humility was as admirable as it was misplaced, for in truth I wasn't worthy of him.

'I never did find anyone better. I spent the rest of my life regretting what I did. I thought about him often, but after the way I treated him I never dared to track him down.'

Laura shook her head and stared dolefully into her coffee.

'How did you find each other again?'

'That's a story in itself,' she smiled. 'My parents moved house and then I met an Australian and went to live in Sydney. We got married and ten years later we got divorced. I came back to England, had a few relationships here and there, some lasted longer than others. And then one day I switched on the television and there he was – Roger Kerry – a self-made millionaire talking about a huge donation he had made to a spine disease charity. He'd set up a recycling business a few years before the idea of recycling had entered the national consciousness and had capitalised on the interest in it. He was as handsome as ever. Suddenly all that pent-up desire came flooding back.'

'After so long,' I said, pouring myself a cup of stewed tea from the pot.

'I know. It surprised me too. I hadn't seen the guy for twenty years. I mean, he was long gone. It only took seeing him once to trigger all those feelings again. Maybe he really was the guy for me, but then why would he be interested in me? After all, he was now a millionaire and I was nothing.

'Seven or eight years later, I decided to set up as a freelance photographer. I got a little website off the ground, showing my work, and I put a cute self-portrait on the home page. One day I got a call from a lady who wanted to know if I would consider doing a brochure for an ethical beauty product business. I told her that it wasn't really my bag; I was more landscapes and portraiture and besides I wasn't particularly good at graphics, but she insisted, saying that they wanted the brochure to be full of photos and that I had come highly recommended by her boss. I took the job and as you've probably guessed, the boss turned out to be Roger Kerry.

'He invited me to his home. He lived in a mansion in Surrey with a swimming pool and an orchard. I was so nervous that day, but he quickly put me at ease. He was as charming and unassuming as ever. He was very keen to show me around his house. I wondered if he hadn't invited me as some kind of revenge to show me how far he had come. At the end of the tour he showed me his bedroom. It was a magnificent room overlooking the lawns and then I saw a small framed photograph next to his bed. "Take a look," he said. I sat on the bed and picked it up. It was a picture of the two of us aged eighteen, his arm proudly around my shoulder. That was why he had invited me: to show me that I had never left his bedside. He had spent his whole life working his guts out so that he would never feel that shame again. He said he'd been trying to find me for many years. He had no idea I was in Australia. With the advent of the internet he would occasionally google my name without any luck. It was only when I started using my maiden name again that he found me.'

'And you immediately got together?'

'Yes. I wasn't about to let him go a second time.'

'How did he die?' I asked.

Her eyes turned down and a dark shadow fell across her face. 'You're an amazing listener, aren't you, Josh? That's rare in a man. For six months we were like two teenagers in love. Then we began to take things for granted, we moved in together and grew a little more domesticated. One day we were out shopping and we had a huge argument. I was angry because I thought he was spending too much time at work and he was always travelling. We hardly saw enough of each other. I felt like I was the least of his priorities and I accused him of being obsessed with money. He objected and we had a stand up row in Bond Street. He was in the middle of telling me that I was a hypocrite because I had rejected him when he was penniless and come running now that he was rich, when he suddenly keeled over backwards and died. It was terrible ... so unexpected. A huge crowd of people gathered round to watch. At first I thought he had fainted but his body hadn't gone limp, it was hard like a plank. He was having some kind of seizure. I screamed at someone to call an ambulance but within a minute he was dead. The worst part of it was that in the heat of this argument I remember thinking, "I wish you were dead, and I'd never met you." I didn't say it but I thought it.'

Laura sighed deeply and her eyes swivelled upwards as if she were still apologising for what she had done.

'Everyone thinks things like that in an argument. It was a coincidence. You mustn't blame yourself for it,' I said sympathetically.

'I know but you can't help thinking ... I mean he was fit ... never had any health problems before that ... it came from nowhere. We lost twenty-five years, we were so lucky to get another chance. I loved him madly and then I made a fuss over a stupid thing like that.'

'But it's normal to have concerns like that,' I said.

'I know. I try not to beat myself up about it, but now I can't help but be superstitious about what I wish for. When he was young I wished him wealthy and when he was wealthy I wished him dead. Regret is a corrosive beast. I don't know if I'll ever get over it.'

'I know how you feel, Laura.'

My mind was turning to my own regrets, and as one confession draws another, I was reminded of the story of Miranda Wilks, a story I had replayed a thousand times but never told.

'I fell in love once ... '

So began my tragic tale ...

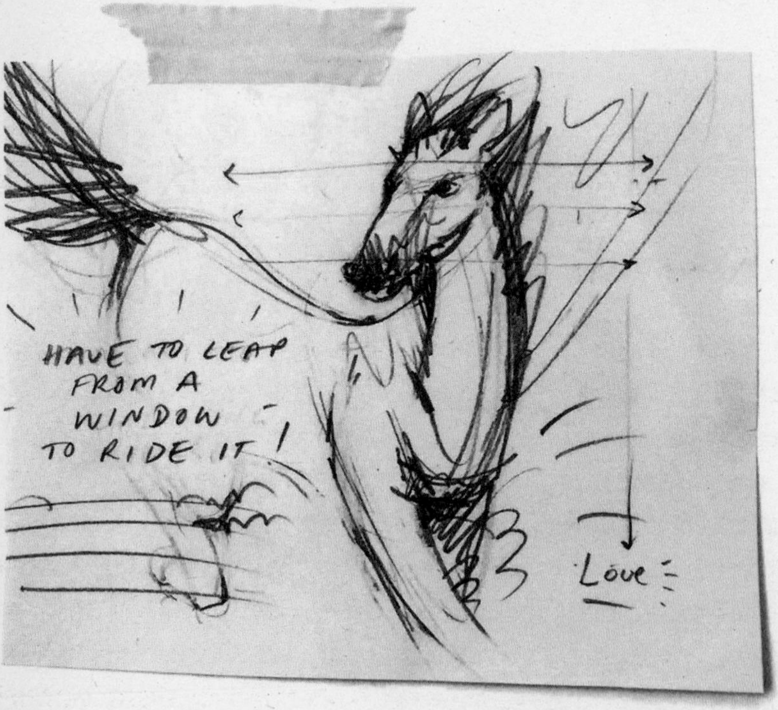
HAVE TO LEAP
FROM A
WINDOW
TO RIDE IT!
Love

CHAPTER 10

The first time I saw Miranda it was 5.28 pm on the 20th June 2000. I know this because every day I used to catch the 5.28 train from Harlow Mill, where I worked, to Liverpool Street. It was a busy train and I didn't normally get a seat, but on that day, for some reason, there was one seat free. I sat down and there opposite me was this tall, elegant girl reading some printed notes. I could say she was beautiful but there are many beautiful women and none before or since have had a similar effect as this woman had on me. For the thirty-eight minutes that the train took to get to Liverpool Street station I felt almost dizzy with lust. When we arrived and the passengers poured on to the platform, I followed her as she strode towards the barriers. I wanted her to notice me but didn't quite have the courage to cross her eye line. She headed towards the tube and I watched her stride down the steps and disappear in the crowd.

The following day I found myself fussing over what to wear to work in case I saw her. I went to the same carriage but she wasn't there. All week I boarded the same carriage in a vain hope that she would be there. I'd pretty much given up hope when, exactly one week later, I saw her again in that very carriage in the same seat. This time there was nowhere for me to sit, so I stood in the aisle near her. Over a period of a month or so I worked out that she only took that train on a Tuesday. For several Tuesdays I stood near her, too embarrassed to say a word but secretly willing something to happen. Then one day she appeared to recognise me and she smiled at me in the polite way that you would to anyone you saw regularly.

Each week we smiled at each other and one day I noticed that, as the train was pulling to a standstill on the platform where I boarded, she lifted her head to seek me out. From that moment forth I felt a spark each time our eyes met. My heart would race and I'd spend the whole thirty-eight minutes in a self-conscious flurry. Neither of us had the courage to start a conversation; if anything, we made a play of nonchalance, pretending to have something to read, not wishing to make our interest too obvious. More often than not I stood by the door rather than give my feelings away by edging too close. Then one Tuesday I had to go to our office in Birmingham. I felt bereft that I would miss her but it acted as some kind of trigger, because the following Tuesday she was standing right by the door where I boarded and she greeted me with a broad smile. For thirty-eight wonderful minutes we talked. She was everything I had imagined: intelligent, flirtatious and witty. Each week from then on we chatted on the way back from work. One day she told me that she was changing jobs and would no longer be taking the 5.28 on a Tuesday evening. We only had one Tuesday left. That whole week I was anxious. I was terrified that this would be our last trip together. I was desperate to take her number or ask her out – anything so it wouldn't end. When the day came I made an extra-special effort to look good. At 5pm I put on aftershave, brushed my teeth and left work for the station. I waited on the platform in the evening sun. I was breathless when I heard the train approach; the story of my life would be shaped in the next thirty-eight minutes. As the train drew up to the platform I squirted some breath freshener into my mouth despite having only just brushed my teeth.

She was there, by the door as usual, wearing a flowery low-cut red dress which clung tightly to her curvaceous body like an exotic vine. My eyes landed on the milky white skin of her upper breasts and slid into her cleavage. A hint of lavender washed over me.

'Hello, Josh,' she said.

I blushed, quickly lifted my gaze like a rabbit breaking cover and smiled nervously. I saw that she too was nervous. I had prepared a speech and, if courage failed, a declaration. I had envisioned a delicate brush of the hands, a kiss, a hotel room, a seduction, and from there, a marriage, a family and a life of boundless love. I had gone to the end of the road. Yet, despite all this mental preparation I struggled to make conversation. I had the endgame but no opening gambit. The clock was ticking down. The stops at Harlow Town and Broxbourne came and went. We stood pressed against the door staring hopelessly at the suburban streets. In the reflection of the window I saw a pale, indistinct version of myself, crippled by my inability to act. I dared myself to break through the chronic passivity which blights my life. We drew into Cheshunt.

'So,' I ventured at last, 'are you excited about the new job?'

'Yes, yes, it's going to be terrific,' she said. 'I'll have a lot more responsibility than I have now.'

'Oh, that's good. You must be excited,' I said, relieved to have begun something.

'Yes, it's going to be exciting. I'll be doing a lot more chemistry in this place. They specialise in Prostaglandins. It's my ... my speciality,' she bumbled.

'Oh, that's exciting, and what exactly are Prostaglandins?'

I could have kicked myself. What was I talking about Prostaglandins for? Then she went into a long explanation about lipids and receptor sites in the body, cures for peptic ulcers and glaucomas and by the time we had finished we had passed Tottenham Hale. There were no more stops and we had nine minutes left. There was a painful two minute silence.

Eventually she said, 'Have you seen *Gladiator*?'

'Yes,' I replied. 'I loved that movie.'

'What about *Erin Brockovich*?' she asked.

'That was good too,' I said, 'but I preferred *Gladiator*.'

She asked me why and halfway through explaining I realised she hadn't seen either film. I wanted to die on the spot. I had just hurdled over two chances to invite her to the cinema. We talked pointlessly about movies until the train pulled into Liverpool Street station. We walked down the platform in silence. When we got to the entrance of the underground we looked at each other longingly and she said, 'Goodbye then.' She held out her hand and I shook it. 'Good luck, I hope it goes well,' I said. She smiled and said, 'Yes, well it was nice to have met you.'

I smiled back. 'And you,' I said.

For a second we stood staring at each other. This was it. Our last possible chance. We both knew it. A small eternity passed in a second. We were both rooted to the spot. The pregnant silence between us tipped into awkwardness and the magic evaporated. As one we both turned away. I felt her slope off down the steps. I headed into the concourse. I was choked.

I turned round but she was gone. There was nothing I could do so I went home.

'You never saw her again?' Laura asked.

'No.'

'You know, Josh, if I've learnt anything it's that love is like a horse that gallops past your window. You have to leap to catch hold of it. You might fall and hurt yourself, but if you don't jump you don't get to ride the horse. It doesn't come by very often.'

'I know. It's amazing how often I think about her.'

'In that case you should call her. What was her name again?'

'Miranda Wilks. I doubt she'll even remember me.'

We chatted a while longer until the conversation came to a natural end. Laura paid the bill and we walked out of the café together into a blaze of sunlight. 'Hey, would you like to come back to my place?' she asked.

Some days everyone wants to sleep with you. It happens once a year. You can feel ugly for months on end and then one morning your petals open and everyone wants to put you on their mantelpiece. You don't even know it's happened.

'No, thank you, there's some business I have to attend to but I'm so grateful for your story, it has got me thinking.'

Laura smiled sadly and her crooked face reorganised itself around her nose.

'You're a nice guy – for a ghost,' she laughed. 'Good luck, Josh.'

She gave me a peck on the cheek and wandered off up the hill. I turned back down Highgate Road and strode determinedly back towards the hospital. I could hear the sound of galloping hooves. I had to catch that horse, but when I got to Angela's bed it was empty.

CHAPTER 11

Had she been discharged? Had she died? My heart began to race. I ran back down the ward until I found a nurse.

'What happened to Angela?'

The nurse looked at me blankly.

'She was third on the right – in that bed there,' I said, pointing to the empty bed.

'Oh I'm afraid, there were some complications. She's in intensive care.'

'Oh Christ!' I gasped. 'What happened?'

'She never came round after the operation. She fell into a coma.'

'What?'

'Yesterday she had surgery to relieve a clot on her brain.'

'Can I see her?'

The nurse explained where I could find the critical care ward and I hurried off through the hospital in a breathless haze, a feeling of nausea mounting in the pit of my stomach.

*

I found her caught in a web of tubes, drips and leads which shot out from her nose, arms, chest and bladder to banks of monitors and bags of fluid.

A woman doctor approached the bed; she was in her fifties. Like everyone else in the hospital she looked tired, her face was creased and rumpled like a badly ironed shirt. Her lips were chewed up like old gum and her nose jutted out accusingly from a pair of metal rimmed spectacles which were pressed so firmly into her skull that her eyebrows sat on top of them like two hairy caterpillars. She looked like she hadn't smiled since the beginning of time.

'Is she going to be OK?' I asked.

'We found a sub-dural haematoma in the left hemisphere of her brain. It was creating a lot of pressure. We have removed the clot, and the scans show that the operation has done what it was meant to do. The trouble with these scans is that although they show us if there is a structural problem in the brain they don't tell us anything about the functioning of the brain. Until she comes round we can't really tell if it is has been a success. But we are optimistic, she is young and the odds are in her favour.'

There was too much uncertainty in the doctor's words for me to have faith in her optimism. To my eye, Angela looked like she was slipping away.

I waited for the doctor to leave and sat down dejectedly by the bed.

'Hi, it's me again.'

A depressing silence.

'Angela, I've got nothing in the world except you. Nothing. I'm almost embarrassed to say that – given I hardly know you – but it's true. You and me, we're like a couple of penguins that showed up at the South Pole at the wrong time of year. It's just the two of us in a wilderness of ice, we have to stick together.'

Silence.

'Come on, I need you, it's time to wake up.'

For some time I stroked her hand rhythmically in time to the peaks on the heart monitor. It was something to do. I found it comforting. Then her finger twitched. It took me by surprise.

'Was that you? Can you hear me?'

Another twitch.

'Is it nice where you are?'

Again she twitched.

'Oh good. Are you ready to wake up yet?'

I detected a little tremor.

'Was that a no? You're not ready? Well I've had a miserable week, I've spent most of it in a dark box with a few ornaments and pieces of furniture from my past. It was like living inside a rotting memory. I imagine that being in a coma is not dissimilar.'

Angela was floating just under the surface of the real world, unable to broach the impenetrable membrane between consciousness and subconsciousness. What if she was trying to communicate with me in the same way I was trying to communicate with her? Would we ever understand each other? We couldn't even hear each other. She spoke a language beyond logic. It was the language of sleep. She occupied a mosaic world built from broken pieces of memory and reality randomly reconfigured to constitute a dream from which she could not escape.

Was the dream she now found herself in more beautiful than the life she had tried to flee? Perhaps she was running free like a gazelle on green savannah. Is it a mistake to assume, in a rather imperialistic way, that the conscious world is superior to the subconscious? The ultimate goal of the medical profession is to bring the coma patient back to our world but what if we were to head in the other direction and try to enter the world of the coma? I wondered if I could establish, through the tiny twitches of her finger, what she was dreaming about.

I asked her if she would like to play twenty questions. The rules were that she could only respond yes or no to my questions and that she was not allowed to give me any clues. I began by trying to establish if she was on land, to which she responded that she was not. At length it became clear she was at sea, but that she was neither swimming nor in a boat or any other vessel I could care to name. At this point I nearly abandoned the game, half-convinced that I was reading far too much into what might have been merely random movement. Then I asked if she were flying and she seemed to respond that she was. To which I said triumphantly, 'So you are flying over a beautiful blue sea.'

She twitched twice in disagreement and I realised that I had introduced a new element that she had not agreed to. A green sea? Red? Yellow? It turned out to be orange.

She was flying over an orange sea.

How I longed to be with her, to leave the troubled land behind and fly into the eternal sunset of her dreams. To conquer gravity with love and glide on the eddies and currents of an orange wind. Greedily I asked her more questions, having long since passed the regulatory twenty, but there were no more responses. After a long pause I was filled with doubt. Had I constructed a fiction from the mechanical movements of her broken body? Might I have asked a wholly different set of questions and received the exact same sequence of twitches?

Either way, if I were going to pass the day with her, I might as well play such games to keep myself amused. In the spirit of the game I decided that it was now her turn, and she could now ask me questions and I would duly answer as best I could. I took hold of her right hand and tried to synchronise my breathing with hers. I imagined myself falling into her heart like a stone falling in a bottomless well. Faster and faster I fell, until through the darkness came light and a feeling of weightlessness.

Bizarrely, as I tried to open my being to the vibrations emanating from beyond the divide, the first thing I heard in my mind was the voice of my mother: 'I need you back home, Joshua.' She was worrying about me, crying and telling me stories about my childhood that I had long forgotten. What on earth was my mother doing down there? Nevertheless I decided to take this as a sign from Angela. She wanted to know about my mother. So I told her everything. How since the loss of my father – which became the subject of a long digression in itself – she had lost her courage like the lion in *The Wizard of Oz*. How I had grown to protect her and despise her in equal measure. And how at this very moment I found myself in a terrible moral dilemma as I had not been able to tell her the truth of my plight, because I knew it would upset her and make her ill with worry. The fact I was constantly hiding the truth from her in turn made me feel bad about myself for it was a form of cowardice, and not only did it deprive her of the opportunity to fulfil her protective role as a mother but it perpetuated a falsity between us which only exacerbated her anxiety when problems did arise. Now I had left her in a state of limbo because I had not contacted her once since I promised I would arrange a time to meet up.

I don't know how Angela received these musings in her world. Perhaps they were nothing more than ripples from which she had to intuit my meaning, rather as her twitches were for me. Nevertheless, once the subject of my mother had been fully explored I felt as if she were telling me to see my mother and tell her the truth of my situation.

I dived back down to meet her once more and was immediately confronted with the thorny issue of my wife. Sheryl. Again I heard Sheryl's voice; it was as if she were saying goodbye to me over and over again. I explained to Angela how we met and the relief I felt at being with someone, who on the surface at least, appeared to demonstrate an equanimity in her emotions that was in stark contrast to my mother. Sheryl was organised, efficient and above all rational. She was pretty, in an understated way, and she expressed her feelings in a calm restrained manner that I could handle without the inner turmoil inflicted on me by the matriarch. Only when she left me did I realise that she was horribly repressed, never natural, never free. Our marriage fell into a kind of tragic repetition of routine and ritual. And yet if she had not put a stop to it I would have spent my life with her. Angela then seemed to ask the question that I most asked myself. Did I love her?

'Love? I don't know. I liked her a lot. I liked her more than anyone else I had ever been out with. If I loved her I loved her rather as a drowning man loves the piece of wood to which he clings. When I was cut adrift, I floundered horribly and then I loved her all the more. Even now I hold her in high esteem because she gave me a structure and a modest aspiration of the nest building variety. The truth is I haven't recovered, even though I realise that what we had was as much based on fear as it was on love. It was only at the end that I discovered she was cheating on me and for all I know she could have been cheating on me for years.

'Was I faithful to her? Another good question. Yes and no. I don't know. It depends how you define faithful. I never touched another woman if that's what you mean. It's a long story, but I don't think either of us have anything else in the diary for today so I might as well tell it. It's a bit embarrassing and I hardly know you but I think secrets are safer shared with strangers than friends.

'It happened about four years into our relationship. We went through a period where we stopped having sex ... oh God, why am I telling you this ... anyway nothing in particular had happened, we just stopped having sex. It was almost imperceptible, we just slipped out of the routine of it. We never seemed to get round to it and then it was almost as if we had forgotten how to initiate it. I was kind of waiting for her to break the ice and she was waiting for me and for three or four months nothing happened. I didn't even notice until a couple of months had passed. Then one day it occurred to me that we hadn't had sex in ages. Nor had I had a single erection in the intervening period. This coincided with an inexplicable deterioration in my ability to control my bladder. I couldn't get through the night without going to the toilet. I began to wonder if I hadn't become middle-aged before my time. Maybe I had dried up.

'Round about that time there was a TV campaign about prostate cancer encouraging men to check for lumps on their testicles. I had never checked for lumps in my life and I became convinced that I did indeed have a lump on my left testicle, but I could not be sure because I had nothing to compare it with. I don't mean that I didn't have a right testicle to compare it with, I mean I had no idea if this lump had always been there or if, in fact, all left testicles had a lump there. I went to the doctor and complained that I was worried there was something wrong, and that perhaps this was the cause of my loss of libido and slight incontinence.

'It was an extremely embarrassing experience because it just so happened that, when I walked into his room at the appointed

119

time, there was a lady with him. She was about twenty-three years old and oddly, for one whose chosen profession should have taught her moderation, she was of a size that takes up two seats on the bus and can't fit through a turnstile. Before I had a chance to reveal my predicament the doctor explained that the lady, whose name was Miss Bullen, was a student doctor on placement for the day and would I mind if she sat in on our meeting. Given the nature of the problem, I didn't feel comfortable with this but I didn't have the courage to say so. The doctor said it was very important for her to learn what general practice was like, so I reluctantly agreed.

'My doctor is very professional and understanding. I must say I am quite fond of him, but Miss Bullen had probably never sat in front of a real patient and she was a little too eager for my liking. Her enormous buttocks were spilling over the edge of her flimsy wooden chair and I wondered if she hadn't put too much faith in it as she leant forward enthusiastically to listen to my complaint. I tried to ignore her and focus on the doctor as I explained the problem. He nodded sympathetically and asked me to lower my trousers and lie on the bed so he could examine my testicles. I unbuckled my trousers and did as requested whilst the doctor slipped on a pair of rubber gloves. The student stood up and followed him to the bed. I couldn't help notice the faintest of smiles cross her lips. This was the second appointment of the day and there she was in front of a young man – I was 29 at the time – who had just pulled his trousers down. It would make a great story at the university. The doctor carefully felt around my left testicle before comparing it with the other. I don't know why the presence of an observer should have made the situation more humiliating than it already was. Perhaps it was because the witnessing of this necessary yet strangely intimate moment between two men transformed it into something that felt perverse. The room was hot, a bead of sweat lined Miss Bullen's forehead. She edged closer to get a better view of the procedure. A flush of crimson crept into her cheeks. I was mortified. I wanted it to be over as quick as possible but the doctor took his time. Why hadn't I been honest from the outset and asked her to leave? Why am I always embarrassed to speak my mind?

'"Well," said the doctor, pulling off his rubber gloves and throwing them in the bin, "there's nothing to worry about; that little lump is perfectly normal. You don't have prostate cancer but you were wise to have it checked."

'Perhaps if he had found something I would have felt wise but now I felt like an idiot. I'd had my balls fondled for nothing. He said I might be suffering from stress or tiredness. It was true that I had been doing some overtime, but I had done overtime before and never felt a loss of libido. I dressed hastily and left. The whole experience left me feeling degraded and dissatisfied. I was convinced something was wrong with me but I didn't know what it was. I had to do something. I no longer felt attractive to women and I couldn't bear the thought that I had lost my sex appeal. I became obsessed with the idea of trying to seduce someone, not because I wanted to be unfaithful but because I needed to prove I could still do it.'

CHAPTER 12

'I started browsing through the dating pages in *Time Out* and found a sporty brunette with good sense of humour in her late twenties who wanted to meet a tall man with own hair for fun evenings out and possible relationship. Non-smoker.

'I responded. It was an aberration of character, a sign of how worried I must have been. We met up and went for dinner at Le Mercury in Islington. We had a few drinks and got on well. Of course I didn't tell her I was married but at no point during the evening did I get turned on. She was attractive enough and made me laugh but I wasn't aroused. All I wanted was one tiny erection and I would have been happy.

'I went on several more dates after this but none of the women gave me any physical sensation whatsoever. I became so desperate that I realised I would have to go further. I would have to get one of these women into the bedroom, and yet I still didn't wish to be unfaithful. So I called the lady with whom I thought I had the best chance – she was my third date – and we arranged to meet again. I flirted as best I could and managed to get an invite back to her flat. She was a yoga teacher called Greta from Germany. She had a terrific figure and long shoulder-length dark hair. According to her posting she enjoyed fell-walking, origami and crime fiction but all of this was by the by. When we got back to her place I was in no doubt that she wanted to sleep with me. Even with this thought in mind I was limp. After a coffee she pressed against me on the sofa and tried to kiss me. "Wait," I said, "not yet," and I gently pushed her back. I was thinking about Sheryl. I would never have been able to face her if I'd kissed another woman.

'"Let's go to the bedroom," I said.

Greta was impossibly attractive, her face was sculpted from alabaster, her eyes a delightful turquoise. She led me into her bedroom and jumped onto her bed, waiting for me to join her. "Let's do this differently," I said. She smiled gamely. "Take off your top," I said. Obediently she took off her shirt. "Now the skirt," she removed her skirt. "Stockings" – she unrolled her stockings. She was breathless with excitement but there was still no sign of my erection. She was wearing a red lacy bra and a thong. "Take them off." She unclasped her bra, threw it on to a chair and then slowly pulled down her knickers. I was desperate to make love to her. "Now it's your turn," she said. "Not yet," I insisted. My heart was thumping, I began to sweat, every pore of my body was aroused but still I couldn't get it up. What was wrong with me? "Open your legs." With toes pointed like a ballerina, she lifted her left leg high and stretched it up and outwards as if she were reaching for the light switch on the wall, then, with yogic control she unfolded her right leg to a similar angle. It was like the unveiling of a plaque at the grand opening of a new municipal building, a leisure centre or place of worship, but I may as well have been staring down the barrel of a gun, for even this seemed to provoke no response in me. By now I was fearful that I would never have another erection for the rest of my life. I stepped closer to the bed, she reached out to me but I asked her not to touch me, not to lay a single finger on me. For some reason this seemed to turn her on and she relaxed back on to the bed and awaited her next instruction. I told her to stretch out her arms like a starfish and close her eyes. I drew as close as I could without touching her, I probed every inch of her skin with my eyes, I let my warm breath breeze against her nipples, I brought my face to within a centimetre of her crotch and a sweet musk filled my nostrils. But still nothing. "Touch yourself," I said. She brought her hand down between her legs and began to gently massage her clitoris. I was burning with temptation but my penis was stubbornly inert. All I wanted was an erection, you understand, just a tiny erection, anything, but nothing came. She was breathing heavily, desperate for me to make love to her. It was intolerable, I had to get out of there. Without a word of explanation or apology, I turned on my heels and fled.

'It was only on the bus on the way home, the image of the gorgeous Greta tattooed to my eyelids, that I felt a shot between my legs like an injection. I had that erection for a whole week. Every time I thought about Greta I got hard. And I couldn't stop thinking about her. I was erect at the hairdressers, at work, in the supermarket. Everywhere I went I was having erections. It became quite painful after a while. Sheryl and I began to make love again and everything got back to normal.

'The next day I changed my mobile number. I never spoke to Greta again. Poor Greta, I never gave her any explanation. Nothing.

'I have often wondered whether this counted as infidelity. I think if I was Sheryl I would definitely say it was. She'd probably feel jealous and hurt and ask herself why she hadn't been able to arouse me. She might feel inadequate in comparison to the loose-limbed Greta. But on the other hand, everything I did, I did for Sheryl. I acted with a perverse sense of fidelity. I didn't touch Greta. The crime was in the mind and not in the body. In that respect you might say there were mitigating circumstances.

'I never told Sheryl about it, not even when we split up. I didn't want to complicate things. I guess that's the surest sign of guilt. I knew I'd done something wrong. Maybe if I'd told her she wouldn't have accused me of being so dull, although I'm sure she would have found other words. I've never spoken about this to anyone. You're the only one, Angela.'

I felt an approach behind me and was surprised to see Lord and Lady Morton being led towards us by a female doctor. They were dressed formally as if attending a state function. The grotesque figure of Lord Morton was clothed in a dark three-piece suit and I could just make out between his lolling head and waistcoat a navy tie with what might have been a school or university insignia beneath the knot. Lady Morton wore a floral dress which hung shapelessly from her neck as if it were held only by a coat hanger. Her expression, frozen in permanent surprise, a testimony to the surgeon's art. As a pair they would have made a fine exhibit at the London Dungeon; wax monstrosities to scare the children and give them nightmares.

Instinctively I stood up and backed away to allow the procession access to Angela. They registered my presence with the faintest of nods and drew up, one on either side of the bed. They stood in silence contemplating their daughter. Who knows what emotions and memories were stirring in their dark souls but I'm certain I saw the old man's lip tremble. The Lady did not blink, there was no movement other than the slow rise and fall of her throat as she swallowed once then twice then three times in quick succession.

'When will she come round?' Lord Morton inquired dolefully.

'We're a little concerned. We reduced the sedative to encourage her to wake up but it clearly hasn't worked,' said the doctor.

'What if she doesn't wake up?' Lady Morton asked.

'We will go for another scan later today to try to assess her brain activity,' answered the doctor.

'Could she die?' I heard myself whisper.

'Let's not get ahead of ourselves. We have every reason to hope she will come through.'

The Mortons continued quizzing the doctor about her chances of survival until at length she said: 'I'm afraid we can't guarantee that she won't die and if she doesn't die we can't guarantee the quality of her life.'

'Which means?' Lord Morton asked, swinging his head towards the doctor like a demolition ball.

'A possibility of permanent and severe brain damage, but I'm sure it won't come to this.'

From which all present could surmise that she wasn't sure at all.

The Mortons turned their attention back to their daughter and then something happened which I wasn't at all expecting. Lady Morton collapsed. It was like watching the fall of one of the Twin Towers. Her insides suddenly yielded and within a few moments all the pride and majesty of the edifice came tumbling down, almost as if there had been nothing holding her up in the first place, other than the collective imagination of those who feared her. The two hundred and six bones in this most unlikely of bipeds had finally realised the absurdity of stacking themselves on top of each other in order to elevate the heaviest bone of all to the highest point. And with the buckling of her knees came a high pitched gurgle from the back of her throat which sounded like the hasty exit of a demon through her windpipe.

I managed to catch her before she hit the floor. The doctor grabbed a chair and we tried to sit her down, but she slid off it like a runny egg and we had to allow her to sit on the floor while I knelt behind her and held her up between her arms. Her faint was only momentary. She came round and looked at me in bewilderment. We brought her back to the chair and then she began to cry uncontrollably.

'What have we done? What have we done to you?' she sobbed.

Lord Morton hurriedly drew the curtains around the bed and asked the doctor and I to let them be alone as a family.

Lady Morton's sorrow made me realise that I had behaved selfishly with my own mum. I felt guilty that I still hadn't seen her. I found a phone box outside the hospital and called her. We arranged to meet that evening in her favourite restaurant and she proceeded to use up the little credit I had to berate me for not calling her sooner. My fifty pence was slowly draining away, counting down time on her admonishments, when she mentioned that Sheryl had called her and was trying to track me down but the phone went dead before I could ask her why.

I made a reverse charge call to Sheryl, which annoyed her. She said she wanted to see me as soon as possible so we arranged to meet that very afternoon.

CHAPTER 13

I stood trembling in the heat by the café at the boating pond in Regent's Park. Sheryl was already ten minutes late. The longer the delay, the more nervous I felt. I watched two young men powerjet layers of bird shit off the pedallos and rowing boats. A job designed by the devil for, even as they worked, scores of pigeons were perched in long lines along the plastic and wood mouldings of the other boats in the fleet and, with little ruffles of their feathers and wiggles of their rears, were surreptitiously adding to the men's labours as if mocking them.

'Hello, Josh,' a familiar voice intoned.

I turned to see the anxious face of Sheryl. She was wearing a white summer dress festooned with blood red poppies. Her auburn hair was tied up in two cute bunches like dogs' ears standing to attention and she was, unusually for her, devoid of make-up. Indeed I don't think I had ever seen her in public without a mask of eyeliner, lipstick and mascara. For the entirety of our marriage this little pancake of colours was applied religiously every morning before breakfast and removed a minute before bedtime. Sheryl only allowed herself to look like this in the dark. The denuding of her face signified a profound shift. What I had seen all those years was not Sheryl at all but a projection of her, a lie that she wanted the world to believe. Without make-up her face appeared rounder, less austere, and with the shedding of this particular insecurity, more confident.

'How are you, Sheryl?'

'Very well, thank you. And you? You've lost a bit of weight.' She took a step back and scanned me up and down like a farmer at a cattle auction. 'You look exhausted. I bumped into Jean a couple of weeks ago and she said she was worried about you. She said you'd not been out for a month.'

'You know Jean, she's so over the top,' I joked.

Sheryl looked at me dubiously. Jean, the curtain twitcher from next door, knew the comings and goings of the entire street. She could usually be relied on for accuracy.

'Shall we take a boat?' I asked, desperately trying to change the subject. 'It's a lovely day.'

'No, I'd rather walk,' she said. So we set off around the lake at a leisurely pace.

'So, are you happy with whatshername, Margaret?' I asked.

'Look, I don't want to waste your time, Josh. I've done a lot of thinking over the past couple of months. I need to take responsibility for the break-up. I'm sorry for the things I said. It was unfair of me. You didn't do anything wrong. I turned you into the enemy because I couldn't understand what was happening inside me. For years I felt uneasy with myself, like I was an intruder in my own life. You were not the first man I blamed for it. Margaret helped me see myself differently. I know it's difficult for you to accept. It's been an immensely difficult journey for me too ... still is ... but it's one I know I have to make.'

An unexpected wave of venom erupted in my spleen. 'But why didn't you talk to me about it? For Christ's sake, I had no idea what the fuck was going on. I didn't see it coming. I'd just lost my job, and you kicked me when I was down.'

'Don't get cross with me. The signs were there, you chose to ignore them. Besides, you weren't exactly Mr Communicative either. Remember that time I asked you if you loved me? You said, of course I do, and I said, well, why don't you ever tell me, and you said that you shouldn't need to tell me – I think you said, "I married you didn't I, so stop asking." Do you remember that, Josh?'

'Well, it was true, I did love you but it didn't seem enough to you. You wanted daily affirmations and that would have been fine except you pestered me on a routine basis and it made everything feel fake. What are you meant to say when someone constantly demands that you declare your love for them? You turned what was natural into a chore. Besides, it wasn't me that broke it, remember. You were the one that admitted that you had never loved me, that you only married me because I was "nice", so why the fuck were you so obsessed with getting me to say it every day? It was all one way traffic ... flat hypocrisy ... take, take, take.'

'Josh, what's happened to you? I've never heard you talk like this before.'

'Shall I tell you what happened, Sheryl? Shall I? I wasn't going to tell you but if you really want to know I will. Jean was right, I didn't leave that flat for four weeks; in fact I didn't leave it for seven weeks. I stared at the fucking wall until I didn't know what time of day it was and I prayed that you would come back. I ate what was left in the cupboards: stale pitta bread, old cheese, tins of chick peas and anchovies that had passed their expiry date, any old shit. I made soup from stock cubes, I

133

finished off the rice and the pasta. I ate everything until there was nothing left but a few manky herbs and half a bottle of malt vinegar then, if I got really hungry, I ordered Indian or Chinese takeaways, pizzas and kebabs. Night and day became the same. I lost all track of time. I almost lost my mind. Maybe I did lose my mind. Then I realised that you were never going to come back. That you were gone for good and that I would have to start again. And I thought about the things that you said when you left, and I hated you for it, I hated you because you were right, we had wasted seven years of our lives and, yes, we were living a sham. I hated you because I thought I loved you, and I thought you loved me. I hated you because you destroyed my delusions and left me with nothing. Absolutely nothing.'

'I don't need this, Josh.'

'Oh you do, you fucking do. You need to know what a cruel, heartless bitch you really are. You ruined my life, Sheryl. Did I ever say a mean word to you?'

I was shouting. She looked around, embarrassed. 'Not so loud, Josh.'

'WELL, DID I?' I yelled.

'No, you didn't.'

'Did I ever hit you, or hurt you?'

'Josh ... '

'DID I?'

'No.'

'Did I ever humiliate you or walk away when you needed me?'

'No. Josh, stop ... '

'So what did I do to deserve this? Why did you cheat on me? Why did you leave me?'

'Because you didn't know how to love me, because you didn't love yourself, because you've spent your life hiding from

134

anything that might make you lose control. Look Josh, this is pointless. I told you it was my fault. I didn't come here to argue with you.'

'So why did you come?' I demanded.

She stopped in her tracks and took a deep breath.

'I want a divorce.'

'Granted. I never want to see you again.'

'And I want my share of the flat. You can buy me out if you want.'

I spat out an ironic laugh. 'Don't you know?'

'Know what?'

'The flat has been repossessed.'

Her mouth fell open. 'You're joking.'

'No, ask Jean. I'm sure she was watching from behind the net curtains.'

'When?'

'Ten days ago.'

'I don't believe it. Why didn't you tell me? How could you let that happen? It was our flat,' she said in disbelief.

'It was in my name. I had no money and you fucked off. What did you think would happen?'

'But half of it was mine, that's what we agreed. So what if the mortgage came from your account. I paid for everything else.'

'What does the bank care about that? The law is an ass. There's nothing I can do.'

She was horrified. 'You should have told me, Josh, we could have sorted something out.'

'Yeah, well, you should have thought about it when you left.'

'Why didn't you go to the Citizens Advice Bureau or try to renegotiate with the bank?'

'It would have made no difference. You know what I realised, as I sat there waiting for you? I realised that we were conned. Conned into borrowing more money than we could ever pay back. We borrowed ten times our earnings. The broker fiddled it for us ... God knows how. We were hoodwinked into thinking we could afford it by that tracker deal that NBS sold us. But I had no idea what would happen to our payments when NBS put the rates up 3.8% at the end of the three year period. No one really went through that with us, did they? We bought into the hype. There was no way I could service the debt on my own. And you know what I found out? That we owed £6,000 more than we borrowed and where did that £6,000 come from? It was the broker's fee. He got £6,000. It was added to the mortgage and I didn't even realise. I know it was in the small print somewhere but I didn't read it and all he said was that NBS paid him a percentage for bringing in the business. I feel like an idiot.'

'But now we've lost any money we had.' She bit her lip and tears welled into her eyes. The force of my earlier aggression rebounded on me and I felt bad.

'I'm sorry, Sheryl.'

'So where are you living then?'

'In the storage container.'

'Oh Josh, is that why you look terrible?'

I nodded.

'Why don't you stay with your mum?'

'She doesn't know I'm homeless, I'm seeing her later. Don't worry about me. I'll sort something out.' I assured her.

'Promise me you'll stay there tonight. I'm angry about the house, Josh, but I don't want anything bad to happen to you.'

'Thank you, I'm sorry. One day I'll pay you back, I promise.'

But we both knew that would never happen.

'I don't think we should meet again,' she said and turned to leave. We had barely spent ten minutes together. It was as if her familiar form was already dissolving into a memory, a piece of the past slowly departing the present. She walked across the grass towards Baker Street and then she was gone.

I stood at the water's edge and watched a toddler on a lead throw pellets of bread towards a swan, but the feeble child's throws never reached the water and the pigeons snapped up every morsel. He strained on his leash to get closer to the edge but his mother held him back. 'I know it's pretty,' she said, 'but it will bite you if you get too close.' The boy began to cry. I turned around and headed back towards the café. My legs were shaking.

The one thing I didn't tell Sheryl about those seven weeks of solitude after she deserted me was that on some nights – long, never-ending nights – people would crawl out of the wall and talk to me. Prophets and demons, soothsayers and sorcerors. Strange people whispering strange messages, which confused and upset me. They tricked me and insulted me. They passed judgments and decrees. Perhaps I was hallucinating, or perhaps in the stillness of my self-imposed meditation, I had become adept at conjuring company. Rather like Moses or Jesus in the desert had conjured God. Who were these people? I have no idea. But I have learnt that if you stare long enough at a wall, you will see them.

CHAPTER 14

The Hilal Curry House on Elgin Avenue was my mum's favourite restaurant. It had gained this lofty status because my mother rarely ate out and had nothing to compare it with. She had eaten there once twenty years ago while on a date with a caretaker from a school where she cleaned. The relationship lasted all of a week but she had found the food perfectly acceptable. She was not a curious person, she had no interest in trying other Indian restaurants, nor was she inclined to go to a Chinese or Italian restaurant. She shunned variety. Whenever I suggested going somewhere else, her nose would curl up and she would say, 'But I don't know that place,' which would exasperate me because how would she ever get to know any other place unless she was prepared to eat in it?

The Hilal was, in truth, a terrible restaurant, a relic of the seventies where almost every curry contained as much pineapple, peas and raisins as it did mutton and diced chicken. The décor of Anaglyptic wallpaper, trellised booths and kaleidoscope red carpets was beyond redemption. The merciful people of Maida Vale should have demolished it years ago and put it out of its misery once and for all.

I was there fifteen minutes early. My mum couldn't tolerate lateness. Not because it made her angry but because it made her worry. She would worry about what had become of the latecomer. Perhaps they had died. Or worse.

The restaurant was empty. Three waiters came to greet me. One of them recognised me from my teenage years.

'Hello, sir, and how are you?'

'Fine, thank you, Amit. And you?'

Amit wobbled his head and gave me a look which seemed to say sometimes life is good, sometimes it is bad, we have no customers any more so I am worried how I am going to survive, the meat in the kitchen has been in the freezer for three months but don't worry, we can defrost it in the microwave, my children have grown up and have married white girls, my wife has acute angina, the chef has got Parkinson's, I don't like the other waiters but they are my third cousins so what can I do? I have a leaky roof and no friends but I am very pleased to see you.

'I haven't seen you for a long time. Why don't you come to see us any more?'

I didn't know where to begin so I said, 'I've moved out of the area.'

One of the waiters took my jacket, the other gestured meaninglessly towards the gaudy belly of the restaurant as if something spectacular were about to happen there like a sound and light show.

Amit led me to my mother's favourite booth. It was her favourite because my mother had sat in it once and found it perfectly acceptable, even though all the other booths were exactly the same.

My mum hadn't arrived yet which surprised me; it was the first time I had ever got somewhere before her. No matter how early I was she would always be there waiting like a piece of furniture. I began to worry what had become of her. Perhaps she had died. Or worse.

All three waiters were now standing around the table, which was slightly disconcerting. I ordered a beer. Poppadoms and spices appeared. The waiters watched me eat. The crunch of poppadoms echoed off the walls. Amit went out onto the street to keep the non-existent queue in order.

The others were watching my every mouthful with the unwavering glare of two loyal mastiffs awaiting an order from their master. If I so much as lifted my head they came bounding in to ask if I needed anything.

I noticed Amit on the street trying to usher a reluctant young couple towards the restaurant as if his granddaughter's dowry depended on it. They nodded unenthusiastically, smiled politely, looked through the window and walked away. He may as well have been recruiting volunteers for a gruesome scientific experiment.

Then I saw my mother scurrying across the street in the fading light. Amit greeted her in a pitiful obsequious manner like she was royalty, although she looked anything but regal. She was wearing a dowdy brown knee-length coat offset by a green leather handbag. With age, her spine and stomach had rounded in equal proportion so that her body was shaped like a barrel supported by two spindly legs, which bowed outwards at such an angle they looked like they couldn't possibly meet at her waist. Her greying hair hung lifelessly down to her shoulders. She seemed agitated.

'Hello, Mum,' I said, standing to kiss her.

'Oh, Josh, I've been so worried I couldn't sleep. Why didn't you call me earlier?' She hugged me. Then gave her coat to Amit and sat down opposite me.

'Sorry, Mum.'

'You said you were coming last week and then I didn't hear from you for a week. Did you know your home phone wasn't working? I must have left a hundred messages on your mobile. Why didn't you call me?'

I felt the unwelcome presence of Amit and his two cousins hovering around us like a trio of bored children looking for something to do.

'My home phone has been cut off.'

'You need to get it repaired. They'll do that for free, you know.'

'I know, I haven't got round to it.'

'Oh, have you been busy?' she probed.

'Er ... sort of.'

'And your mobile?'

'It's not charged up.'

'For a week? Why don't you plug it in?'

'I've been busy.'

'Josh, are you avoiding me? Have I done something wrong? What did I do? Tell me?'

'Mum, it's nothing to do with you. Really.'

'Then what's going on, Josh? It's not like you to ignore my calls. You know that I needed to speak to you about something very important. And then you don't call. How do you think that makes me feel?' she asked, with a feeble tremor in her voice, which I knew was the precursor to tears.

'Look, Mum, I meant to tell you but I was worried that you'd get upset.'

'What?'

'I was evicted last week.'

From the corner of my eye I saw Amit wobble his head in sympathy.

'What do you mean evicted?' she cried.

'Evicted ... you know ... evicted from my home. Repossessed ... by the bank.'

Her face dropped in disbelief, 'Oh, Josh, that's awful. So where have you been sleeping?'

'Here and there.'

'Why didn't you come home?'

'Shall we order?' I asked. 'I'm hungry.'

'Have you been eating properly?' she inquired worriedly.

I turned to Amit. 'What can you recommend?'

'You must try the chicken tikka masala, it is fresh yesterday.'

'All right,' I said dubiously.

'Will Madam have her usual?' Amit asked.

'Yes please, Amit.'

With the waiters occupied at last, I felt more able to talk freely. I tried to explain to her that I hadn't come home because it didn't feel right, but then she wanted to know what didn't feel right. Was it her? Was it my bedroom? Was her cooking no good? Was it because she lived in a council block? Was there someone who had bullied me from round there? Was there someone I didn't want to see? Had I been abused? Was Mr Lockheart from number 43 a pervert? Didn't I think he was a weirdo with his long coat? Had he ever had a go at me? Did I want to see a doctor? A therapist? A psychoanalyst? A marriage councillor? Was she a bad mother? Where had she gone wrong? What could she have done better? Was I embarrassed that she was a cleaner? Did I remember I once said she had bad breath? Does she still have bad breath?

On and on it went, an endless daisy chain of randomly generated questions from the four corners of her brain. Every answer I gave led to more questions. And then we got on to the subject of Sheryl and she wanted to know if I was hiding anything else from her. Was I gay? Was Tom Cruise gay? Was my marriage a facade? Did I remember the time she caught me playing doctors with Harry Lumden when we were four? He had his trousers down and I was looking at his bottom? Did I think she cared if I was gay?

There seemed to be no answers I could give that satisfied her. Like a rabbit caught in the firing line of a machine gun, I hopped left and right dodging the bullets until eventually I could take it no longer and I screamed at her to leave me alone.

'This is why I didn't want to come home,' I shouted in exasperation.

She fell into a shocked silence but after a few seconds the questions began to whir again quietly in the back of her mind. Even when she wasn't speaking I could hear them scuttling around her brain. Why was I shouting at her? What had she done wrong? How long did she have to leave me alone for? Did I still want to be her son? Didn't I love her anymore? What would my dad say if he were alive?

She didn't have to open her mouth for me to know exactly what she was thinking.

My curry had long since arrived and now it was staring at me sadly from its silver tureen, daring me to eat it. I broke the congealed surface with a spoon and ladled it on to my plate. We ate without speaking until I noticed a tear roll down my mother's cheek and fall into her food.

'Sorry, Mum,' I said sheepishly, 'I shouldn't have said that. I don't want to upset you. I'm having a difficult time. Do you want to tell me what it was you wanted to talk to me about?'

'No.'

'Please, Mum. I said I'm sorry ... I'd really like to stay over tonight?'

'Would you, sweetie?' Her face brightened. 'Your bed is all made and ready for you. It'll be nice ... just the two of us again.'

I tried my best to smile.

'So,' she said, shifting uncomfortably in her seat, 'the reason I wanted to talk to you was because ... because they found your dad's helmet.'

'What?' I felt a trapdoor open in my stomach and all the old emotions came flooding back.

'I got a call from the South Wales Caving Club.'

'After all this time? I don't believe it. Where was it?' I asked.

'At the bottom of a sump. I want you to go and collect it for me.'

'Oh Mum, I'm not going back there.'

'Why not?'

'Because he's dead, Mum. It's taken us so long to get over it. I don't want to revisit that part of my life again.'

'I told them you were coming.'

'What do you mean, when?'

'This weekend.'

'What did you do that for? I told you I don't think it's a good idea.'

'Shall we talk about it at home?' she said, throwing a nod to Amit for the bill.

I never spoke about Dad with my mum after he died. She hid away all the photos of him and got rid of anything that could possibly remind me of him. Perhaps she thought it would stop me from crying so much. She told me we just had to get on with it and for a long time I thought that was what adults did when someone died. They just got on with it. As if nothing had happened. As if the deceased had never existed. My mum never grieved in front of me. She didn't bring him up in conversation. It was like she had lost nothing more significant than a glove, which made my own feelings all the more baffling. I wondered if there wasn't something wrong with me that I should feel so bereft. Gradually I learnt to hide my feelings from Mum because I thought this was what she wanted.

One day, many years later, when I was perhaps ten or eleven, I found the key to my mother's bedside cupboard. She had said it contained medicines and other dangerous things but when I opened it I discovered a shrine to my father. There were piles of dog-eared photos, and love letters. There was some aftershave, an old scarf, a pair of sunglasses, a wallet and perhaps more tellingly a half-used box of tissues. I felt deceived. Why had my mother kept this treasure from me? I confronted her about my discovery. At first she shouted at me for having the audacity to open her cupboard but the following day the photos appeared on the shelves. Not a word was spoken about them. It was as if they had been there all along. And so my father once again took pride of place in our home.

I was standing in the living room looking at the pictures. My mother was busy in the kitchen. There was one particular photograph that caught my eye. My father was wearing the recently found bright yellow helmet and the caving suit that had disappeared with him on that fateful day. He held me in his right arm and was tickling me with his left. We were both lost in laughter. My mother was standing on the right edge of the frame watching us with a look of beaming pride. The strangest thing about it was that my father, whom I hardly knew, was instantly recognisable as a face frozen in time, whereas it was my mother who looked like a stranger; I didn't recognise her at all. It was taken in a golden time before my mother had become immobilised with worry, before she had lost all sense of adventure. Back then she was a confident, beautiful woman with open shoulders and an ever-present smile. Now she was more like a withered fruit that stubbornly clings on to its stalk. It was impossible to imagine the woman that my mother has become ever allowing her husband to go caving. I don't know who took the picture.

'He loved you so much, Josh,' my mum said as she entered with a tray of tea.

And yet I felt more abandoned than loved. How was it possible that the pain of his loss was still etched in my heart but the love he once gave me was too long ago for me to remember?

'What was he like?' I asked.

'Vince was a good man. A moral man. People found him aloof because he was quite shy with strangers but when you got to know him he was all heart ... loving, loyal, resolute. Don't you remember him at all?'

Given her usual reticence to talk about him, I was agreeably surprised by her question.

'I have a vague sense of him,' I said. 'I measure him more by his absence than his presence. I can't remember his voice or anything else about him, I just feel there's a dark hole inside me, like I swallowed the cave.'

'I know, I know.' My mother shook her head and sighed heavily. She came to my side and together we stared nostalgically at the pictures. 'It's a shame you don't remember him.'

She stooped down to the bottom shelf and picked out a thin red photo album. 'Here, I want you to take this.'

I was grateful for the gift, I had so little to remind me of him. As I flicked through the album, past picture upon picture of my father cuddling me as a baby or proudly gripping my mother outside some church or standing on an old cobbled bridge over a river, or covered up to his neck in sand with seaweed on his head, I came to one picture that stole the air from my lungs and made the skin on the nape of my neck prickle with shock. There was my father with a group of men gathered round a table in a restaurant holding up their glasses of wine to the camera as if toasting something. On one side of him sat the caver who had come to our cottage on the night of my father's death and on the other side was the administrator-cum-detective from the hospital, the same man who I had seen on the train from Norwich.

'Who is that man?' I stammered.

My mother peered at the photograph. 'Oh, probably some climbing buddy of your father's. Why?'

'He reminds me of someone I know. What's his name?'

'I don't know. I can't remember. I haven't seen any of them since your father died.'

'When was the picture taken?'

'I think it was the night before he died. He went out a few times with the guys from the club while I stayed in the cottage looking after you. He has a very distinctive face, doesn't he?'

The picture was twenty-five years old and yet disturbingly the man in the photo looked the exact same age as the administrator. It was as if he had a twin in the past. I hurriedly closed the album and walked over to the table. I sat down with my mother and watched her pour the tea and, in the quiet but loving way she handed me the cup, I saw a woman who had endured her best years in loneliness and whose only hopes rested on my shoulders.

'I'll go and get the helmet, Mum, if that's what you want.'

'You're a good boy, Josh.' She reached over the table and squeezed my arm.

My bedroom was like a mausoleum to my lost youth. My doodle-filled school books lined the shelves, some of my old clothes hung in the wardrobe, my stand up punch bag still languished in the corner, all gathering dust. I headed for the chest of drawers at the foot of my bed, wondering if the things I had once hidden there were still hiding. I pulled open the top drawer and found my old sketch pads, pencil cases, shells, marbles, swimming badges, some Arsenal memorabilia and other evidence of my boyhood interests. There were scarves and tracksuits and table tennis bats. I pulled out the bottom drawer and there at the back was an old pornographic photograph ripped from *Mayfair* or *Playboy*. Goodness knows how often I had masturbated over that picture. And next to it were the objects of my search. An old hand-drawn survey of the Ogof Ffynnon Ddu cave system and a tiny troll with red hair that my dad had given me in Wales. I had kept them hidden at the back of my drawer for fear my mum would find them and take them away from me.

In the early days, shortly after my father's death, I would sometimes study the survey at night and stroke the troll's wild hair, before carefully hiding them away again before morning. Eventually, as my life got back to normal, I had forgotten about my precious keepsakes and, never having cause to remove my drawers from the chest, not rediscovered them. Strange that for years both Mum and I had conducted our nightly rituals in secret for fear of upsetting each other, she weeping over photographs and me over my map. The cave survey looked like an unintelligible scribble, a crisscrossing doodle of passageways and dead ends which meandered across the page from a squiggle labelled 'Resurgence' via a tightly tangled web of runs around the so-called Skeleton Chamber, through Pluto's Bath and Dip Sump, past something called the Marble Showers, along Gnome Passage, up Smith's Armoury to a final squiggle called simply 'Sink'. A place that had swallowed its own definite article. It was easy to dream into these bizarrely named places and imagine that my father was still down there, somewhere, ploughing deeper and deeper into the earth through fantastical crystal caverns and dinosaur burial grounds to another world filled with gnomes and moles. A place so alluring perhaps that he chose not to return. I've heard it said that we have done more exploration of outer space than we have of the first kilometre of the earth's crust. Who knows what secrets are hidden down there? My father was never dead in my child mind, he was lost. Wandering. Discovering. The survey, which was held together by bits of tape that I had stuck on myself whenever it was required, was the only tangible record of his whereabouts and many a night I vowed that I would go there one day and find him. I had long since squashed that childish notion and rather dreaded the idea of going, but now it seemed the call of my father was finally forcing me to make the trip and in a couple of days, I would find myself at the jaws of the cavern that had engulfed him.

As for the troll, it had a calming familiarity about it, with its bulbous tummy and little fingers. I stroked its mane of synthetic hair as I had done so often as a child and that night slept with it once more at my bedside.

The following morning, clean and well slept, and with a shameful pocket full of Mum's savings, I found myself back

150

at the hospital. Back at Angela's bedside. Alone with her once more.

'You're like Sleeping Beauty, aren't you, just waiting for some metaphorical prince to wake you up. How does the story go? A hundred years of slumber ... he cuts through a forest of thorns, slays the dragon. Is there a dragon? Or is that a different fairy tale? Maybe it's the Disney version. I'm sure there's a dragon protecting her. Well, my little angel of sleep, if I could do that for you I would. I'd tear that dragon to pieces with my fingernails and I'd hack through the briar until I found you and I'd kiss you so tenderly that your little heart would stir once more.'

I looked around the ward. All the nurses were momentarily preoccupied with another patient who they were moving to a private room. I traced my fingers around the oval of her face.

'If Sheryl could hear me now she'd be laughing her head off. She'd be saying, why did you never say such things to me? Where was the poetry and the romance in our relationship? But it's different with you, Angela. You will never judge me and you will never disappoint me, will you?'

I leant forward and kissed her in the stray hope that she might just wake up, as if the fairy tale might come true, for when Sleeping Beauty wakes, the whole kingdom wakes, and the prince will free himself of sadness. I felt a hand on my shoulder, and the next thing I knew I had been hurled across the ward and Mikey was standing over me with a face as dark as thunder.

CHAPTER 15

Mikey's lips scrunched up into a tight, wrinkled hoop like a cat's anus and his eyes bulged demonically. I tried to get up but he pushed me back to the ground. I was vaguely aware of raised voices further down the ward. Two nurses were running to see what all the commotion was.

'I caught this man sexually assaulting my girlfriend,' he said.

'She's not your girlfriend. You told me yourself. You said it was over. You don't own her.'

'He was forcing himself on a woman in a coma. It's not right.'

'I wasn't forcing myself on her, I was kissing her.'

'She's in a fucking coma. She couldn't exactly say no.'

'It's not what you think. We've kissed before.'

'What? When?' Mikey looked appalled.

'Before she tried to kill herself. I love her, I'm trying to help.'

'What do you mean you love her? You said you had only just met her.'

A hefty security guard was ploughing his way through the ward towards us.

'What's going on?' he said.

'This man was assaulting a patient. He was kissing her and had his hand between her legs,' Mikey hissed.

I stared at him in disbelief.

'He's lying,' I protested.

The security guard looked from Mikey to me, trying to assess who was guilty before turning to the nurses for guidance.

'I saw him kissing her,' one of the nurses said, 'but I was too far away to see anything else.'

'I admit I gave her a kiss. Is that a crime? As for the rest, it's a total fabrication.'

I brought myself up on to my feet. 'He's jealous.'

Mikey shook his head angrily. 'Jealousy has got nothing to do with it. He doesn't know her, he has no right to even touch her, let alone do what he did. Look, I've known Angela for years ... ' He pulled out his wallet and produced a photograph of the two of them arm in arm on a park bench, ' ... and I've never seen this man until I met him here.'

This somewhat tenuous documentary evidence seemed to persuade the guard and he cupped my arm in his.

'I am going to have to ask you to leave the hospital,' he said, in the kind of officious voice that is the reserve of those with an over-inflated opinion of their limited power.

'I will not leave,' I said, pulling away from him. 'Angela needs me.'

'Needs?' Mikey bridled.

'I'm the only one who talks to her. She communicates to me.'

'Don't you see what is happening here?' Mikey said to the security guard, the nurses and all the other visitors who had gathered round to listen. 'This man has the misfortune to witness the suicide attempt of an extremely beautiful girl and then fantasises that he is her boyfriend. Somehow he inveigles himself into the ambulance and finds himself at the hospital and now he thinks he can do whatever he wants with her, when in reality he is nothing more than a stalker.'

'That is your version of the truth,' I retorted, 'but you don't know the half of it. Angela threw herself on me. It was she that initiated it. She kissed me. She needs me. Whereas you are just a selfish thug. You and her are no longer together and you can't come to terms with it. Can you?'

Mikey laughed. 'Oh that is pathetic, I've never heard such drivel. If she needed you then why did she throw herself in front of a bus within an hour of meeting you? The last thing she was thinking about was you.'

The security guard had heard enough. He took hold of my arm again, this time with greater force.

'I asked you to leave the hospital, sir. Now either you do so quietly or I will have to call the police and have you arrested. I don't know the ins and outs of your little squabble but something is clearly not right here. So I'm warning you not to show your face in this hospital again – or at least not until you can prove to us that you are a relative or friend of this lady.'

He frog-marched me out of the ward.

'But I've honestly done nothing wrong,' I bleated in vain.

I was pushed into the lift and escorted on to the street. I paced up and down outside fuming at the injustice. I was damned if I was going to let that fool get the upper hand over me. The security guard stood by the entrance watching me implacably until at length I crept away like a wounded kitten.

I skirted the hospital until I was out of his view and found a wall in the car park, where I planted myself and considered what I should do next. I felt something vibrate in my pocket. I put my hand inside and pulled out the wooden box. It was shaking like an old fashioned alarm clock. What was this wretched thing that periodically reminded me of its presence and demanded attention? I wished I could open it and see what was inside, maybe then it would stop scaring me.

I saw a black, chauffeur-driven Bentley turn into the car park. Harvey was at the wheel; the Mortons in the rear. He pulled in opposite the entrance to Accident and Emergency and allowed his passengers to discharge. The distinctive figure of Lord Morton, with his head thrown forward, emerged first, followed by his wife. Both looked withered and drawn. I watched as they hurried into the hospital and Harvey found himself a parking spot.

Harvey got out of the car and lit a cigarette. I made my way towards him. When he saw me approaching, he threw me a tired smile.

'Hello, Josh.'

'Hello, Harvey.' I offered my hand and he shook it firmly.

'What's happening? Have you seen her yet today? Is there any change?' he asked, a look of sorrow in his eyes.

'I saw her briefly, I didn't get a chance to talk to the doctor. Have you managed to see her yet?'

'No, they won't be wanting me in there, they wouldn't have it. It's not my place. But I will ask them if I can pay my respects if they decide to turn the machine off. I hope they won't begrudge me that.'

'Why would they do that?' I asked in shock.

'Weren't you there yesterday?'

'When?'

'When they discussed her latest scan?'

'No, I must have gone by then. What did they say?'

'Well, I can't rightly tell you all the details, I was picking up titbits of what they was saying in the car but I gathered that the doctors were not optimistic from what they saw. Apparently

156

they had a conversation about when they might think about turning it off.'

'And what ... and what did they decide?' I stammered.

'Doctors said to hang on another day or so but if there was no sign of improvement they might want to consider their options.'

'Surely they wouldn't turn her off. I mean, people have come round after months sometimes.'

'I'm with you but they decided it wouldn't be fair on her if she had severe brain damage and I have to say that if it came to that I'm inclined to agree.'

'But they don't know, no one can know, can they?'

Harvey took a deep drag on his cigarette and shook his head dolefully. 'As I said, the doctors weren't very confident, I'm praying for some improvement over the next few hours. We all are, Josh. I'm trying not to think about it. I loved that girl more than anyone but I can't bear the thought of her suffering for the rest of her life neither.'

'Oh God, Harvey, what are we going to do? I'm not even allowed to see her any more.'

'Why on earth not?' he asked.

'Because I'm not family. Because her twit of an ex-boyfriend doesn't want me around.'

Harvey sighed. 'It's in the lap of the gods ... the lap of the gods.'

It was a couple of hours before we saw the Mortons emerge from the foyer. I made a hasty departure so as not to embarrass Harvey in front of his employers. After they had gone, I was emboldened to make my way back to the entrance of the hospital. I couldn't bear the thought that I would never see Angela again but as I approached the door, I saw that the security guard was hovering and, cursing my luck, I decided to go home to my mother's.

I spent a torrid night, unable to sleep, now mingling thoughts of losing Angela with a deep fear for the future, the two somehow inextricably entwined.

In the morning I batted away a torrent of questions from my mother about a myriad of unrelated topics from lesbianism to my wayward hairstyle and then, like a fool, I returned to the hospital. Of course it was a pointless exercise, I would never gain access to that ward again, I would never see Angela again but I simply couldn't sit at home or be anywhere other than as near to Angela as I could possibly get.

I found the same wall in the car park and watched the visitors come and go wishing desperately to be among them. Then from afar I saw Mikey walking towards the entrance. I tried to duck down behind the wall but he had already seen me. It was pointless trying to hide now.

I could see from the way he strode towards me that he was furious. Scary visions of my first encounter with him in his bandanna at the bank rushed into my mind. Instinctively I began to retreat. He broke into a run. I turned on my heels and fled into the car park.

He was much faster than me. I tried to up my pace but I realised that I had trapped myself in a corner of the car park with high walls on all sides. There was a dark rubbish bin store under one of the buildings and, in a vain and stupid attempt to escape, I ran inside. There were seven or eight tall cylindrical containers on wheels. I headed into the darker depths and, panting, hunkered down behind one of them. There was an odour of rotten food and blood. I prayed for a miracle. In the gloom I saw a broken-down bedstead. I picked up one of the metal legs and clutched it to my chest. I heard the thudding of running feet. They slowed down and came to a standstill by the entrance to the store. There was a long silence. I sensed his presence close by. The veins in my neck began to throb in fear. Then I heard the scrunch of an empty plastic wrapper on the other side of the container. I leapt up and tried to push the bin on to him with my shoulder but the wheels were locked and it wouldn't budge.

'Show yourself, you coward,' he hissed.

I could feel him edging round towards me. I panicked and made a run for it, but he caught hold of my jacket and threw me back into the depths of the bin store, sending me sprawling into a pile of empty boxes. I screamed for help but there was no one around. I scrambled to my feet and gripped the metal leg tightly in my right hand.

'Leave me alone,' I begged.

'What are you doing here? You were told to stay away.'

'I ... I just wanted to find out how she was,' I stammered.

'You don't get it, do you? You need to be taught a fucking lesson.'

He closed in on me menacingly and, terrified, I raised the piece of broken bed above my head to protect myself but, before I could bring it down on him, I felt his fist slam into my stomach. I doubled up and he grabbed hold of my wrist and prised the weapon from my hands. It clattered on to the concrete. I took a knee in the chest and a couple of karate kicks which propelled me with a thump against the damp wall. He flew at me with a flurry of punches. There was no sign of the violence abating. The next thing I knew, he had his hands around my neck and was throttling me. There was a burning pain in my throat as the flow of air halted and his vice-like fingers tightened their hold. I tried in vain to pull his hands off me. He had me pressed up against the wall, his face straining with the effort.

'It's over, Josh, not just for you, but for Angela. If she doesn't come round by tomorrow her parents will turn off the machine. Then what are you going to do, you fucking pervert? Stalk some other sick girl?'

My stomach convulsed involuntarily, and a galaxy of red dots blurred my vision as my body slowly ran out of oxygen. Mikey's hands seemed only to tighten, and tighten and tighten. I was fading, the muscles in my legs were beginning to spasm. My arms fell away from his and I went limp. The dots in my eyes were turning white.

CHAPTER 16

Mikey's fingers were sinking deep into my neck. My life force was ebbing away, but at the last gasp came an unexpectedly violent surge of anger. I wasn't angry with Mikey, I was angry with myself. I couldn't let it all end without achieving at least one thing of true value. I wasn't done with life. I had unfinished business and there were people who needed me.

A sudden and final rush of blood powered through my body. My arm lurched out and I managed to grab Mikey by the balls and crunch them tightly in my fist. He winced and his grip loosened. I felt the honey flow of air seep into my lungs and I squeezed harder until he released me. He was doubled up in pain. I saw a brick on the floor by my feet and in a blur I picked it up and brought it down on his head. A hot splash of blood hit my face. He tottered and fell to the ground. I felt weak and dizzy, but I held on to the brick and staggered over to him. I was about to strike him again when he swiped at my legs with his right arm and I fell on top of him. For a moment we rolled hopelessly one on top of the other, neither able to get the upper hand, until he managed to scramble away. He tried to get to his feet but he lost his balance, tripped backwards over a piece of wood and careered into the wall. His head jarred against something and he let forth a high pitched scream as he tried to free himself. His legs began to twitch manically and then, like an abandoned puppet, his body sagged abruptly and fell still.

I pulled myself up and took a step towards him. A rivulet of blood was dribbling down the wall and pooling by his feet. A large rusty hook in the brickwork had penetrated the back of his skull. I listened for his breath but there was nothing.

A cold terror swept over me. What had I done? Trembling, I hauled him off the hook, lowered him to the ground and tried, with my limited knowledge of the art, to resuscitate him. His lips were dry and dusty and my breath returned with the stench of marijuana and alcohol. All I could think was 'Don't die on me. Don't fucking die on me.' I have no idea how long I tried; two minutes, five minutes, perhaps ten, but there was nothing I could do. I felt sick.

Now what?

I floundered for a plan of action. Nothing came. If I called the police, I would get arrested and then what would happen to Angela? If I ran away, a porter would surely discover the body within minutes. I needed time and I could only win time if I could find a way to dispose of his body. The next moment I found myself dragging the corpse towards the nearest bin. It was taller than me, designed to catch rubbish from the chutes. I lugged him on to my shoulders and, with strength I didn't know I possessed, I pushed him over the side. The bin was empty and he hit the bottom with a metallic thud. I scrabbled around in the dark looking for bits of rubbish to hide his body. I grabbed a large strip of blue tarpaulin and hurled it into the bin on top of him. I was like a dog kicking soil over its excrement. It was more instinctive than methodical and no sooner was it done when I realised I was behaving as if I was guilty of the crime. When the rubbish trucks came in the morning, the bin would be wheeled out, hoisted up by the hydraulic lift and the contents tipped into the grinder. Mikey's corpse would tumble out for all to see. What I was doing was ridiculous.

In a daze I lurched out into the light of the car park. A paramedic was getting into a van. He turned to look at me. I felt something damp against my chest. A bright red blood stain marked my shirt. There was another on my jeans. Shit. How was I going to explain my way out of this?

'Are you alright?' the paramedic asked.

'A man attacked me.'

'You know where A&E is?'

I felt like the captain of a sinking ship whose last lifeboat had been launched and was disappearing on the horizon without him. For seven weeks after Sheryl left I had fallen into a mental black hole. The encounter with Angela had unwittingly pulled me out and now I could feel myself looking into the darkness all over again, but I was damned if I was going to let myself fall. How long would it be before suspicion for Mikey's death fell on me? I was certain that within a couple of days I would be in police custody, and who would believe that I hadn't killed Mikey when all the evidence would indicate that I had.

I had no time and nothing to lose. I had to get to Angela before they turned off the life support.

CHAPTER 17

I made my way to the main entrance and cautiously peered in. The security guard who had turfed me out the previous day was standing by the front desk. Even if I managed to get past him I doubted whether the nurses on Angela's ward would let me see her, especially not in the state I was in.

My only chance of seeing Angela now would be to wait until nightfall, when there would be different staff on the ward. I would somehow have to procure myself some hospital clothing, so as not to raise suspicion when visiting after hours. At the very least, I had to get rid of the blood-stained clothes I was currently wearing.

I skirted the building looking for an alternative way in. There was a security door on the west side of the building through which staff members seemed to pass on a regular basis. I hovered at a discreet distance, watching them swipe their cards to gain access. The door was on a self-closer which took two or three seconds to shut after each use. I walked purposefully towards the door and, as I approached, a woman exited. I turned my back and pretended to be searching my jacket for a staff card. As she walked away, I caught hold of the door and slipped into the hospital. I found myself in what must have been the administrative centre of the building, with open plan offices to my right and a staff canteen to my left. Doctors and nurses were chatting noisily over the clinking of cutlery. I hurried past them, nervous about my bloody appearance, until I came to a set of lifts.

I pressed the call button and waited. A couple of nurses joined me by the lift. I kept my back to them. They were too busy talking about a patient to pay any attention to me.

'It's such a shame, he's still so young,' said the first.

'And isn't he handsome?' commented the second.

'I'll say. But there's nothing more they can do. The doctor said they've done everything.'

'I'll be sad if he goes,' said the second.

'Don't get involved, Tia.'

'I know, I know, but I can't help it with him.'

The lift pinged and the door opened. I hesitated, not wishing to share a lift in my current state.

'Go ahead,' I said, 'I'm going down,' not even sure if there was a down.

They bustled past me into the lift.

'You know he hasn't got a chance,' the first nurse said as the door closed and their conversation faded away.

I waited for the next lift and got in. In the mirror I noticed a splatter of blood on my face. I rubbed it frenetically with my sleeve and spat on my fingers to wash away the last stubborn spots. The lift came to a halt.

I found myself in a basement clearly not intended for patients or the general public. There were no ward signs and the floor was shabbily decked with grey tiles that hadn't been cleaned for some time. There had to be a laundry somewhere down here or a place where the surgeons or cleaners changed. Somewhere I could find some hospital clothes.

There were two sets of double doors, one to the left, one to the right. I had a strange sense that one of these doors would lead to something good and one to something bad; I can't explain why I felt this way. There was the distant rumbling sound of giant boilers pumping hot water around the building. Through one door the devil himself would be stoking a great furnace, through the other, people in togas would be lounging on chaise-longues eating grapes. Instinctively I wanted to go right but it felt too obvious – a reflex choice. My father had been right-handed, he would have gone right. My mother is ambidextrous – which way would she have gone? There was something alluring about the left, a magnetic force pulled me toward the doors. A naughty playful energy emanated from that side that wasn't entirely trustworthy. I knew that in my old life I wouldn't have noticed this energy and would have turned right.

Of course there was nothing to stop me looking through both of these doors but at that moment I was caught in an existential crisis. All my life I had followed a path without thinking and look where I had ended up, turning right had got me nowhere. It occurred to me that if, from now on, I did the opposite of what I would normally do I might lead a more exciting life, or at least a less unthinking life.

The lift door suddenly opened again behind me. With its arrival came the expansion of choice. Now I could also go up and possibly even further down into the Minotaur's labyrinth. Life was so complicated. I ascertained from the display inside the lift that I was on floor minus two. I remembered from school that minus numbers don't really exist, they are purely a mathematical construct. You can't, for example, have minus two elephants. You probably can't have any elephants – well not in a London flat at least – but even if you lived in the zoo you definitely can't have minus two. Setting aside this mathematical conundrum, which could only lead me to the scary conclusion that I had slipped beneath reality and was inhabiting a non-existent, metaphysical underworld, I decided to ignore the lift. It was clearly a red herring – whatever that means.

I walked through the double doors on the left and entered a seemingly endless corridor with a long line of doors on either side. The corridor was lit by strips of neon lights but at the furthest end of the corridor the lights were not working and it disappeared ominously into darkness.

It reminded me of one of Rabbi Feldenberg's stories. As I remember it, God lived in a palace and one day he invited the people to come and meet him. The people arrived at the palace. Some were so struck by the ornate ironwork and carvings on the gate that they stayed behind to admire its beauty, others pressed on, a few lost themselves in the splendour of the gardens but the rest entered the palace and found themselves in a very long corridor, at the end of which God was waiting with open arms. As the people walked down the corridor they couldn't help but look into the rooms on either side. In one room, there were exquisite treasures, jewels and diamonds; many people thronged here to adorn themselves from head to foot. In another room, hordes of people swarmed around neatly stacked piles of gold ingots and mountains of silver coins. Those who were hungry gathered in a third room which offered food of every kind – finely cooked meats, exotic fruits and rare wines – and there they ate greedily. A fourth room was adorned with art and fine furnishing, a fifth with delicately embroidered clothing, and a sixth with nubile men and women engaged in bawdy entertainment. Each room was more interesting than the next and the people flocked into them, forgetting why they had come to the palace in the first place, until there was no one left in the corridor and it is said that, to this day, God is still waiting.

Even as an atheist I wasn't going to make the same mistake as all those people. I was going to go to the very end of this corridor where, I was now convinced, a pair of trousers and a hospital coat would be waiting for me. I passed through the light and into the dark extremities of the corridor. At the very end was a plain white door without any distinguishing features. With mounting trepidation I pushed it open.

I entered a room the size of a municipal library with columns of shelves stretching from the floor to the ceiling. They were crammed full of files that were uniformly manila and dusty. The shelves were so tightly aligned that there was virtually no space between them. It would have been impossible for a person to walk down the aisles and retrieve the files. To combat this the shelves were on rollers and at the end of each row was a wooden wheel rather like the steering wheel on a boat. Presumably by turning the wheel you could move the shelves to one side or the other to get to the files. I could have been inside a computer chip with all the information neatly catalogued but accessible only to an expert.

The room was lit by the ubiquitous hospital strip lights. There were precisely minus two windows and there were no trousers or people in sight. I was about to leave when I heard a heavily accented voice.

'I have been waiting for you.'

It was a high-pitched male voice from the Indian sub-continent. It sounded as if it was coming from the other side of the room. I walked along the rows of shelves looking for a gap I could squeeze through, but there was none. An eerie grinding sound caught me unawares and I was surprised to see the shelves part like the Red Sea. An old man appeared on the far side. He was bald with a perfectly round, mahogany brown scalp. An impressively bushy, triangular white beard made up for the lack of hair on his head. Give the man a fishing rod and a red hat and he might have been a gnome. He waddled towards me with a box of files in his arms.

'Here,' he said, 'you can begin with these.'

'Sorry?'

I was somewhat confused; this man was addressing me like I worked for him.

'These are all deceased,' he intoned.

I looked at the box in dismay.

'Deceased?'

'Yes, sir. Dead. All the deceased are beginning on row sixteen.' He thrust the box in my arms and pointed me back in the direction I had come. 'Alphabetically please.'

'Excuse me, but ... '

'You know how to do filing, sir?' he interrupted.

'Yes, of course I do, but ... '

'Well then, off you be going. We have so much to be doing. By the way, my name is Arjuna.'

'I'm Josh.'

'OK, Josh.' He patted my back and chivvied me along towards row sixteen. I accompanied him if only because it was my new creed to do the opposite of what I wanted to do. The man rolled back a couple of rows of shelves to make space for me and then promptly disappeared. I put the box on the ground and gazed at the sea of files on the shelves.

So many dead people. So many lives reduced to data. I rifled through the box at my feet and picked out one at random. Andrew Burgess, 74, cardiac arrest. I put Andrew in his place in between Zoe Brown, 56, cancer of the colon and Amy Burnett, 85, pneumonia. Next was Emily Hargreaves. I skimmed the file and was brought to an immediate halt. Emily was aged 4; she had died of anaphylactic shock after eating a peanut. I imagined a little honey-eyed girl at a birthday party. How awful it must have been for her mother to see her daughter's face swell up and her eyes roll into her head; the panic as they rushed to hospital, the desperation when it was too late. I swallowed hard and felt my eyes well up. I thought about the ladder of scars on Angela's arms and how acutely she must have felt the pain of the world. Something inside me was peeling away. I ploughed on through the box, through the tragedies of a hundred strangers, even finding a namesake, J. Jones, who I instinctively folded and put in my jacket pocket out of defiant solidarity.

As I placed the last file on the shelf I was overcome with grief. I slumped on the floor and wept for all that had happened. A wave of exhaustion washed over me, I could have lain down and slept right there, but instead, I dutifully picked up the empty box and went to look for Arjuna.

I found him doing some filing of his own on row forty-six.

'I've finished,' I said, throwing the box to the ground.

The old man laughed. 'Young sir, you have never finished. I myself am doing this since forty-two years. Now please take another box.'

'Actually, I am not here to do filing.'

'What? You mean they are not sending you to me?'

'No.'

'Oh.' Arjuna looked surprised. 'Then why are you here?'

173

'I was looking for some new clothes.'

The old man almost fell over backwards. 'It is not possible, my God, my God.'

He brought his hands together in front of his third eye and bowed deeply. He began to recite something in what I presumed was Hindi or Sanskrit.

'Oh, babaji, you have come at last.' He whispered and, dropping to his knees, he began to kiss my feet. 'I have waited so long for you.'

'Have you?' I said.

He jumped to his feet. 'I must be asking you one question, sir.'

I nodded my permission.

'You are not wearing under garment – is this right?' he asked.

I was astonished. 'No. I'm not.' I had run out of clean underwear. 'How did you know?'

'This was the prophecy. There is no doubting.' He began to loosen his trousers. 'Please take all my clothes ... '

'No, no, really,' I jumped in, 'I really couldn't take ... no, please, don't take off your ... if you know where the laundry room is or ... '

Despite all my protestations I could not stop him from removing his trousers and revealing a pair of spindly legs latticed with purple veins and cracked with dry skin. He offered up his trousers to me with arms outstretched and head bowed as if he were offering a gift to a Sultan.

'I don't want them, thank you.'

I didn't even like them. They were rather conventional brown cotton trousers with a single well-ironed crease down the front. They were the kind of trousers that you might find at half-price at the back of a stall in Uttar Pradesh.

He looked at me pleadingly. 'You must, babaji. Or my curse will not be lifted.'

My eyes widened. 'You're under a curse?'

It was the same word Lord Morton had used in Norfolk.

He nodded sadly. 'When I was a young man living in India, I did a terrible thing. I am stealing a Sadhu's arbandh while he is bathing in the Ganges during the Kumbh Mela at Haridwar.'

'What's a Sadhu's arbandh?' I asked.

'It is the small rope and cloth that cover the genitals of a man who is renouncing all worldly possessions.'

'Why did you steal it?'

'I was a very poor man and I was knowing that if I am wearing this I would be treated as a holy man and given food and charity by devotees. There are many false holy men who are living this way in India but I was caught with red hands by another Sadhu, and when the victim is coming out of the river and seeing me, he cursed me. He told me that in my next incarnation I will be a mollusc. This is one of the lowliest incarnations possible. I begged him not to be putting me under such a terrible curse. Eventually, after a great deal of loud wailing, he took pity on me. He told me that if I wanted to be escaping the curse I must exile myself to a foreign land, far away from the Ganges and that there I should perform ascetic austerities for forty years, and then Shiva would be appearing to me in the form of a man with no possessions other than the dirty robes he is standing up in and this man would ask me for clothes and I would be recognizing this man for, like the Sadhu who stood before me, he would not be wearing an arbandh of any kind and when this man comes to me I must to show charity and be removing my own clothing and give them to him. Then and only then would the curse be lifted and I am to be allowed to return to my beloved Ganges where

I might die in peace. So I came to England and I am realising that in England it is not possible to survive as an ascetic here, one cannot be standing on one leg or crawling the streets on all fours. In India people will feed you, but here you will be arrested, so I was seeking another kind of austerity. I took this job and I have spent forty years in this room. I have been doing nothing but filing, I am doing it with an open heart and as a form of meditation. I have found peace, but never, never am I thinking you will find me here. Thank you, babaji, for coming.'

His face shone with excitement and he smiled so broadly that I thought his lips would reach his ears and his face would crack in two. I didn't know what to say; I had never released a man from his curse before. Was there some formal language or holy gesture that should be used? I thought it best to say and do nothing.

The man removed his underpants which looked as old as their owner and, as before, held them out to me in a deep bow. I took them from him, holding them at arm's length between finger and thumb and wondered what I should do next.

'You must be putting these on,' he said as if reading my thoughts.

I nodded. For forty years this man had been waiting for me. I could not let him down. In a slow, almost ritualistic manner I removed my blood-stained trousers and put on his underpants. They felt warm and lived in, there was a lifetime of penance in those pants. Miraculously, they fit perfectly. I slipped on the brown cotton trousers from the imagined stall in Uttar Pradesh and they too fitted so perfectly that they might as well have been hand-made for me by a tailor in Savile Row. I transferred all my possessions into my new trousers. I took off my shirt and jacket. He then removed his grey hospital coat and I put it on.

Any misgivings I may have had about wearing another man's pants were easily offset by the childlike pleasure I had bestowed upon this man. A great burden had been lifted from his shoulders. He hopped from one leg to the other in glee. His small wrinkled penis lolloped from side to side, slapping against his thigh like a fish marooned on the deck of a boat.

'I may not be the person you are looking for,' I said.

Arjuna stopped hopping. His penis slowly came to rest. 'How can you be saying this?'

'I'm not Shiva. I'm no one. Just an ordinary fool.'

He laughed. 'And how would you be knowing this?'

'Believe me, I know,' I said wistfully.

'Do you know the story of Karna and Kunti?' he asked.

'Karna and who?'

'Kunti was a little girl when a great sage was coming to stay at her home. She was serving him and attending his every need with patience and diligence for a whole year. The sage was so pleased with her devotion that he gave her a divine mantra. With this mantra she could summon any god and that god would bless her with a child who would possess exceptional qualities.

'One day Kunti was basking in the sun. The warm rays enveloped her body and she was overcome with the desire to test her new mantra. She repeated the words softly to herself and at once the sky was clouding over and Surya, the sun god, appeared before her. She was begging him to be going back because she was, as yet, unmarried, but the words had been spoken and Surya was under their spell. There was a blinding flash, and the god disappeared, leaving in his place a beautiful boy covered in golden armour. Kunti was most mortified, she could not be telling anyone of this child. Who would believe her story? So she placed the baby in a basket and put the basket in the river. The basket was found by a poor charioteer who brought the baby home to his wife. They were calling the boy Karna and raised him as their own. He was an extraordinary boy but he was scorned by those of noble birth. He never knew he was the son of a god, not until much later when his father Surya was appearing to him in a dream and revealing the truth.' The old man smiled. 'I could tell you a hundred stories like this.'

I could have listened to them too.

'What are you saying?' I asked.

'Who is your father, babaji?'

'I never really knew him. He disappeared when I was six. He was into potholing. He was down some huge cave network in Wales when a ferocious storm struck up. There was torrential rain, which caused an underground flood. He didn't come home that evening. In the morning they sent out a search party but he was never seen again.'

Arjuna nodded sagely. 'I don't know who you are, young man, but what I am saying is that people, even from humble origin, must be living with the possibility that they may be greater than they think they are.'

I fell silent as I let this thought expand inside me like the birth of a new universe.

'But I don't believe in God,' I said at length.

'Which god don't you believe in?'

I was puzzled. 'What do you mean?'

'There are many gods, not everyone is believing in every god. Which god are you not believing in?'

'I don't believe in any god,' I asserted.

The Indian burst out laughing. 'That is plainly ridiculous,'

'I'm an atheist.'

'Then you are believing in the atheist God.'

'Atheists don't have a god,' I maintained.

'But you are plainly believing in something.'

'Yes, that there is no god.'

'Then this is your God. Every man has his God. It is not possible to be believing in nothing, for this in itself is a belief.'

He grinned at me beatifically and continued. 'At the end of every belief there is a God waiting. When you are desiring to do the right thing, there is Dharma, God of rightful conduct. When you are believing in your erotic prowess, there is Kama. When you are worshipping the sun, like Kunti, there is Surya. When you are lighting a match, you are summoning Agni. When you are showing compassion, there is Shiva.'

'You don't understand; I am not looking for any God. I don't need a God,' I insisted, though I was no longer sure what I needed.

'Then you are the God that you don't believe in,' he said triumphantly.

My head was beginning to spin. That was a statement I could spend the rest of my life thinking about and still not understand. He was too clever for me. His arguments had such deep appeal that I was almost ready to believe that there was a god for atheists. My mind was opening to magical new thinking. We had somehow released each other. Instinctively I reached forward and hugged him and I felt his compassion and his gratitude in my arms.

From the depths of this embrace I heard the door to the room swing open. A pair of women's heels clicked along the floor from somewhere behind the shelves. 'Hellooo,' she called out, 'is anyone here? I've come to help with the filing.'

Before we knew it she had found us in row forty-six. She stood at the end of the aisle and stared at us. Her mouth dropped open. She clearly wasn't expecting to see two men hugging, one of whom was completely naked.

'Oh … oh,' she stammered, eyeing us with suspicion, 'what on earth are you doing?'

We stepped away from each other guiltily. I looked at Arjuna, embarrassed, and then turned abruptly, ran out of the file room past the flabbergasted girl and back into the corridor where, for a moment, I stood bewildered in my new underpants, trousers and hospital coat.

I wended my way down through the dark end of the corridor into the light and tried not to think about the genitals that had previously inhabited my pants but the more I tried not to think about it the bigger those genitals grew, until they were like a great hairy road block in my mind; there was no way I could get round them, my head was in my pants. Our testicles were gently rubbing against each other through a sliver of cotton as I walked. The follicles of my pubic hair were quietly capturing the groinal odours of the previous occupant, my penis was sashaying rhythmically in the Y front as his had done, my buttocks were pressing the fabric in his precise imprint. I am quite a squeamish person and there are certain intimacies I would rather not share. My focus was drawn away from this unsavoury subject by the sudden appearance of a man blocking my route to the lift. It was the administrator with his notebook.

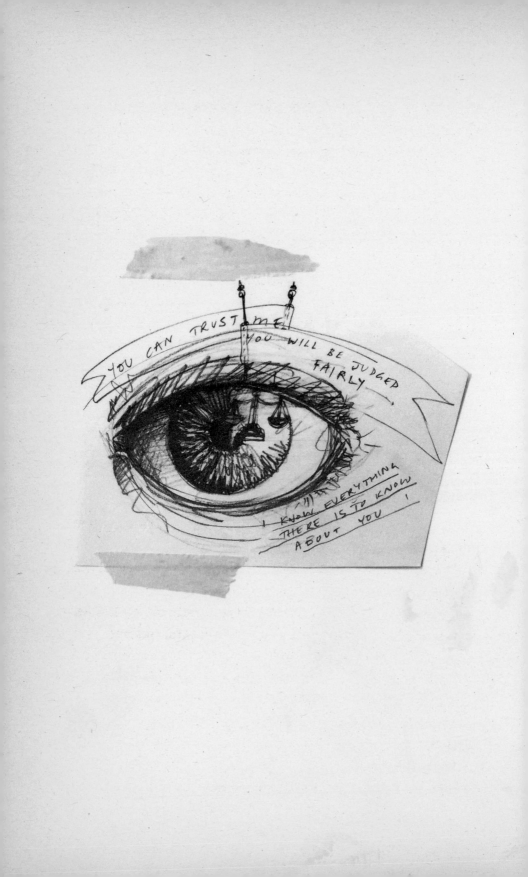

CHAPTER 18

The administrator glared at me with his impenetrable eyes.

'What do you want from me?' I demanded.

'I think you know why I'm here,' he intoned in a smooth caramel voice.

Was it because of Mikey?

'I don't know what you're talking about,' I said, holding tight my nerve.

'Mr Jones,' he sighed sympathetically. I was perturbed that he knew my name.

'I know everything there is to know about you, even down to the wooden box that you are carrying in your pocket.'

'What?'

'You picked it up off the table in the cafe after the suicide attempt.'

I stopped breathing, a chill went down my spine. 'You were there?'

He nodded.

'But I … I don't remember seeing you.'

'I was there.'

'I've never looked inside. It's locked. I don't know what's in it.'

The administrator opened his hand. There was a small gold key in his palm.

'I do,' he said. 'Why don't you give it to me?'

I took it out of my pocket. The administrator's eyes sparkled with anticipation.

'I promise that you will be judged fairly,' he said.

I was desperate to be rid of it. I should have handed it to him there and then but I hesitated. I didn't want to betray Angela or get her into trouble.

I shook my head decisively. 'I can't.'

'It's all right, I'm here to help you. You can trust me.'

I began to feel dizzy. The box was heavy in my hand like compressed matter, as if the entire universe were contained inside it. Rabbi Feldenberg once told us that all the secrets of the universe were held in a single grain of sand. The story of our planet, from the primeval swamp to the formation of continents, from single cell life-forms to man, could be mapped in its journey. Each grain held the breath of God from the beginning of time. Such a burden for one small granule to carry. Similarly my little box felt like it contained the pain and suffering of a thousand generations and with it the entirety of their wisdom and knowledge. Oh, the sheer weight and beauty of it all. How could I possibly give that away? I withdrew my hand.

'It's not mine to give.'

The man sighed with disappointment.

'Do you know what is happening?' he asked gently.

This question echoed deep inside me. I knew the answer but I couldn't access it. Skulking down in my guts there was an understanding of my situation that I could not quite grasp. No matter how far I dug I could not surface the truth. I scraped the inside of my brain for an answer but nothing came. Perhaps I was losing my mind, but after the seven crazy weeks I had spent when Sheryl left me I didn't want to open up that thought.

I shook my head. 'No, I don't know what is happening.'

'Do you know where you are?'

'I'm in a hospital ... aren't I?' I was now doubting the veracity of everything.

The administrator put his hands on my shoulders in a fatherly way. His clothes smelt of mothballs and camphor, like they belonged to someone who had been dead a long time.

'Yes and you have to come to terms with this,' he said. 'You know who Angela is, you have to accept the truth about her.'

'No,' I shouted, 'I don't want to know the truth, leave me alone.'

'You're running out of time, Josh. What you decide now could be life or death. We can't let this situation drag on much longer. It's time to come over to our side.'

'But I don't know anything. I can't help you. Listen, let me think about it.'

He shook his head.

'Please,' I begged.

'All right,' he relented, 'you have one day and that's it.'

I nodded meekly and put the box back in my pocket. He stepped to one side and let me pass. In a daze I walked down the corridor to the lift. I pressed the call button. Minus two was upsetting my mental equilibrium, I was desperate to escape.

I found a quiet place to sit outside the maternity ward where I could wait for a shift change in the critical care unit. After

185

a while I was beginning to attract stray glances from staff, who must have been wondering why an employee should be loitering for so long without showing any sign of doing work. I got up and wandered off until I found another waiting room in ophthalmology and so it went from waiting room to waiting room until the small hours.

Hoping that none of the night staff on Angela's ward would recognise me, I made my way up to her floor. Angela had been moved to one of the private rooms in the critical care unit, maybe because they intended to turn off the machine, but I didn't know for sure. There was a nurse at the end of Angela's bed watching over her. I stepped into the room.

'Are you Joanne Hall?' I asked, reading her name badge.

'Yes,' she replied.

'You have to go down to A&E immediately. There's been a big accident, they've got more victims than they can deal with right now,' I said breathlessly.

'But I'm not supposed to leave here,' she said.

'I know, it's highly irregular, but believe me it's chaos down there and Doctor Strang sent me to get someone from critical care.'

'Who is Doctor Strang?'

'He's the new guy. Look, please hurry. It's all hands on deck. I can keep an eye on your patient if you tell me what to do,' I said, pointing at Angela.

'There's nothing to do. If any of the readings become irregular the alarms will go off. Here I'll put them on for you.' She fiddled with a knob on the monitor to the right of Angela's head. 'I'll be back as soon as I can.' She rushed away.

'Be quick,' I called after her.

There was a folded wheelchair up against the back wall. I quickly opened it and wheeled it to Angela's bedside.

'Hello, my lovely, it's me again.' I whispered. 'I don't think anyone believes that you'll ever come back. Mikey said they were going to turn you off in the morning. I don't know if he was saying that to make me go away or if he was telling the truth but I'm not prepared to take that chance. You understand what I'm saying? I'm not going to let you die like this without one more taste of life. I mean, if you're going to die anyway then you may as well die somewhere beautiful with the sound of birds in your ears – not here, not in this shit hole. I'm going to take you away, but I need your help. I need to know that this is what you want. You have to give me a sign, Angela.'

I watched her carefully but nothing came. Not even a twitch from her finger.

'OK, Angela, I know you can hear me, I know you can. You have to hear me. Listen to me, you're in a coma, Angela, and they're going to take you off life support. Do you understand me? It's now or never, sweetheart.' I put my hands on her shoulders and shook her. The rhythm of her breathing appeared to alter as she took in more air. I mirrored her breath. Anything to enter her world and bring her out. Then I changed the rhythm to see if she would go with me, but it had no effect.

'Come on, we don't have much time. Give me a sign, come on, or it will be too late. Are you with me? Can you hear me?'

Nothing.

'OK, I'm just going to do it anyway. OK? I'm going to be the God I don't believe in. I'm going to do it. I'm just going to do it. Oh shit, I can't believe I'm going to do this but I'm going to do it anyway. You're not staying here a minute longer.'

I looked at the tubes and the monitors, not knowing where to begin. I turned down the volume on the screen and then, carefully but inexpertly, I began to detach her from the paraphernalia that ensnared her.

Now denuded of everything, I leant over and hugged her. 'Oh my darling, what have I done?'

I should have known better, but I could not help myself; I brought my lips to hers and kissed her gently. A fountain of tiny electrical impulses spilt down my body making my flesh tingle. Her sleeping breast heaved against my chest. A flush of blood flooded into my groin. It was wrong, so wrong.

A great cavern opened up inside me, I was falling deeper and deeper inside myself. There was no end to it, a terrific free-dive into the depths of a well without limit. I never wanted to breathe again. I felt a droplet roll down my cheek. Then another and another. Something moved. A pair of hands locked on to my shoulders like clamps. Perhaps the nurse had witnessed my indiscretion, except the hands were not pulling me away, they were hauling me in. Angela's mouth opened and her tongue jolted into life and entwined around mine. Her whole body went into spasm and her grip tightened as if she were clinging to a buoy in a storm swept ocean. She was holding on for dear life as the waves crashed around her. A ferocious passion was unleashed inside her as she sucked me in. Her need was overwhelming. I would have given her everything I had but I didn't understand what was happening, whether she was dying or coming back to life. I tried to pull away from her but her arms were unyielding and then suddenly her eyes opened wide and her body went limp.

CHAPTER 19

I retreated, terrified that I had killed her but then I saw her chest move; she was still breathing.

I sprung into action. I picked her up and put her into the wheel chair and lifted the leg rest for her broken leg. Her head lolled forward. I noticed some bindings on the chair and quickly tied them round her chest to prevent her from slumping forward. I threw a couple of blankets over her and pushed her down the ward as fast as I could.

I remembered that I had seen an exit by the maternity ward on the ground floor. It would be a less obvious way to leave the building. Once out into the car park I pushed the wheelchair up a ramp to a small pedestrian side exit on to Dartmouth Park Hill. I glanced over anxiously towards the bin area where Mikey lay dead. There was police tape blocking off that part of the car park and a solitary officer standing guard. It was approaching dawn, a puddle of pink light was rising in the east. Angela's absence would already have been discovered, the police already called. Soon security officers and nurses would be giving their testimony. Connections to Mikey's death would quickly be made and a major manhunt would soon begin, even though there wasn't a shred of ill intent in my actions and I had done nothing wrong. Besides, Angela appeared to be waking up; she had been jolted back to life. Shouldn't I be given credit for that at least?

I could think of only one place to go: Hampstead Heath. There, we could enjoy the early morning rays, breathe the grassy air and listen to birdsong. We could hide for a while and then what? First I had to do the thing I had promised my mother. I would hire a car and go to Wales to retrieve my father's helmet. I would bring it to my mum and then I would hand myself in. And what about Angela? I would look after her as long as I could, until I had shown her the swans gliding on the ponds; the strange green parakeets nesting in the hollow stumps of dying trees; the dappled woods under Kenwood House; the panorama from the top of Parliament Hill where it is said Guy Fawkes waited to watch the Houses of Parliament burn. I would collect her flowers from the meadow; we would marvel at the intricacies of spider's webs and track down owl pellets. We would live out a life in a few golden hours and I would talk to her about love and death and the universe and what it all meant to me. We would be the King and Queen of England, and then I would do what needed to be done before the police caught up with me and the noose finally closed around my neck.

As I pushed her towards the Heath I wanted to speak to her wakening mind but I didn't know what to say, so I described in every detail the conveyor belt of life that swept past her wheelchair, as if I were creating the world by the magic of language. Rabbi Feldenberg told the story of a man who woke up one day and everything he had ever known was gone. A desolate waste stretched out before him, leaking into an indistinct horizon which contained neither land, sea or sky but was nothing more than a muddy haze. Where was his bed, his room, his home, his family? Where were all the objects that brought him comfort? Where was nature? Where in hell was he? For a long time the man did not know what to do, indeed he could not even think of all the things that he had lost, so innumerable were they. At length he began to recite the alphabet, for it was the only thing he could remember and with each sound, each combination of letters, things began to reappear until, by the time he had voiced every consonant and every vowel, the whole universe had been reborn. Nothing exists without the possibility of its name and vibration.

For Angela, might this be a gentle reintroduction to the world? A moment to allow the jumbled contents of her mind to resettle and find focus?

'On your left side is a low wall made from red bricks, held together by cement and in front of us is a black and white metal pole with a round orange ball on top. Inside the ball is a light which shines at night. The pole shows people where they can cross the road safely. Sticking out of the pavement ahead of us are two London plane trees. The bright colourful objects going past us at speed are called cars, they take people from one place to another. A lady is walking towards us with a small creature on the end of a rope. The creature has four legs and black fur and is known as a dog. To the right are some concrete boxes stacked on top of each other. Each box contains a family. The boxes are called flats and people pay huge amounts of money to own them. I used to have one. We are walking past a school, which is a place where children learn how to read and write. There is no one there yet. Most people are still asleep.'

On it went until we were in the park. She did not speak but her eyes flicked from side to side as she slowly came to terms with her surroundings. She seemed to register my presence with some curiosity but no sign of recognition.

I found a bench on the outer edge of a ring of trees which stood like sentinels on the brow of a grassy hillock. I sat down. I was tired from pushing Angela up the hill. Ahead of us a meadow swept down towards a shimmering pond beyond which rose the half hidden lawns and houses of wealthy Londoners reaching their pinnacle in Highgate village where the mismatched spires of a church and a communication beacon scratched the cloudless sky. A crisp light breeze was sweeping the night air into the trees and swallowing up the moisture from the morning dew. I described it all in great detail before falling silent to catch my breath.

'Did you get on the ship?'

Her words took me by surprise. They dropped out of her mouth slowly in little jaggedy nuggets of sound as if she were regurgitating crystals of shattered glass.

'What ship?' I asked, puzzled.

'The big ship.'

'Er … no, I didn't get on the ship … did you?

'It was such a beautiful ship.'

'Was it?'

'They wouldn't let me on. I was begging them. Let me on, let me on. I didn't have a ticket.'

'Maybe another time.'

'Yeah maybe another time.'

She reached up and touched the bandage on her head. Then she looked at me strangely, blinked hard and rubbed her eyes. 'It is lovely here, in the trees. Are we dead?'

I wasn't sure whether she would rather I answered in the

affirmative or the negative. I didn't want to disappoint her either way. Something in my hesitation must have betrayed the truth for she sighed heavily as if life were the greatest of all ailments.

'I know your voice. Who are you?' she asked.

'Don't you remember me?'

She shook her head vacantly.

'I was there when you tried to commit suicide.'

Angela nodded and her eyes moistened. 'Oh.'

'We met after you got evicted, remember? Outside your house. I'd just been evicted too. We went to a café.'

'Did we?'

'Yes, remember? We went to the café to console ourselves.'

Angela's brow furrowed. It dismayed me that, whilst she had made such a huge impression on me, I had not had a similar effect on her.

'Do you know what happened? Do you know how close you came? You died in the road and a doctor brought you back. You've been out cold for more than a week.'

'Really?' Her gaze lifted skyward as if she were straining to recall something. 'I had a sense of passing through a wormhole into another universe.'

Her words were slow and measured, each sentence punctuated by long pauses.

'It was as if time had lost its chronology; everything was happening at once. Past, present and future were indistinguishable.' She marvelled at the memory. 'I was above and beyond time. A baby, a child, a woman, an elder – all things equally and simultaneously. As a child I carried the wisdom of age and as an old woman I carried the vigour of youth.'

'Like you were in heaven?'

'Not as such ... '

I could see she was struggling to marshal her thoughts and yet, with the effort, came a simple articulacy.

'... it felt more like a perception shift ... like I had suddenly become aware of a way of seeing that I didn't even know existed and I was thinking: "oh this is how to see", and I couldn't understand why I hadn't noticed it before ... like discovering a new function on your computer which would have made all your labours so much easier had you known about it. Everything was impossibly bright and clear. I have never felt so free, so limitless, so powerful. I was not bound by memory. For the first time in my life I had a sense of achievement, but those achievements were not in the world of work, they did not involve ego or fame, but simple things ... like that I could walk or build a tower from blocks or hang upside down from a tree branch, or read a book. I was immensely proud of these things as if all my tiny accomplishments in life had just happened and still carried their glow of satisfaction. The mechanism of forgetting is so cruel. We forget our sense of wonder.

'I was a toddler in a playground by the seaside. I was looking out to sea, "ship, ship, SHIP," I was shouting. I was filled with awe and excitement. The ship came closer until it dropped anchor close to shore and a small boat emerged from it. There was a man on board rowing through the silent water towards me. I was pointing and screaming: "baby ship, baby ship, SHIP". My whole body was engaged ... invested in what was happening. I wanted to get on. I was literally jumping up and down. My amazement never waned.'

She sighed heavily.

'I have forgotten how to wonder. Nothing makes me jump up and down any more. Why don't we accumulate wonder as we grow old until we die of astonishment?'

She raised her arms in a gesture of supplication to the gods. 'I guess we can't ... we just can't do it.'

Her nightie slid up her arm and again I caught sight of the patchwork of scars that criss-crossed her wrists and arms like notches on a tree. She followed my eyes.

'I've been cutting myself for years,' she said. 'Sometimes I get so angry, so frustrated with everything and I can't speak with anyone about it and then I cut myself and it sort of takes the other pain away. It takes my mind off my troubles. It gives me a kind of focus when my mind is spinning out of control. I don't expect you to understand. I know I shouldn't do it but I almost enjoy it. While I'm doing it I feel in control. Afterwards I feel ashamed.'

'I like your scars,' I said

'What?'

'I like your scars'

She was taken aback. There was a long pause and then she said:

'No one has ever said that before. People get upset by them, they want to cure me. What is there to like?'

'It's so courageous, I could never cut myself. I'm far too squeamish. I never get that angry, I never feel that much pain. I have to say I'm almost jealous. You've felt things that I have never felt, you have been to the very edge of what a human being can tolerate. It's ennobling.'

She was flabbergasted. 'You're quite something, aren't you? What was your name again?'

'Josh,' I said.

'Josh. You've just gone and turned everything on its head. I don't know what to say. Courageous, huh? Ennobling?' She began to laugh. 'You're an extraordinary person.'

'You think so?'

'Yes, did no one ever tell you?'

'No. My wife said I was dull. And she should know – we were together seven years, married for six,' I said.

'She said that! I think I remember you telling me about her now. And you told me about a tree and a rabbit. That was a beautiful story.'

'You heard all that. I wasn't sure … '

'Sometimes I could hear people talking to me. Sometimes I must have been dreaming, going on adventures of my own. I can't really describe it.'

'How are you feeling now?'

'I've got a headache but that's by the by. My leg hurts, my ribs ache, I've got bruises all over and I feel exhausted beyond belief, but aside from all that I feel fucking fantastic, Josh. What about you?'

I laughed. 'Well, it's been the strangest week of my life but I haven't felt as excited as I feel now about anything since … since I can remember.'

There were so many questions I wanted to ask her. There were so many answers I needed for myself.

'Why did you kiss me in the café?' I asked.

At first she looked surprised but slowly the memory came to her.

'I guess I wanted to feel something for the last time. I was saying goodbye to life.'

'But what about me? Didn't you think about what that would do to me?'

She shook her head. 'I wasn't thinking about you at the time. I am sorry that I put you through that. It was selfish … I am selfish.'

'Why did you want to die?' I asked.

'Because I have always felt incomplete, like half of me was missing.'

I nodded. I knew exactly what she meant.

'Mikey said you had an argument.'

'You know Mikey?'

'I met him at your bedside. I didn't like him much.'

Now was not the moment to tell her of his death.

'We always argued, he thinks everything is about him; even my suicide is about him.'

'Wasn't it?'

'No. The way I see it, death is not the enemy ... it's not the end. It's an opportunity.'

'Would you do it again?'

A shadow crossed her eyes. 'I don't know, maybe.'

'But Angela, you've got your whole death to be dead, if you know what I mean, you don't have to hurry to get there, it's going to happen anyway. There has to be something on this side of the line, some beauty, some love, some fun, something that makes it all worthwhile.'

A deep well of sadness seemed to overflow inside her. 'Don't you think I've already thought that, don't you think I've already tried? But it's hopeless, I can't make it work. I don't even think it *can* work – at least not for me.'

'But what makes you say that? Where's your evidence?' I persisted.

With some effort she turned her chair towards me. 'People like you live your whole lives under anaesthetic. You are so numb that you don't feel what's going on around you. You build a dam inside you so that you can withstand the pressures of the outside world. You don't get hurt by the injustice in the world. I'm sure like everyone else you see the starving children in Africa and you say "isn't that awful", but then you carry on as if nothing happened. When you watch the polar ice caps slip away into the sea, you throw up your arms and say "we should be doing more", and then promptly forget all about it. Or when you see the organised mass murder that goes unpunished in warzones and hellholes across the world you wish it didn't have to be like this. You are not unthinking, you are not unfeeling but these things hardly make a dent in your psyche, you are deadened to the suffering. People build cocoons in which they accumulate privilege, and so a whole nation absolves itself of responsibility. We tell ourselves that our individual impact on global events is insignificant, and we transfer the blame to politicians or big business and forget that we are working for these businesses, that we are buying their products, that we are sanctioning their abuses. It is we who hold all the aces and it is they who are serving our insatiable needs and, in the final analysis, We are They. When we point the finger at Them we are pointing it at ourselves. The problem is we don't know how to live otherwise. I don't have answers, I just don't want to be part of it. People say they care but they don't. If they really cared, their hearts would bleed and they wouldn't stop bleeding. They wouldn't be able to sleep or eat for the rage inside them.

'For the life of me, Josh, I wish I was like you and everyone else. I need a voice of sanity. I wish I had a layer of blubber that made me impenetrable to all this, but I don't. I spend my life in horror. I feel every bomb that falls as if it fell on me. Every baby that dies of hunger has been ripped from my own womb. Everywhere I go I see energy pissing away, CO_2 billowing into the atmosphere. Every light, every car, every machine, every bit of plastic, every slab of concrete; look around you Josh, virtually everything we touch is tainted. We can't stop ourselves, we are addicted to waste. We can't help but abuse each other.

'Maybe I stepped in front of that bus because I realised that nothing will ever change, and that even radical action won't work. In thirty years there'll be ten billion people on the planet, there'll be nothing to drink, Southern Spain will be like the Sahara, the permafrost in Siberia will have melted, there will be no coral, no glaciers, no polar bears, the Pacific Islands will be under water, we will have wrecked it all and no one really cares. We are nothing more than a plague on this planet.'

She was talking as if the responsibility for all this rested on her shoulders alone, as if Atlas had relinquished his duties and given her the onerous task of keeping the planet aloft. The survival angst of every living organism had been tipped into her fragile soul and she couldn't live with the burden a moment longer. I wished I could slip into a phone box, put on a pair of Superman's pants and make the world spin backwards like Christopher Reeve did in the movie. Back to a time of innocence, to a time when we worshipped the sun and moon and earth and lived in fear of their powers. If only it were that simple.

'I can't reconcile myself to it,' she went on. 'That's when I cut myself; when the pain of living is so intolerable that I have to divert myself away from it. Yes, I feel all right now but it is transitory, I know it won't be long before I sink again, because that's the story of my life. Look. Each cut has a story. This first one here,' she pointed to a slash on her forearm, 'I did after the massacres at Srebrenica, I was still a teenager. This one I did after I watched a huge piece of the Antarctic coastal shelf collapse into the sea. This one I did when I read about the mass rapes in the Congo.'

She went on like this for some time, hopping, almost randomly, from one cause to another as if they were all connected; matching each scar with something that made her furious. The longer she related these stories the more I began to tune out. She was right, I was numb to the pain. That side of me had long since been suppressed. I found myself focussing not so much on what she said but the way she said it. Her eyes were stretched wide open, almost unblinking, her pale cheeks flushed red and she made emphatic sweeps of her arms every few sentences as if she were clearing the air of doubt. Her voice, no longer hesitant, seemed to find an extra octave. She was the passion I craved for myself, the conscience of my dormant soul.

As she spoke, a gravitational-like force was sucking me towards her. I was spiralling headlong into Angela's world like a piece of driftwood in a whirlpool. I wanted her to be part of me and me to be part of her. I leant forward and kissed her. I could not stop myself. She responded by pulling me tightly towards her as though she never wanted to let me go.

She was all I had. I was all she had.

We left our vantage point and wandered along a meandering path through thickets and woods. We talked and talked as if the entirety of what needed to be said had to be said in a heartbeat. She told me about her repressed childhood, her family and her political activities and I told her about everything that had happened to me since I met her, about the riot, the meeting with her parents, the photographer in the cemetery and the strange encounter with Arjuna. I told her about my father and the mysterious reappearance of his helmet and, when all this had been recounted, I showed her the box I had found in the cafe.

'It's not mine,' she said, turning it in her fingers.

'Really?' I exclaimed. 'But didn't you leave it on the table?'

'I've never seen it in my life,' she assured me.

'So whose is it then?' I asked.

'I've no idea.'

A shiver of anxiety ran through me. Now I knew something had happened in that café which my mind would not let me remember. If the box did not belong to Angela could it actually be mine? Why was the administrator following me and why was he so intent on having the box if it wasn't Angela's? This led to a far more disturbing question: why did I have the growing feeling that I could not trust myself anymore? That my actions, though logical to me, were not necessarily those of a sane human being?

CHAPTER 20

We drifted up the hill into the grounds of Kenwood House and came across a pond nestling between the lower reaches of the lawn and woodland. A couple of brilliant blue dragonflies hovered over the still waters.

I decided to come clean about the death of Mikey. She would find out soon enough and it wouldn't serve me not to tell her. Better she heard it from me than be told by another and consequently grow suspicious of my motives for not telling her.

She tutted angrily when I explained how he had lied to the security guards to get me evicted from the hospital. She was shocked to hear how he had chased and attacked me, but when I told her the tragic denouement, her emotions bubbled over and she began to cry, which made me worry that I would lose her and that maybe I shouldn't have told her.

A gust of wind caught the top of the trees and sent ripples across the pond. I stopped pushing and waited for her to find some equilibrium.

'I'm sorry,' I said simply.

'Why should you be sorry, he almost killed you.'

'Did you love him very much?' I asked.

'Actually I hated him. I hated him and I loved him.'

'It sounds like a complicated relationship. How did you meet him?'

'On a protest march at the G7 summit. He was a monument of a man, ferocious and fearless. He led a charge against the police and nearly got through to Merkel's car. I found myself gravitating towards him in the melee. I remember thinking: here is a true revolutionary, a Danton, a man who would die for the change he sought. I threw myself at him that day and took him home. I can be terribly impulsive when it comes to men. We made love and in our passion we exorcised all the frustration and anger of the riot; but I was wrong about him, he was more Robespierre than Danton, more of a narrow-minded puritan than a freedom fighter. He would turn against his own friends if they disagreed with him. He was a bully and he represented everything that's wrong with the movement. Maybe every belief has its shadow – a seductive Darth Vader figure who stalks and ultimately undermines it. He was fighting against the forces of darkness in the world but he couldn't control the forces of darkness in himself. He was the mirror image of the people we abhorred, the polar opposite. One day I realised that the people we were fighting against or seeking to persuade would never join our ranks, because what they saw in us was as ugly as what we saw in them. Mikey wanted to get results by any means and for a long time I went with him, but if you sully your belief, if you use it to justify morally questionable acts, then your cause is lost in the eyes of others. In the end I couldn't support Mikey's position any more. Violence was in his nature; all his life he grappled with that side of himself and it was only when he found a cause, that he could justify his aggression. If he hadn't found politics he would have been a criminal. The politics was just an excuse. I think he got a perverse pleasure from violence – almost a sexual pleasure. He didn't want peaceful outcomes. He was the same with me, that's why we argued all the time. Later we would make up and everything would taste like honey compared with what went on before. I lived for these meagre drops of honey but, oh God, how much shit did I have to swallow in between. This time I was through with him for good. I guess his death was fitting of his life. I shouldn't be so sad, but I am … I really am.'

'I'm so sorry,' I said again, 'I didn't mean to hurt him, he tripped and fell, but I know I'll get the blame.'

'What are you going to do?'

'I'm going to collect my father's helmet for my mum and hand myself in. If I run away it will be taken as a sign of guilt. I think if I come forward I'll have a chance of explaining myself. Maybe they'll believe me, but even if they do, I think I'll be in a lot of trouble for taking you from the hospital.'

She nodded gravely. 'I'll stand by you.'

I heard something move in the grass and a toad leapt up and landed close by. I knelt down and caught it in my hands.

'If you kiss it, maybe a prince will appear,' I said.

She looked at me wryly. 'Do you believe in fairy tales?'

I was about to say 'no', but then I thought about the magnificent Rabbi Feldenberg, and I changed my mind. His belief in the redeeming nature of story was absolute.

'Not literally, of course, but I think they mean something.'

'What is the toad and the princess about then?'

'The power of transformation? The toad is cursed, he feels ugly and useless, then along comes a girl who is very pretty, but terribly lonely. She recognises the toad for what he really is, and that's all it takes for the toad to realise his inner beauty and for the princess to lose her loneliness. It's so simple, isn't it? Two people transform each other in the act of love.'

'I don't believe in romantic love,' Angela replied. 'I think the princess and the toad are the same person. You know, like we all have a toad and a princess inside us, we all have a repressed part to our character. Call it what you want: light and dark, yin and yang; it's only when the one embraces the other that we become complete. It's about self-love and self-acceptance.'

'Maybe you're right,' I reflected. 'All the more reason to kiss it.'

I opened my palm and brought it up to my lips, but before I could kiss it, the toad leapt out of my hand and hopped into the long grass.

'Damn,' I exclaimed. 'There goes my chance.'

When I turned back to Angela, something had changed in her face, she seemed momentarily lost and bewildered, then her muscles spasmed sharply as if a flash of lightening were passing through her. Her brow furrowed and her body shuddered before slowly releasing as she came back to herself.

'What was that?' I asked with concern.

'I don't know. Like a shooting pain. I'm OK.'

'You're not OK. I'm going to take you back to the hospital.'

'No, please don't make me go back, I want to stay with you. I'm fine, really I am.' She smiled feebly to prove the point.

'Let's not take risks, Angela. It's a miracle you've come round, a miracle you can even talk. We need to get you checked over and make sure you recover as best you can.'

'Josh, you're not hearing me. I don't want to go back,' she said forcefully.

'And you're not hearing me,' I asserted.

She sighed deeply. 'All right, let's make a deal: take me with you to get the helmet and then I promise I'll go back to the hospital.'

'Why are you being so insistent?'

'Do you honestly think they'll let you stay with me? This could be the only day we have.'

I grimaced at the thought. She was right.

'OK, but as soon as the shops open, I'm going to buy you a dress. You can't go around dressed in a blanket.'

The South Wales Caving Club Centre was housed in a limestone grey row of shabby terraced cottages, which stood as a solitary outpost of humanity half way up the western slope of some nameless hill in the Brecon Beacons National Park across the valley from the Black Mountain. The car struggled up the potholed track, past a disused quarry and through a clump of trees into the car park. Angela, who had been sleeping for most of the journey, awoke with a jolt. She looked pale and confused. I watched her in the mirror as she rubbed her eyes in the rear seat and adjusted her broken leg which was stretched out across the black upholstery.

'Are we here?' she asked.

I nodded and pulled into the car park.

As I got out, I was filled with a terrible sense of foreboding. Beneath my feet was the ogre that had swallowed my father: Ogof Ffynnon Ddu, one of the longest, deepest caves in Britain. Twenty-eight miles of caverns, phreatic tubes and streamways sculpted out of limestone by the slow percolation of rainwater and the penetrating curiosity of an underground river over many millions of years.

Somewhere down there my father had disappeared and now, a quarter of a century later, the dozing ogre had spat out his helmet like a piece of indigestible gristle. I surveyed the earth and the hills around; if this hill was my father's burial ground then the Black Mountain was his gravestone. I took a deep breath and went round to the boot to get the wheelchair. I brought it round to the rear door and helped Angela into it. Then we headed towards the main entrance of the club.

Each cottage had two tiny windows, one upstairs and one downstairs, like two scrunched up eyes that looked out cheerlessly over the green undulating landscape. From the outside they looked austere and unwelcoming but inside it was altogether different. The cottages had been knocked through to create more open spaces. It had the feel of a lively youth hostel filled with spectacular photographs of underground canyons, lakes and rock formations.

The entrance led straight into a kitchen with a long stretch of metal worktop over cheap formica cupboards. A half-eaten loaf of bread stood abandoned on a wooden chopping board next to an open tub of margarine. Steam was rising from a recently boiled kettle.

'Hello,' I called, 'is anyone here?'

'In the common room,' a voice called back.

We followed the voice down a corridor past a couple of flights of stairs and a small room with a telephone and chair, to another much larger room. It was full of old mismatched armchairs and there was a giant survey map of the caves which ran the length of the near wall. There were three men and a woman sitting around an old wooden table which bore four mugs of tea and a bowl of sugar. The woman must have been in her mid-forties, her face was as craggy as the caves she explored but her eyes were a luminous blue and shone out like a couple of sapphires in the rock. The men were variously

aged in their twenties, forties and sixties. The youngest of
them jumped to his feet and stretched out his hand.

'Are you Josh?' he asked.

'Yes,' I said shaking his hand. 'And this is Angela.'

'I'm Gerry.'

I had been expecting a Welsh accent and was a little
surprised to hear well-tutored vowels from the Home
Counties. He introduced the middle-aged man and woman
as Glenda and Alan. The older man was called Arthur. He
was a tall athletic chap with a full head of unkempt grey hair.
He appeared to jolt upright when I said hello as if he had
accidentally touched an electrified fence.

'Did you bring sleeping bags?' asked Gerry

'No, I didn't know we needed them. We may not stick
around too long. I may drive straight back, if I've got the
energy,' I replied.

I threw a glance at Angela to see if she had any preferences.
Her face looked strained, as if she was battling against
a migraine.

'I don't think I could face driving straight back,' she said.
'Why don't we stay over, it will be lovely to wake up in the hills.'

'It's up to you,' Gerry said, 'it's a warm night, you could easily
sleep in your clothes. We've got three dormitories upstairs,
one for members, one for women, one for men. There's also
one family room, which is free tonight, if you wanted to be
together. Just a warning though – it's very basic.'

'Can we take the family room?' Angela asked.

'Absolutely. The rooms are upstairs. Will you manage that?'

'I'll find a way.' Angela forced a pained smile. She
was suffering.

'Arthur, do you want to get Josh and Angela a cup of tea?
They must be thirsty after the drive.'

Arthur sprang to his feet and stared at me strangely as he walked past. He was unnerving me and I was glad to see him leave the room. In the brief time since I had met him he had already succeeded in making me feel very uncomfortable.

I sat down in a chair which had seen better days and felt the springs press into my backside. They asked me if we had found the place all right and we made light conversation until Arthur returned with our tea. As he put the tea on the table he studied my face and shuddered involuntarily. I felt the hairs on the back of my neck bristle like a threatened cat.

Gerry produced a plastic bag from under his seat and pulled out my father's battered helmet. The yellow plastic had faded and was stained green with algae. Two of the rivets that held the lamp in place had sheered off, a third was loose and the rusted light clung forlornly to its final fixing. The strappings had long since rotted away and the inner webbing was all but destroyed. I took the helmet from Gerry and ran my fingers over it. It took me hurtling back to that final day, when Dad had held me in his arms before disappearing into the cave, and to the moment when we had taken the photograph of the three of us laughing together that was on the mantelpiece in Mum's flat.

Now that I held the helmet in my hand I couldn't ever remember my father without it. Whether this impression came from that photograph or from time spent at potholing and climbing weekends during which Mum and I would have picnics whilst he hovered above us on the end of a rope or disappeared into a cave for a couple of hours, I cannot say. Perhaps it was a combination of the two, for such is the flimsy nature of memory that I could easily have imposed the photographic image that eventually took pride of place on our mantelpiece on to every one of those vague and distant childhood remembrances.

On the back of the helmet, I could make out the faded letters V and N where he had written his name. Vince.

'Where did you find it?' I asked.

'It was wedged between a couple of rocks at the bottom of a sump,' said Gerry. 'I've dived down there a couple of times and never seen anything before so I was surprised when I saw it. I didn't know whose it was at first. I figured someone must have dropped it in the streamway, except that it looked so old. It was my uncle who told me it was your dad's.' He gestured to the older man.

Arthur nodded, 'I knew immediately.'

'How?'

'I knew your dad very well, Josh. He came here many times before you were born and a couple of times after. I was there when he died. When you walked in earlier my heart skipped a beat, I thought I'd seen a ghost. You look exactly like him – I would have recognised you immediately.'

Only then did I realise Arthur was the man who had come to the cottage with the policeman on that dreadful night of the accident to tell my mum what had happened. His face had cracked and shifted so much over the years.

'You were in the cave with him when he died, weren't you?'

Arthur nodded. 'He was right behind me.' A troubled look crossed his brow as he was transported back to the fateful moment when my father was washed away.

'What happened?' I asked.

He shook his head forlornly, he opened his mouth but no words came out. He blinked rapidly a few times and then got up and left the room. I looked at the others for reassurance.

'He's been carrying a heavy burden all these years,' said Glenda.

'He's not been himself ever since we found the helmet,' Gerry added.

'I don't understand why his helmet should suddenly appear now? After twenty-five years?' Angela said.

'There are a lot of inaccessible places down there where the water disappears under the rocks and emerges further down the cave. He could easily have got carried down river and trapped in one of those places and we would never have found him. A cave can change shape in a flood; a lot of rocks move around. He could have been wedged in by a boulder which is probably why they couldn't find him. There was a guy who died in France in Gouffre Berger. Oh, what was his name, Glenda?'

'Alex Miller?'

'Yes that's it; Alex Miller. He disappeared down there and they searched everywhere for him. It's a huge pothole – drops more than a kilometre underground – it can take days to get to the bottom. They turned over every stone, explored every passageway and even dived the sump pools. Then two years later an expedition discovered a previously unknown gallery in a dead-end, side passage about a hundred meters below the ground. At the end of this gallery was a small vertical pitch – a hole; and at the bottom of that hole they found Alex Miller under a boulder. He must have fallen down it and dislodged some rocks as he fell. In the case of your father they couldn't explore the waterways until the flood water dropped but there are plenty of dry passages that they would have scoured. If he'd managed to get out of the water they would have found him – if not in the days following the accident then soon after. There's a couple of sumps which are pretty easy to dive which they will have checked but the general policy on a rescue is not to risk anyone's life trying to recover someone who we know is dead. It's just not worth it. We'll search the places we can get to but we won't do anything stupid. Over time stuff has shifted and maybe the helmet came free and got washed into the pool where I found it. We had a flood a month back, it could have happened then,' Gerry said.

'But we haven't had much rain since, so right now the water level is very low. It's possible that over the coming weeks we'll find more things,' Glenda added.

'Really,' my heart was thumping, 'you mean we might find his body?'

Gerry shifted uncomfortably at the prospect. 'I don't know. What do you think, Alan?'

Alan shook his head. 'I doubt it, not after all this time. The current's strong; the bones would separate from each other. They'd probably pass through the cave, they could be anywhere downstream. I'm sorry, Josh, I don't think we'll find him.'

'But what about that diver they found in South Africa?' Glenda wondered. 'Some of the bones were still inside the wetsuit after ten years.'

Alan shrugged his shoulders. 'Different kind of wetsuit. Caving suits are much looser. Look, I suppose it's technically possible but I wouldn't know where to start.'

'At the place you found the helmet?' I offered.

'I very much doubt they'll be together. Besides, what would be the point?'

The others nodded in agreement.

'All this gory talk! Josh is going to get the wrong impression about us,' Gerry said jovially. 'It's not half as dangerous as it sounds. Most caves we go down are perfectly safe, they are well explored. They've been there for millions of years. Rocks don't suddenly fall on your head. There are a few tight squeezes; sometimes you have to crawl, but on the whole you're on your feet. It's terrific fun. Obviously the press go to town every time there is an accident but actually your father's experience is very rare. There are a few intrepid souls who want to be the first to uncover a new system and they will take more risks, but for most of us, it is just a sport and we wouldn't do it if we thought it was that dangerous.'

I was desperate to understand why my father had enjoyed potholing but nothing Gerry could say would make me believe it was safe. For me it would always be a killer no matter what the statistics.

Arthur appeared in the doorway.

'Josh, I'd like to take you for a little walk. We need to talk.'

I glanced at Angela.

'You go. I'm going to get some rest. I'll get these guys to help me up the stairs,' she said.

'Are you sure you're OK?'

'Yes, I'll be fine. It's been a long day, that's all.'

Arthur led me out of the centre. The sun was dropping fast. We walked slowly up the hill behind the cottages, pushing our giant shadows before us.

'I've never told anyone what really happened down there,' Arthur said. 'Your father's death was my fault. I ... I killed him.'

I stopped. I could push my shadow no further, it had suddenly become too long and heavy.

'What?'

He turned to face me. I searched his sad eyes.

'We were in the streamway, the water level was already quite high ... well above our knees. At that height you can walk against the current but if you tried to go downstream you would lose your footing. We were making steady progress upstream, using hand holds on the walls of the tunnel to help us keep our balance, when our leader, Gareth, suddenly yelled for us to hold on. Before I could even think, a wall of water

216

came crashing over me. Within seconds I was up to my neck. I lost my footing and my whole body lifted off the ground. Fortunately I had a good grip on the rock face and was able to hang on. Your father managed to catch hold of my leg and the two of us clung on like spiders in a drain. The water level rose rapidly and I realised that we were in the lowest part of the tunnel, and that within a few seconds we would be completely engulfed. Up ahead I knew that the roof got higher and that we had to edge towards it before it was too late, but with your father hanging on to me I didn't have the strength to pull myself forward. Suddenly the water was over our heads. I began to kick at your father, desperately trying to get him off me. I felt him grip me even tighter, I couldn't breathe. I kicked him in the head and felt one of his arms come away. I kicked again and he let go. With the last of my breath, I managed to pull myself along the tunnel to the higher opening ... '

'You kicked him off?' I said incredulously. 'How could you do that? Jesus!'

'I don't know. I have relived it a thousand times. I don't know. The terrible thing was I kicked him really hard. At that moment I didn't care. I wanted him off me, that was all.'

My body stiffened. A wave of revulsion came over me. I could feel my fists clench. I raised my arm to strike him. He looked at me pathetically, almost imploring me to thrash the guilt out of him, but I couldn't do it. I dropped my arm and turned away.

He sighed forlornly. 'I'm sorry. It was only later that I felt bad. As soon as I got air in my lungs again, I knew I had to go back for him. I went looking for him day after day and I kept going down long after it was obvious that he couldn't have survived. I was desperate to find his body. I grieved so much I felt like I'd lost my brother. I thought a lot about you and your mum. If I could find his body then at least you could have a funeral. It was the least I could do ... but he vanished ... it's unheard of ... not a sign ... like he'd been plucked off the earth ... I've never come to terms with it. I often wondered how you were getting on ... how you were managing without him.'

'Oh really,' I shouted, swivelling towards him, 'then why didn't you get in touch ... if you cared so much ... you could have called any time and said it was old uncle Arthur phoning to see how we were after you'd kicked my dad in the face when he was drowning.'

Arthur bit his lip. 'You have every right to be angry.'

'I want you to take me down there, Arthur, I want you to show me where it happened,' I said at length.

He was incredulous. 'You've got what you came for, don't you think you should leave?'

'No. I need to pay my respects. It's the very least you owe me,' I insisted.

He looked at me pleadingly as if to say: ask me anything but not this. I had no intention of relenting. There was a long silence before he sighed deeply and shook his head in defeat.

'All right, if you must. I'll cobble together some kit for you. We'll go down in half an hour.'

He turned round and started to drag his shadow back down the hill.

'It's getting a bit dark, isn't it? We could go in the morning,' I called after him.

'It makes no difference down there. The conditions are fine. Let's get it over and done with.' So saying, he sloped off in the direction of the cottage.

I began to shake uncontrollably. A raw, feral energy sprang up from the ground like a squall. The cave was sucking me in.

Angela was no longer in the common room. The others said

218

they had helped her upstairs and she had gone to bed. I went up to check on her. The family room was a tiny blue box with two narrow homemade bunks, each comprising three single beds stacked on top of each other, the lowest on the floor and the highest a close head bang from the ceiling. I looked dubiously at the matchstick-thin pine frames and wondered how three people could possibly sleep in one of these bunks without it collapsing under the weight. The mattresses, made from pancake thin foam and covered in grime, looked anything but enticing.

Angela lay sprawled on the bottom left bunk, her eyes already closed. I didn't know if it was a good or bad thing that she was sleeping so much. Taking her away from the hospital may have been the trigger for her awakening but, without the doctors and the medication, how could I assess how much danger she was in? I watched her chest rise and fall. She was breathing without any trouble. A gnawing guilt was eating at me. I should never have agreed to bring her to Wales. I was tempted to wake her up, if for no other reason than to reassure myself that she *could* wake up and hadn't fallen back into an endless sleep. I hovered over her for a moment, unsure what to do, before eventually deciding it would be best to let her rest.

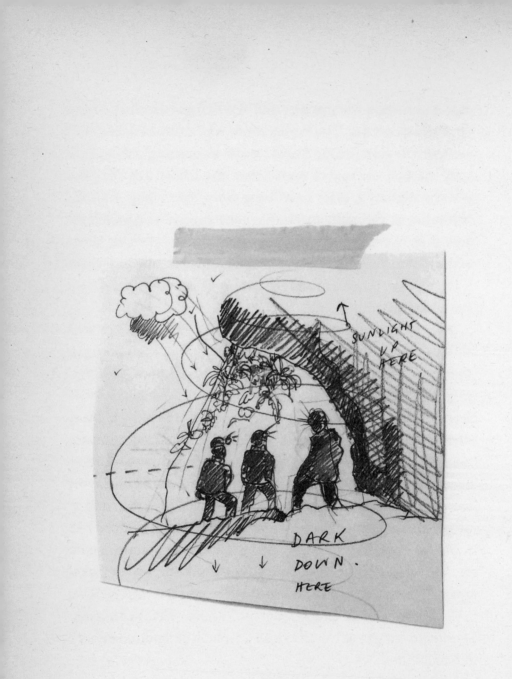

CHAPTER 21

Gerry, Arthur and I strode down the road towards the bottom entrance of Ogof Ffynnon Ddu. Dusk was in its death throes. We walked through a blanket of gloom. There was scarcely enough light for us to see as we veered off the road on to a path that descended gently into the valley. The others continued at full pace as if they could have made the walk blindfolded but I was less confident and switched on my head lamp to guide me. We came to a fence, which we climbed over, and dropped down another twenty metres, before the path doubled back on itself and came to an end in front of a familiar cleft in the rock. My breath caught in my throat as I momentarily lurched back into childhood.

'This is it,' Gerry pronounced.

He went on to explain that in 1946 a couple of bright-eyed cavers had noticed how the interweaving streams on the high slopes of Fan Gyhirych came to an abrupt halt as they flowed into a bog and filtered through the rock and mud. They wondered where the water was going. The river reemerged blinking into the daylight four kilometres away in the Tawe Valley; a drop of some three hundred metres. The cavers, whose names were Peter Harvey and Ian Nixon, guessed that the hill was riddled with tunnels and caverns where the water had percolated through the rock, but the river resurgence in the valley was too strong and treacherous to afford a route into the underground network. In the neighbouring woods they had noticed water bubbling up through the rocks in heavy rain. Here the underground spring was unable to cope with the sheer volume of water that gushed through the hillside and was bursting through every crack and crevasse. So in the summer of 1946 they began to dig. Within a few months they had tunnelled their way in and discovered a stunning river cave which wound its way through the black limestone deep into the hillside. This cave came to an abrupt halt after eight hundred metres where huge boulders blocked the passage. It wasn't until the sixties that anyone managed to find a way through, but they were immediately confronted with a deep sump pool which they called Dip Sump. In 1966 they managed to get beyond the sump into a second section of caves which rose steadily for a couple of kilometres and a year later a top entrance to the cave was found, creating a spectacular through trip. Yet there was more to come and over the following years a third network was discovered.

In the eighties, when my father was coming, potholers from all over the country were converging on the cave looking for new routes. My father had wanted to plant his flag in caving history; ironically, he accomplished his goal but not in the way he had imagined.

'If you look over the fence there,' Gerry continued, 'you can see where they originally got in but the farmer who owns that bit of land wouldn't give us access so we've moved the entrance to this side where the landlord is far more tolerant.'

'So who owns the cave?' I asked.

'Officially caves belong to the land where the entrance is, even if the cave extends under another person's land but where there is more than one entrance, it's owned by all the parties with access according to the normal boundaries above ground. Some landlords charge entrance fees but we've been lucky.'

In front of the cleft in the rock was a deep hole with a rusty metal ladder descending into the darkness. I shone my lamp down the hole and saw the metal door that covered the entrance into the cave. I felt nauseous; I could see my father disappearing in the cave. My little self happily waving him goodbye. Arthur produced a key from his waterproof bag and climbed down the ladder. He unlocked the door and swung it open. Beyond him was blackness.

'There's another ladder once you get through here. Be careful as you come through; it's a bit of a drop.'

I watched as his light disappeared into the cave and then began to climb down after him. Gerry waited at the top and shone his light down the shaft to help me. As I passed beyond the door and dropped into the cave, I imagined my mother begging me not to go in. She would be choked with anxiety if she could see me. It wasn't too late to walk away, but an overwhelming force was driving me into the belly of the hillside. Gerry followed me down and slammed the door shut above his head. The sound of the clanging metal made me jump with fright.

'Are we locked in?' I asked.

'No, you can open it from the inside but not from the outside. Don't worry.'

We were standing in a high-ceilinged passageway. In front

of us was a large tunnel, to our right was a middle-sized tunnel that came to a dead end by the resurgence and behind us was a much smaller one about a metre high, which led to the original entrance to the cave. We set off down the large tunnel. It was not as claustrophobic as I imagined it would be, the ground was dry under foot, the tube was a comfortable three metres wide and our lamps created plenty of light, but I hadn't anticipated the sudden drop in temperature. It must have been ten degrees colder than the surface.

'This is the way we came in with your father,' Arthur said. 'When it gets very wet, some of these tunnels fill with water and it becomes impassable, but there's no chance of rain tonight so there's nothing to worry about.'

It was the second time I had been told not to worry in as many minutes. I guessed they felt uneasy about bringing me down here. As we progressed along the passageway, Gerry chirped on amiably about the history of the cave and the various rock formations. Ogof Ffynnon Ddu had been circling around my dreams like a vulture for a quarter of a century. I had always known that one day I would have to venture inside. There was no other place on Earth that would bring me closer to the memory of my father, no other way to understand his passions. There were periods when the pull was so strong that I read books and scoured the internet in preparation for a visit; but these were mere flirtations that I always managed to resist. Gerry wasn't telling me anything I didn't know and I rather hoped he would be quiet and leave me to my thoughts. I suspected Arthur felt the same but Gerry sought to excavate the silence from every crevice of the cave. His prattling irritated me because the spirit of my father sheltered in those ancient silences; or so it felt to me. Perhaps Gerry thought he was doing us a service. Perhaps, as the only person not directly affected by his death, he felt it was his duty to chase away my father's sombre presence. He didn't seem to understand that sometimes the bereaved *want* to commune with the dead. We don't need protecting from our grief, for grief cleanses the soul and does not sully it.

We reached another fork in the tunnel. A luminous creamy flow stone adorned the cave wall to our right. At its foot was a series of shallow gour pools with white calcite rims resembling basins of water. Steady drips fell from the roof and I was aware of the distant thunder of an underground river.

'On our left here is Skeleton Chamber,' Gerry said. 'When Harvey and Nixon came down this tunnel they found a skeleton at the end. They called him Smith and to this day no one knows how Smith got there or how old he was. There were no modern accoutrements or metal objects nearby – which would suggest he was several hundred years old – but he might have been a lot older. Carbon dating hadn't been discovered, so the local museum took him out and varnished his bones, which means they can't date him at all now. They found him in a sitting position with no broken bones so the theory is he got lost … had no light and couldn't find his way out.'

'But how did he get in if there was no entrance?' I asked.

'It's a mystery; but in the local folklore there is a story that the valley was once terrorised by the sound of screaming which they thought came from a monster that lived inside the hill.'

If Smith was the legendary monster, he would have been screaming for his wife, his children, his friends, anyone to come and rescue him, his incomprehensible howls of despair carried by gusting winds down the mountain into the scattered villages and hamlets of the valley, filling the superstitious

225

Celts with dread. If my father had been washed on to some inaccessible subterranean ledge and left to perish, he would no doubt have done the same. To imagine my father screaming himself to death was unbearable.

I wondered if the spirit of the abandoned Smith still haunted the cave and if so, was it good or bad that my father was not alone down here?

We continued past Skeleton Chamber into a narrow high section called The Nave. The sound of the river was growing louder and the air felt damp and cold. We passed a series of fluted stalactites hanging down like matted dreadlocks and came to a giant flowstone which looked like a frozen waterfall. A ladder had been bolted into it. As I remembered from my old survey of the cave, it was called the Toast Rack and to the right was a sump pool called Pluto's Bath. I stared into the deep black water of the pool. Only a diver could get through there. If, in a flood, you got washed into a sump pool you would find yourself trapped under the rock. You might try to swim out, but would you know which way to go in the blackness and would you have the breath to swim twenty, thirty, forty, fifty metres to the next opening?

We climbed up the Toast Rack and clambered over the slippy, smooth calcite at the top, then followed the cave round until we came to an opening which looked down on to the roaring streamway three or four metres below. The sound was deafening; Gerry broke off his commentary for the first time. Arthur, who had hardly said a word up to this point, began to shout in my ear.

'To get to the place we found the helmet we have to wade upstream. It's only ankle deep here but in places it will come to your knees. Are you OK with that?'

I nodded. 'How deep is it when it floods?' I yelled.

He pointed to the roof of the cave. 'It can fill up, but don't worry.'

I wished they would stop saying that.

It was staggering to think that even where I stood, which seemed so high above the water, I could be submerged. We descended towards the streamway and began to wade upstream. I felt the torrent press against my wellies and I put my hands on the black cold walls of the cave to steady myself. It was narrower here and often I could touch both walls at once. In some parts, the ceiling of the cave stretched high above us like a cathedral and in others, we had to watch we didn't bang our heads. It was easy to imagine how a body of water could amass and flood a constricted part of the cave in seconds.

We meandered through the streamway for what felt like a very long time. It was the central artery of the network. We were a long way underground now and the deeper we went, the more I had the sense that I was trapped inside my father's soul with its plunging hollows, rectilinear caverns and dark squeezes. His ghostly presence seeped through the rock like the luminous white moon milk that coated the black grotto walls. His tears dripped from stalactites, hope clung to crags and fissures and there was love gathering in frothy pools and forcing its way into the tiniest of cracks – but, like any man's soul, there were traps and pitfalls, bizarre idiosyncrasies in the rock face and dark duplicities that threatened to break your bones and hold you hostage. Some of these manifested themselves on the riverbed, which was full of basins and troughs that were impossible to see in the black water. Many times I took a step and found myself up to my knees. The water filled my boots and seeped inside my caving suit. While I was flailing away behind them, Arthur and Gerry somehow managed to keep their socks dry. They knew exactly where to put their feet.

We came to a well-rounded phreatic tube; a perfectly hewn tunnel, where the walls were striped with white calcite veins. Gerry told me to be careful as there were some very deep pots under the water.

'There's a metal bar in the water which crosses over the top of them. You need to edge sideways along the bar and use your hands on the wall to balance.'

I shone my headlamp down into the depths and could just make out the edge of a scaffolding bar which disappeared under the water. I inched along it, terrified that I would slip. I couldn't imagine how difficult it must be when the water level was high. When at last I reached the other side, I felt relieved and exhilarated. I was beginning to understand why my father found this exciting.

'Are you all right?' Gerry asked.

'Yes, how much further?'

Gerry laughed. 'Don't worry, it's not far now.'

Enough with the worry.

We followed the streamway a little further until we came to an arc in the river. Here, three metres above our heads, was a large opening. A rope hung down from the opening into the water.

'This is the escape route,' Gerry yelled. 'Once you get here, you can climb up and get out of the cave without going through the waterway. We'll show you on the way back.'

We continued past the rope and at length came to a path that led away from the streamway. My boots were heavy with water and my feet sodden and cold. We ploughed on until we came to a huge cavern that was blocked from top to bottom by a mountain of giant boulders. This was Boulder Chamber, the furthest point that Harvey and Nixon reached in 1946. At some point in prehistory the roof must have collapsed. The river was now a distant echo. It looked as if there was no way on from here but Arthur scampered up the rocks like a goat and edged through a tiny gap halfway up to the right. I squelched up after him with Gerry taking the rear. On the other side we came to a patch of damp sand which dropped into an ominous looking sump pool.

'I found the helmet down there,' Gerry said.

I stared into the murky impenetrable darkness.

'Is this where you were when it happened?' I asked Arthur.

'No, we were in the Marble Showers – further upstream, it's another hour or so from here,' he said.

I nodded. I didn't want to go any further. I was exhausted and I had an overpowering sense that I was where I needed to be, except I couldn't relax with these two strangers at my side: the one who could not stop talking and the other who had kicked my father in the head in his moment of need.

'Can I have some time alone?' I asked.

Gerry ran his hands through his hair nervously and glanced at Arthur. 'I'm sorry, Josh. We can't leave you here.'

'I'll stay here. I won't move. You can come back in an hour. I need time to think.'

Arthur looked aghast. 'There's no way I'm leaving you down here alone. We wouldn't do it for anyone. There are no exceptions.'

I checked my watch; it was ten thirty. I tried again to persuade them but there was no shifting them. I felt incomplete and frustrated; I had been robbed of any sense of closure. Reluctantly, I turned my back on the sump and followed them out of the cave. We took the so-called escape route on the way back, which in truth was no quicker than the other route, but at least it was dryer. At one point I thought we'd taken a wrong turn because we came to a cavern that looked like a dead end. Then I felt a draught on my face coming up from the floor. Gerry got down on his stomach and rolled into an aperture that was no bigger than the gap under a bed. He disappeared.

'Are you kidding?' I said to Arthur.

'It's too narrow to crawl. We call it the rolly polly.'

I got down on my knees and shone my torch under the plate of rock. Gerry was still rolling.

'Jesus,' I exclaimed.

I manoeuvered on to my back. For the first time I felt claustrophobic. There wasn't even enough room to bend my legs so I copied Gerry and started to roll. Both plates of rock were perfectly smooth where the water had forced them apart. The plate above me was only a few centimetres from my nose. What if it slipped? I would be crushed under a million tons of rock. I kept rolling until I began to feel dizzy. After fifteen metres I rolled out into a corridor. More challenges lay ahead. We came to the Pi Chamber, famous for the enormous Greek symbol etched in moon milk on its wall, and then dropped into a tiny tubular descent that helter-skeltered down towards the cave exit. The final ordeal was a high wire traverse some twenty metres above the streamway, for which I had to be cow-tailed on to a wire that was bolted to the wall to prevent me from falling. Eventually we found ourselves back in the corridor near the Skeleton Chamber and we retraced our steps back out of the cave.

We kept our lamps switched on as we climbed back up the hill to the club.

'Tell me, Arthur,' I asked, as we removed our wet clothes in the changing block, 'what do you do in life?'

'I'm a professor at the University of Bristol.'

'What's your subject?'

'Black holes.'

'That's ironic,' I chuckled.

'I guess I'm drawn to the darkness.'

'What exactly is a black hole?'

'It is a place of extreme gravity. It swallows everything in its event horizon. Like a giant vacuum cleaner. Even light can't escape its clutches. At its centre is a singularity that has infinite density, zero volume and incredible mass. Einstein's theory of general relativity suggests that this singularity might even form a bridge to another universe.'

'And time in a black hole?'

'For the external observer, time appears to slow down as you approach it and stop at its centre.'

If I had a superpower this would be it; to be able to freeze time in a moment of happiness. Then I could be with Angela forever.

'Could the earth ever become a black hole?'

'A black hole needs to be incredibly dense. If you compressed the earth to the size of a marble then it would turn into a black hole.'

'Hmm. So if you get sucked into a black hole, you get flattened and crushed by an invisible force, which transforms you into something unrecognisable. You feel infinitely small. Time stops. Then, all of a sudden, you get spat out into a new universe,' I summarised.

'Something like that.'

'Sounds like someone going through depression or personal transformation. And this new universe is the same as ours?' I asked.

'Who knows, but you will be a long way from where you started.'

'Mmm. Do you think the soul is like a black hole?'

'How do you mean?'

'I don't know ... a singularity of zero volume and infinite density ... it contains everything but looks like nothing ... a bridge to another universe.'

'I never thought about it like that, Josh, but I often think about my work when I'm in a cave. I do my best thinking underground. Darkness focuses the mind. Anyway, I hope that going in helped you in some way.'

'Yes, it has. It gave me an insight into my father's passion. Maybe I'll come back one day. Thank you for taking me down.'

'I'm sorry for what happened. I live with it everyday,' he said dolefully.

'If you hadn't done what you did you would probably have died too. I don't think he would begrudge you your life. There was nothing you could do.'

'Thank you, Josh. That means a lot to me,' Arthur said and instinctively put his arm around me and engulfed me in a bear hug. I could almost feel the torment and burden of guilt leaving his body.

CHAPTER 22

I found Angela sitting in the wheelchair by the window, staring at the moon.

'Where have you been?' she asked without turning.

'In the cave. They took me to where they found the helmet.'

'How was it?'

'Good, but Gerry wouldn't shut up. It was like we were on a guided tour. How are you feeling?'

'I've got a weird tingling sensation in these two fingers.'

She held up her right hand. Her third and fourth finger were curled unnaturally. 'They feel kind of weak and fizzy ... and I keep getting shooting pains in my head. It's not like a headache. It comes and goes. One minute it's fine, then it feels like it's going to explode. Like a butter ready to hatch.'

'You mean an egg,' I corrected.

'Yes, what did I say?'

'Butter.'

'Oh ... an egg. Yes. Like there's a ... there's er a ... an aminal trying to get out,' she stammered.

'Animal. There's an animal trying to get out?'

'Yes ... that's what I said ... it's ... er ... the pressure is unbearable.'

'Angela ... '

'I won't go back to hospital,' she said, reading my thoughts.

'Well, you have to go, Angela. Something's wrong.'

'You don't understand,' she insisted.

'It's getting worse. Why won't you go?'

'Because it's ... too late, Josh, it's too late. I know it is. Please don't argue with me.'

She took a couple of deep breaths and blinked hard. After a moment the bombardment in her head seemed to pass.

'Have you ever seen a moon so orange?' she said, changing the subject.

I came over to the window. The moon appeared to be perched on the brow of the hill casting a wondrous amber halo of light into the valley.

'Josh,' she whispered, 'I want to make love to you.'

I was taken aback. 'What, here?' I looked around at the grimy bunk beds.

'Outside in the moonlight.'

'But what about your leg?'

She shrugged as if to say she didn't care.

'You're kidding, right?' I said.

'Don't you want to?'

'Of course I do but you're not feeling well ... '

'Please. Carry me.'

She held out her arms and I picked her up. It was a balmy warm night. I carried her across the car park and into a field where I lay her down under the stars. Each star a black hole in the making, a celestial body waiting to implode and explore its own soul. Angela took hold of my arm and pulled me towards her.

'Kiss me,' she whispered.

Our mouths came together. Inside the kiss was loss beyond compare. The kind of loss one feels before the real loss has even happened. My heart was cracking into a million pieces. There is no word for the nostalgia we feel before something is lost, no word for the longing we feel for a person who is still present, no word for the regret we feel for things beyond our control. No word for the loss before loss. I was losing Angela. The sun would never rise again. I read it in her kiss.

'You turn me inside out,' I said.

We undressed each other and let the tiger moon bathe our naked bodies as we explored each other for the first time. A tawny owl hooted in the distance, while something small ferreted around the undergrowth nearer by. I treated her with infinite care. I was as gentle as a man can be. I never pushed her beyond where she wanted to go. I tried not to put weight on her broken leg. All this I say in my defence. When at last I entered her, she whispered, 'Now we belong to each other,' and began to cry. We made love incredibly slowly. The focus was intense. We teetered on the precipice of a dizzying climax and then I felt her body spasm and tighten. For the first time in my life I felt at one.

Suddenly her neck stiffened and her top lip contorted bizarrely as if she had been caught by an invisible fishing hook. She exhaled a long deep sigh, the muscles in her face slackened and her mouth dropped open.

'Angela? Angela?'

There was no movement in her chest, no rise and fall, no intake of air. Her eyes were staring at me, unblinkingly.

My mind began to fragment.

'Angela! Wake up, for Christ's sake, wake up.'

CHAPTER 23

I tried to shake her awake but I knew she was dead. I recoiled in horror. I had no idea what to do. My thoughts went into overdrive. Should I run? Should I call the police? It would be manslaughter at the very least; life imprisonment. I could see how it must look from the outside. I would be treated as a stalker, a psychopath, a rapist, a murderer. No one would believe anything I had to say, but what had I done wrong? I had brought a sleeping angel back to life, I had followed her wishes; she didn't want to go back to hospital, she had wanted to die in my arms, to be born again inside me. This was how she wanted it to be. I couldn't understand how I had got myself into this situation. Events were unfolding so quickly I couldn't get a handle on them. In the back of my mind I wondered if I wasn't going mad. When Sheryl left me I had imagined people coming out of the wall in my old flat. Subsequently I had met the strangest of characters in the strangest of places. Perhaps I really was insane. My thoughts passed to my mother and how she would take the news. It would devastate her all over again. I didn't think she would ever recover.

I can't explain what happened next. All I remember is that I began to scrabble around in the grass, digging into the soil furiously with my hands. I threw clod after clod over her corpse until she was covered from head to toe with earth and my fingers ached with the effort. From the long grass I yanked out fronds of bracken and heather to decorate the mound. Then I ran to the bushes and tore off the wiry green branches, oblivious to the thorns and sharp twigs that scraped my skin. From the trees I tore off loose limbs and strips of dry bark and piled them all on the pyre. I was a man possessed, my nails were ripped and blood trickled from scratches on my arms and legs. Then without thinking of the consequences I ran back towards the club. I was still naked. The lights were on in the common room and I could hear the sound of distant voices. Through the window I could see the administrator. I had run out of time. The kind man who smelt of death had come to claim me.

There was nobody in the kitchen when I burst through the door, looking for matches and something flammable. I'm not sure that it would have made any difference to me if there had been, for I had turned feral with grief. The authoritative voice of the administrator drifted down the corridor. He must have been telling them about all the terrible things I had done, because he was saying that I had completely lost my mind, and that unfortunately there was no way back for me. Now more than ever, I was convinced he was from the secret service, for why were there no police involved in this manhunt? It was as if they had been deliberately kept away. Mikey and Angela must have been involved in something far murkier than I could ever know. What was he after? Perhaps he had been waiting for

Angela to wake up. Perhaps he wanted to question her. Again I wondered why he wanted the box and what secrets it kept, but now was not the time to speculate.

I found some brandy and firelighters and, armed with a box of matches, I fled the building. I poured the alcohol on the pyre, brought a match to the firelighters and threw them on top. I picked up Angela's new dress, held it to my nose for one last lungful of scent then tore it into strips. These I added to the growing flames before gathering up Arjuna's clothes which had served me so well and flinging them on to the pyre. I fell to my knees and blackened my body with soil and dirt. I had become Shiva, the God of destruction and transformation and for maybe a minute I prayed to all the Gods I didn't believe in.

Now I had to escape. I didn't have time to watch her burn. The administrator, or whoever he was, had me cornered. I had to get away and there was only one place to go. There was nothing to lose. The pull of the cave was stronger than ever. I had unfinished business there. My thoughts flew through the tunnels to the sump where my father lay. I was sure I could find my way back, if only I could get in.

I went to the car and picked up my dad's helmet, the old cave survey and the potbellied troll my father had given me. I saw the little wooden box where I had left it in the drinks holder between the seats. I snatched it up. I was sure that if I left it on show in the car my pursuer would find it. I sprinted to the changing block and put on the wetsuit that Arthur had lent me; it was clammy and damp. I pulled on a caving suit over the top, zipped it up and slipped my feet back into my soaking wellies. I kissed my dad's helmet for good luck and put it on my head; a perfect fit. I found a lamp on a shelf, flicked it on and off to check it was working, packed the survey and the troll into a waterproof bag that I found hanging on the door and set off towards the valley. When I looked back I could see the flicker of flames beginning to emerge over the bushes on the far side of the building. I heard voices; the administrator and a few others were spilling out of the club and running towards the fire. No one looked down the valley in my direction. With our clothes burning and the stench of flesh they might assume we were both dead.

I hardly noticed the distant rumble of thunder and the unanticipated spots of rain that were beginning to fall as I ran down the valley towards the entrance of the cave. I was far more interested in getting away than in the vagaries of the Welsh weather. The official entrance was locked so I climbed over the fence on to the farmer's land where the 1946 entrance was situated. I found it in a clearing not far away, encircled by protective black and yellow police tape. The hole was much smaller than the one Arthur and Gerry had taken me down, but at least there was no door. I attached the lamp to my dad's helmet, flicked it on and crawled in. After twenty metres of crawling I found myself at the metal ladder under the new entrance. I walked, as if pulled by some all-pervading force, back along the tunnel until I found the streamway. I retraced the route we had taken earlier but as I waded resolutely through the water I completely forgot about the hidden potholes and suddenly fell headlong into a deep pool. My knee crashed into the scaffold bar and before I knew it I was completely under water. A jet of icy liquid filled my wetsuit. I managed to grab hold of the bar and pull myself along it until I reached the edge. The lamp flickered. I dragged myself out of the hole. My boots were heavy with water; I took them off and emptied them out. The lamp flickered again and abruptly gave up the ghost. I was plunged into blackness. A black so profound and complete it filled me with terror. I fumbled for the helmet, yanked it off and shook it.

Nothing.

I felt for the battery pack and bashed it with my hand. The lamp sparked back into life. I set off once more, taking greater care with my footing. It was a relief to leave the streamway and take the tunnel to Boulder Chamber. I arrived at Dip Sump hungry, tired and soaked to the skin.

I slumped down and listened to the sound of water plinking on the stone. The cave was alive with drips and plops that echoed off the walls. A rainbow of emotion breached my heart. My father was everywhere. I may have been in a giant underground network of passages and tunnels but there was nowhere to hide. I had reached the epicentre of everything. Ripples danced over the water. Their shadows undulated on the walls high above me. I felt like a fish breathing under the ocean. There was a tingling charge in the air. A battalion of goosebumps stood to attention on my damp arms and legs.

As my listening sharpened in the silence, I was convinced I could hear voices in a distant cavern. Was someone else in the cave? Had they sent a search party or was it Smith and my dad sharing a joke?

I stared into the sump. I wondered how much of my father was down there; ground-down bones, teeth, skull. A floodgate unlocked inside me and I began to cry. I cried for Angela and I cried for the twenty-five years of not crying.

The distant voices babbled away. My lamp flickered again and then died. I shook it and bashed it but this time the lamp would not be beaten into submission. I don't think I had ever experienced a blackness so black. It made no difference if my eyes were open or closed. My tears turned to blind fear. No one knew I was in the cave. I stood up and stretched out my arms and felt for the wall. I took a few steps. There was no way I would be able to find my way out of here.

'Hello!' I shouted.

No response.

'Is anyone there?'

Nothing.

'HELP!'

I remembered that Rabbi Feldenberg had once told us the story of a man lost in the forest. For days and weeks he wandered in a panic, desperately trying to find his way out. Eventually he came across an old woman sitting on a tree stump. The man was overjoyed to see her. 'Please help me get out of this forest, I've been lost for thirty days.' The old woman began to laugh and laugh. 'What's so funny?' said the man. 'Thirty days!' chuckled the woman. 'I've been lost for thirty years!' The man's mouth dropped open. 'So you can't show me the path that leads out of here?' 'No,' she replied, 'but I can show you a thousand paths that lead nowhere.'

The Rabbi said it was the curse of those without faith to constantly seek meaning but never find it. I have never known what to believe. I have never known what I stood for. How long can a man strive before he is eaten by his own pointlessness?

I sat down again. My heart was thrashing frantically against my ribs like a bird trapped inside a house. I tried to keep calm. Best to wait, I told myself. Someone was bound to come down the next day; some expedition, a university club, a couple of members. Someone. It was a busy cave. I didn't care if I got arrested, I just wanted to get out of there. Gerry said the best thing to do if you got into trouble was to find dry ground and wait for rescue. They had a system whereby, if you were not back by the time you said you would be back, they would wait one hour and then send out a search party. Everyone who went into the cave wrote their name on to a notice board in the club with their planned return time. I hadn't put my name on the list. No one had any reason to look for me – at least not until they realised I hadn't burned with Angela. Then maybe someone would notice that their wetsuit was missing and put two and two together. But how long would that take? And, oh my goodness, I was so far underground. Parts of the cave were two hundred million years old. Gerry said it was formed when the land which is now Great Britain was on the equator and Wales was connected to the Appalachian Mountains, now the backbone of New York State. The bedding rock I was sitting on was once part of a desert.

The cave had time. All the time in the world. It was the keeper of time. I was a millionth of a blink. A fossil waiting to happen. A secret that would never be told. My insignificance could not be more profound.

I was cold. So very cold. I lay back and waited. Time lost all sense. After a while I could not tell if I had been waiting ten minutes or several hours. I closed my eyes, though it made no difference.

Hello, Dad, I'm here.

CHAPTER 24

Stare long enough at a wall and the ghosts will crawl out. So now there were two of us waiting. Dad and me. Three with Smith. Four if you included the flame-haired troll in my bag. What were we waiting for? To be found? To find ourselves, perhaps?

I had reached that point of singularity, the very soul of everything, the ultimate energy source from which there could be no return. This was the very lowest place I could be. On the other side, through some worm hole I had yet to discover, a new universe beckoned. Maybe Smith and my dad already knew something about this other place. If ever I were to survive this ordeal, nothing would ever be the same again.

'Dad!' I spoke out loud. 'Help me. Get me out of here.'

I waited for a reply but there was only the constant drip drip of water and the distant burbling echo of the streamway.

I felt as if I had been in the belly of Ogof Ffynnon Ddu for a small eternity. I was shivering helplessly, my mind was drifting and I suddenly became concerned with the very real possibility of my own death. It was time to let go of all I had been and abandon myself to my inevitable fate. Finger by finger I symbolically released my grip on life and, as I watched it float away, an apparition emerged from the blackness. It was my father dressed in his caving suit. I didn't know what was real any more or if I had lost my mind, but why should I care? Only the insane can dispense with the stultifying predictability of a linear existence and wander freely through time. Only the insane can transcend earthly bonds to raid heaven and conjure the dead. Madness was my friend. I would happily forego a hundred lives and ironclad sanity to see my dad again.

He towered over me. I had no memory of ever being taller than his waist; always my bear hug giant, my bucking horse, my monster. I gazed hungrily into his eyes and stretched out my arms as high as they could go. 'Please, Daddy, please carry me. I'm so tired'.

He scooped me off the ground and brought me into his chest. I wrapped my arms and legs around him and nuzzled my face into his neck. He kissed my forehead and enveloped me in his powerful frame. I ached for his love.

'Josh,' he whispered.

My name sounded so reassuring on his lips.

'I miss you, Dad'.

He held me for a long time, speaking soundlessly into my heart. Beautiful words, comforting words that oozed through my veins like honey. He spoke of pride and love and I understood, at last, that he hadn't deserted me, that he had always been with me and always would be.

I remembered the box in my pocket and took it out. When I was very little I would collect beautiful things like malachite and moonstones, or acorns, buttercups and rose petals from the beaches and woods I visited with my mum while we waited for my dad to surface, and I would give them to him as presents. All my tiny heart wanted was to give and give and give. He in turn would bring me fossils and stardust, which he had found deep underground. How we enjoyed these ritual exchanges.

'Dad, I've got a present for you. I don't know what it is. I found it. I think there is something trapped inside it.'

I gave him the box. He examined it carefully.

'I think it's time to let it out, Josh.'

He closed his mighty hand around it and there was a crack like bone snapping. The air moved sharply and we were hit by a tremendous blast of energy. I heard the sound of giant wings beating, as if a mythical creature were coming back to life.

It flapped in a frenzy around our heads before turning its attention on me. It hovered in front of my face for a second, then, with tender force, it penetrated my skull through my ears, mouth and nostrils. My scalp prickled from the inside as it forensically probed my brain, sparking every synapse and unblocking every channel before coursing down my throat, sweeping through my glands and organs, brushing away clots of stale matter and years of inner deadness. It powered through my arteries into the very cavities and ventricles of my core. There the creature found an empty hollow, fluttered a while and settled down to roost. A tingling pleasure coursed through me. Whatever this alien thing was, I knew that it was mine and that it belonged inside me.

'It's all right, it won't hurt you,' dad said.

My body relaxed and we both began to laugh, such was the feeling of liberation and relief.

At length he put me down on the rocks.

'It's time to go, Josh. Go back to Mum. She needs you.'

'I love you, Dad.'

'Me too, son.' He ruffled my hair one last time and disappeared back into the sump.

All was still.

I waited.

I was a heartbeat from death. The noise in my head seemed to burn itself out and, hiding in the wreckage, I found a tranquillity and quiet self-belief.

With huge effort I got to my feet and opened my ears. I pictured the short section of cave that led to the Boulder Chamber and I began to walk, never committing my foot until I had felt the ground beneath it. With my arms stretched out as antennae, I listened to the dripping water and turned my face to where the draught was strongest. I heard the distant rumble of water and made my way towards it. I made friends with the darkness. I was no longer afraid. As I moved, the water in my wetsuit warmed up and I forgot the hunger in my belly. Soon I was at the streamway. I scooped up some water in my hands and drank until I felt replete. Then I stood in the river and felt the pull of the current on my feet. I turned until I felt the pressure on the back of my ankles and began to slide my feet, step by step downstream. It was more difficult walking with the current; if I was not careful it would knock me off balance. I chose not to hurry but to give each step equal concentration. Many times I dipped my foot into a deeper section but I never lost my footing; I was able to withdraw it and feel around for the calcite lips and firmer footholds. I inched along like a snail, clinging to the walls. The faint earthy smell of peat suggested that new water was filtering through the ground into the cave. It must have been raining outside. I touched the rope that led to the 'escape route' but decided that I would have less chance of getting lost in the streamway. The 'escape route' would have taken me high above the water into a system of caves which could only be navigated by inching across ropes attached to the rock wall with anchor bolts. The risk in the dark of falling from these high ropes was far greater than that of drowning in the stream. Even though the water level was beginning to rise above my knees, I continued on until I felt the metal scaffolding bar that crossed the deep potholes. In the rush of water, I imagined I could hear voices and many times called out 'hello' through the tunnels.

I tried to remember the landmark features of the cave as I had experienced them walking upstream. There had been one place where we had to climb over a large rock and another where the tunnel had been extremely narrow. For each of these I tried to imagine what they might feel like in the dark, so that I could recognise them on my return and gain a sense of my progress, but the key feature that I had to find was the place they called The Step, the place where I would have to get out of the waterway and climb a ladder back towards the Toast Rack and ultimately the exit. If I continued beyond The Step I had no idea where I would end up.

Many hours passed; the pressure of water was building on my legs, making me stumble blindly into the rocks. Again I thought I heard voices. This time I didn't call out. By now I had realised it was a trick of the cave and I was best conserving my energy but, a little further on, the voices seemed to grow louder and a flash of torchlight danced on the cave wall. The light grew stronger. The illuminated limestone was beginning to crack and crumble. Without warning, a surge of water hit my back, tossing me forward. Loose rocks thudded into my body but I felt no pain. The tunnel was collapsing all around me and all I could hear were the voices of my mother and Sheryl. I tried to speak but I couldn't move my mouth. The cave was dissolving like a sand castle. Hard, defined edges were softening. Ancient structures were disintegrating. The light was so bright now; I had to scrunch up my eyes.

Then I hear my mother say, 'He's moving.' Her voice is faint and distorted, as if my head were immersed in a bath full of water or she was speaking with a pillow over her mouth.

I try to open my eyes again but I can't. Something is impeding their movement. I am confused. I don't understand what is happening. I can't move.

'Oh my God!'

It is Sheryl speaking.

She is a million miles away. I can't breathe. I am drowning. My lungs inflate and deflate like a balloon. I am not in control of them.

Again I try to talk but no words form. My tongue feels dry and furry like a piece of old carpet. I am scared and confused. Will someone tell me what is happening? Why are Sheryl and Mum in the cave?

I become aware of eerie detached voices hovering above me. They don't make any sense and I can't be bothered to listen to them; I am beyond exhaustion.

I sleep.

Someone is prodding and poking me with hands that are neither delicate nor comforting. They pinch and scratch my flesh, intent on hurting me. Something sticky is pulled from my eyes. It takes the thin skin of my eyelids with it. Now the lights are so bright they hurt my head but I am determined to see. One of them flickers. Blurry shapes rear up in front of me. I blink a few times but everything remains stubbornly out of focus.

I sleep.

When next I open my eyes I can make out indistinct, fuzzy faces floating in cloud like giant gods. I feel a sharp pain under my arm and I flinch. A bright light appears right in front of me and moves slowly from left to right.

'Josh, Josh, can you hear me?'

It's a man.

I can hear him but when I try to reply nothing happens. This annoys me, why can't I speak? I have intention, I have words, but my mouth has forgotten how to open. I've lost the neural pathway from my brain. I search inside, fruitlessly pressing imaginary buttons. I close my eyes. It's all too much. I feel exhausted with the effort.

I become aware of something beeping, and then I notice a deep hum and the sound of a child sucking the last few drops of liquid from a beaker with a straw, before blowing it out and sucking it up again repeatedly. In the distance I hear a radio playing a tune that is vaguely familiar but which has no name in my mind. There is the swish of a curtain rail. I am convinced it is the shower curtain in the flat I used to share with Sheryl. Did she manage to take repossession of our flat? Is that where I am? Who is the child with the straw?

I sleep.

I wake up. It is dark. The child is still sucking on its straw rhythmically, so it can't be a child. Have I slipped through a wormhole into another universe? I can still smell the damp hollows of the cave where my father's spirit lurks. I grieve for Angela. Grateful for her brief awakening.

I sleep.

It's light again and I've never felt so thirsty in all my life. I could drink a lake. My throat is sore, my lips are desiccated. I become aware that I'm lying on a bed. Stainless steel rods rise up above my head from behind me and from either side; four, five of them, maybe six. Various bags, cylinders and tubes hang off them. I note that one of them contains what looks like milkshake. Next to these are various machines and monitors. I follow one of the myriad tubes down from a bag and am shocked to discover that it is coming out of my ribcage, which is when I realise that I am naked and that there is a catheter sticking out of the end of my penis. A sheet, which I presume is intended to cover my dignity, is lying on my right thigh. Beyond this I can see a forearm with a tube sticking out of it and a right leg covered in plaster. As I look down at these horrors and wonder what has happened to me, I have the strange feeling that the body before me is not mine, that it belongs to someone else. This body is nothing but bones with a dry papery skin stretched over it like cellophane, whereas my body is stocky, muscular and smooth.

I ascertain that I have woken up in a hospital, but I have no idea why I am there. I am not ill. Something must have happened in the cave. I must have collapsed down there, or fallen, or been crushed. I don't remember this happening but it is the only thing that makes sense.

Two young women are standing over me.

'Good morning, Josh, welcome to planet Earth,' says one cheerily.

Who is she? How does she know my name?

'I'm Kate, this is Tia.'

They feel familiar; like they have always been there but I have never noticed them before.

They are explaining something to me; they are going to do something; but what they say leaves absolutely no impression, their words evaporate as soon as they are spoken, all meaning washed away like dust in the rain.

Before I know it, Tia peels off a tape that stretches across my nose. It feels as if she is removing a layer of skin with it. Then she begins to pull a tube out of my right nostril. It emerges little by little like a foul creature from the swamp. After about three feet it seems to get stuck. Kate holds my head down whilst Tia tugs. The end of the tube feels much fatter. My nostril is stretching wider and wider, and something wet dribbles down my face. A foul goop, like pond sludge, clings to the outside of the tube. As Tia pulls, more of the detritus inside my stomach emerges encrusted on to the tube as if it has been there a thousand years. It slides out of my nose. I'm snotting up the mother of all mucus and, as the final bit of tubing slithers out, it is followed by a slimy tail of brown seaweed that dribbles all over me. The nurses sponge me down before reinserting a new tube up my nose. A giant syringe is jabbed into my arm and a transparent fluid is injected into me. I scream silently for them to leave me alone. I am frighteningly out of control.

I sleep.

I discover that I can roll my head fully to the left but only partially to the right, because a needle is sticking out of the side of my neck and the needle is connected to something that feels like a lego brick with three tubes snaking into it. At the front of my neck is an incision in my wind pipe; a tracheotomy. The sucking straw sound is coming from a ventilator that breathes for me, which must explain why I can't speak. There are drips and drains protruding from the side of my ribcage under my arms, which prevent me from rolling over. My hands – so skinny it's unbearable – have needles in them; there is some kind of peg on the middle finger of my right hand. My nails are long and yellow like talons. Three black pads stick to my chest like leeches. I don't know how many days have passed since I first woke up. I am vaguely aware that my mother and Sheryl have sometimes been at my side, although I can't remember anything they have said to me. I flicker on and off like a faulty light.

Two physiotherapists come and massage my feet and slowly manipulate my arms; they tell me that I will walk again but that my muscles have wasted away. It will take time. I can move my hand quite easily now. They tell me to tap on the side of the bed once for yes, twice for no, and repeatedly for attention. They also show me a communication card with pictures of toilets, combs, toothbrushes and blankets, and a word list reducing all my basic needs to twenty essentials: lie down, sit up, a glass of water, sleep, leave me alone, don't leave, come back later, pillow, exercise, suction, remove restraints, moisten lips, massage, pen and paper, and prayer. On the reverse is a pain chart where I can describe my pain from one to ten and point to the affected part of the body on a picture. There are also pictograms to express my feelings. I can show them I am feeling sick, tired, hot, cold, dizzy, pain, short of breath, angry, sad, frightened, and frustrated but not happy; there is no picture for happy. No one is ever happy or they would have put it on the card. According to my options, life in the hospital can only be expressed as functional, sad and painful.

They prop me up and put a couple of pillows behind my back. The cool cotton on my back is momentarily lovely. No picture for that. After about ten minutes I slip down the bed again. Throughout the day, and the days that are to follow, an odd cycle repeats. I get propped up; I slide down; my chest begins to rattle as my lungs fill up and won't clear; I tap on the bed; the nurses come and stick a suction straw up my nose and suck out the infection or whatever it is from my lungs – a process which takes about two minutes. Then I am propped up and feel the pleasure of a freshly plumped pillow behind me before inevitably sliding down the bed again. It happens twenty times a day and every time I long for that cool plump pillow.

A doctor comes – she introduces herself as Dr Andrea Knowles – why do I know that name? She bombards me with questions, some of which I answer with a click of the nails, some of which I ignore. She tells me I have been in a coma for seven weeks. I'm lucky to be alive. Blah, blah, blah. After a while I grow angry and close my eyes.

I am more aware of my surroundings now. I wonder why I am in the same room, maybe even the same bed that was Angela's. It is the strangest of all coincidences that I too should find myself in the same situation. Maybe all intensive care units look the same. One difference: Angela came to her senses much more quickly than I did. Perhaps because she was only unconscious for a few days.

I wonder if the police will arrest me when I am back to strength.

I sleep.

Today I am visited by my mum and Sheryl. They can't get close for the paraphernalia surrounding me and sit three quarters of the way down the bed, facing each other like opposing generals across the battlefield of my broken body. They never liked each other. I can't remember ever spending a relaxing evening together, just the three of us. I slide inexorably down the bed.

'Mummy's here, sweetheart.' She squeezes my fingers.

'Hello, Josh,' says Sheryl cheerily.

She isn't angry with me any more and she is back to wearing make-up which I can't help thinking means she is hiding something.

I have been fretting about Dad's helmet. I desperately want to ask Mum if someone has retrieved it and given it to her. It would be terrible if it had been lost in the cave again.

'Can you understand me, Josh?' Mum asks.

I tap once. Yes.

'I love you, Josh. We thought we'd lost you. Oh my God, oh my God. I never thought I'd see you open your eyes. The doctors thought you were done for. They told me they didn't think you would survive. You'd got pneumonia, it was getting worse. You had a terrible fever and they were using ice packs to cool you down. Then you had sepsis. It was damaging your liver and kidneys. I was angry. I didn't really understand how you can get these things in a hospital of all places. There wasn't enough oxygen in your blood; they thought you would be brain-damaged even if you did survive. Do you understand me, Josh?'

I tap once.

'Then one day they said they didn't think you would make it through the night. The hospital chaplain read you your last rites. I sat in the waiting room all night. They wouldn't let me sit with you. But in the morning you were still alive, sweety. It was a miracle. You hung on for a few days. They asked me if I wanted to turn off the machine. I could tell they thought it was pointless keeping you alive so I said yes. We agreed to do it the following day at noon to give me time to prepare myself. I didn't sleep. We came to the hospital. I held your hand. I could feel your pulse; it was so strong, so defiant. I watched the heart monitor for a long while. Your heartbeat was true. Your lungs had been ravaged by the pneumonia, your body was broken, your brain wasn't functioning, you weren't responding to any stimulus, but your heart, your heart was working perfectly and I said to the doctor if Josh's heart is still in it then so is mine. So they kept you alive and after a few more weeks I thought that maybe I had made a terrible mistake, that it was cruel to keep you going like this. And then they came to me again … just when I was cracking and I … I said OK. Turn it off.'

Mum's bottom lip begins to quiver, then her tiny frame shudders and her eyes overflow. I can't bear to see my mum cry. My dried-out eyeballs are growing moist. Even Sheryl seems moved and she doesn't even love me because I am dull, dull, dull and I lost her share of the flat.

'I don't think you should be telling him this story now,'

258

Sheryl says, but my mum ignores her.

'And so we came into the hospital. We'd agreed to do it at midday but that morning ... we started noticing little spasms in your fingers ... it was as if you knew that it was your last chance and then your eyeballs started moving. They were taped closed to protect them from the light. The doctor took off the tape and you opened them, it was incredible. I never gave up hope, Josh. I never gave up hope. Not really.'

I tap repeatedly on the side of the bed. My mum seems confused. Kate comes over and asks if I want to be propped up again. I tap once, but it's not really what I want. I want a pen and paper so I can write something down, but I realise that I can't communicate this without the board so I settle for a little comfort. Kate calls Tia and they haul me up by the top of my arms. They do it effortlessly, which is surprising because I weigh 12 stone. Well, I was 12 stone. Now I weigh as much as a bag of bones. Tia fetches a little damp pink sponge which is attached to a stick and uses it to wipe my eyes and moisten my lips.

My mother talks incessantly about the minutiae of her life because she doesn't know what else to talk about and because she will never talk about anything important in front of Sheryl, and for the first time in my life I enjoy it. I feel nothing but love for her. She has suffered so much over the years. I don't want to be the cause of any more misery. I see that Sheryl wants to speak too, but my mum won't let up for a second. This is deliberate; she wants to punish Sheryl for leaving me. Eventually Sheryl gets up and says she will come back at a quieter time and sneers at my mother behind her back as she walks out. It is a look I have seen so many times; one in which, not so long ago, I would have been complicit.

No sooner has Sheryl gone than my mother relaxes.

'I never liked her, Josh. I told you she wasn't good for you.

Remember how she threw out that present I bought you? You know, that lovely executive office set. I'd rather she wasn't here; I'm sure it must be upsetting you after all she did. Leaving you like that. Disgusting! And when you'd just lost your job. What happened to those vows? For better for worse. Disgraceful. Can I tell you something, Josh? I invited her to the hospital on the day they were going to turn off the machine – even though I blame her for what you did – I invited her because I wanted her to suffer. I wanted her to see the consequence of her selfishness. I'm ashamed I could be so vengeful and small minded – but I wanted her to understand what she had done.'

An alarm sounds by my bed; one of the drips need refilling. My mother carries on, undeterred by the arrival of the nurse.

'I just don't understand. I know things were going badly but ... trying to take your own life? You know it was two days before I found out. I don't know why it took them so long to tell me.'

Is that what she thought? That I'd gone into the cave to join my father in a poetic but failed suicide attempt? Perhaps I did. Perhaps she was right. Why else would I have gone back down there if it wasn't some kind of death wish after I had lost Angela? Except that's not how it felt to me. It was my father who pulled me into that hole. I could not have fought it if I I had tried. I had been locked in his orbit since he died and when I got close he sucked me in. It was as if we had held each other in suspension and needed to release each other.

'Anyway, I don't suppose you want to talk about that. The important thing is you're back and when you feel better you can come back home to me. I'll look after you, sweetheart. I'm so sorry if I haven't been a good mother to you. I'll make up for it, I promise I will.'

I close my eyes.

'Oh, you're tired. I'll let you sleep but do you remember I had something to tell you? Well, ... '

'Mrs Jones,' Nurse Kate interrupts, 'Josh needs to rest now and we have some procedures to do, so perhaps you could come back tomorrow. Why don't you go home and get some rest?'

'All right, I understand ... maybe now isn't the time to tell you anyway, Josh ... I'll wait till you're a bit stronger ... I don't know how you're going to take it ... '

I open my eyes. I am confused by what she has just said, because she already told me her news that Dad's helmet had been found. Why doesn't she remember? I tap on the bed several times.

'Do you want propping up again?' Tia asks.

I tap twice.

'No?'

I look towards the communication card. Tia passes it to me and I point to a picture.

'A pen, you want a pen? You want to write something?'

I tap once.

'It's early days for that, Josh,' Tia says with a warm smile.

I scratch the bedside with my long nails furiously.

'All right, we'll try, crazy man.'

She fetches a pen and a pad from her desk. She puts the pad on my emaciated stomach and lifts my right hand on top of it. Except that I'm left-handed. I'm left-handed, for Christ's sake. Tell her, Mum. My mum doesn't even notice. Tia places the pen in my fingers and steps back. For a second I hold it, wondering if I can do this with my right hand. Where to begin? I have to keep this brief because it will take a monumental effort to even write one word. The pen slips out of my fingers and rolls on to the floor.

'What did I tell you?' Tia chides.

'Let him try again,' my mum urges.

'We really need to be getting on now, Mrs Jones.'

'No, let him try again, he's trying to say something.'

'Last time,' says Tia. She means it.

She picks up the pen and puts it back in my right hand. Damn it. How long have you known me, Mum?

Tia guides the pen on to the paper. I hold on to it as tightly as I can but I am unable to exert enough pressure on to the paper to get any ink out. Fuck this. It's driving me crazy.

'Let me see if I can help you,' Tia says.

She puts her fingers around mine and presses the pen on to the paper like she was teaching a child to write. 'Go on, Shakespeare.'

I summon all my strength to make the shapes. Letter by painful letter we scrawl together. My mum follows each scrape of the pen with rapt anticipation.

hemet

'Hemet,' my mum reads. 'What does that mean? Sounds Turkish. Oh I know, "he met" ... who did you meet sweetheart? Do you mean you or he? You met someone? Or he met someone? Who is he?'

I curse to myself. I've missed out the 'l'.

I tap twice on the bed with my left hand.

'No, he's saying no,' Mum says. 'No what? No it's not he?'

I tap no.

'Is it you then?'

I tap no. I'm getting angry. Why can't she guess what I mean? She bloody well sent me to get it. It's not that complicated, is it?

I try to write again. Tia responds and we manage to scratch out an 'l' above the 'e' and the 'm'

he'met

'I he met,' Mum says, confused. 'It's not making sense, Josh.'

I am so frustrated I want to scream.

'We have to stop this, his blood pressure has gone above 190 over 90,' Tia worries.

With the last of my strength I scrawl out 'dads' so it reads,

dads

he'met

'Dads?'

I tap once, yes, and drop the pen. I am completely exhausted.

'Dads?' Mum repeats.

I tap. Yes, Dad's helmet. At last.

'Dads I hemet.'

It's not a fucking I, it's a fucking l as in lemon. Jesus, Mum.

'I met Dad?' suggests Tia.

'You met Dad?' Mum asks.

NO. I tap hard. I sort of met Dad but that's not what I meant. My God!

I see that my mum is crying. Why on earth is she crying? I'm the one who should be crying, she's driving me nuts. One way or another my mother always ends up stressing me out.

'What's wrong, Mrs Jones?' Tia asks.

'I think he's brain damaged. He doesn't make any sense.'

I close my eyes. I give up. I give up on life. What's the point of living like this?

CHAPTER 25

It is quiet in the hospital again. Apart from the wretched sucking sound of the iron lung, the hum of the machinery, the bloody beep of the heart rate monitors, the fucking alarms. Apart from all this incessant racket, it is quiet. Calm. I go to sleep wondering why my mum thinks she hasn't told me her news.

Days pass, and with each day's passing I can do a little more. Like a newborn, I have to learn everything as if I am doing it for the first time. My bed is my security, my cot. Six nurses, all women, attend my every need. Every day they sponge me down and change my sheets by rolling me from side to side to pull out the linen. They wash my hair, half of which has fallen out, just like a baby's, from lying down for so long, and at last they cut my ghastly nails. I am manipulated and exercised and encouraged to make small movements of my own. It is a source of great anxiety that all this was once so easy. I have a memory of movement but now my brain sends signals that my body ignores. I am all jerks and twitches, an alien to

265

myself, but with each effort my body learns something new. Connections are being made. The process is exhausting. Now I know why newborn babies spend so much time sleeping; the dazzling business of life with its infinite array of stimuli and information is utterly overwhelming. The mastery of the muscles, synapses and circuitry required to produce even the smallest of coordinated movements is a task so monumental it takes us a decade of life before we can successfully cut a slice of bread without making a mess of it. I am beyond exhaustion after my tiny exertions. Worst of all is learning how to breathe. This I must do literally one breath at a time. When they tell me they are going to remove the ventilator I am filled with dread. Tia stands at the ready with what looks like a face mask connected to a little air balloon. She tells me to nod if I need oxygen. I nod and she laughs because she hasn't removed the ventilator yet.

'Very funny,' she says.

It's my first joke.

When the ventilator is removed I panic. I don't know what to do, I have no chest muscles, I have forgotten how to breathe, I think I am going to die and then suddenly my lungs go on a rasping raid for oxygen and for the first time in months a tiny gasp of air passes my lips. Tia puts in the ventilator before I even have time to nod. That one breath knocks me out for the whole afternoon.

My next foray into the complicated world of breathing will involve two breaths, then three, then four. I die a tiny death as I wait for my lungs to draw each breath. I am told it will get easier.

The first time I sit is similarly exhausting. Tia and Kate hoist me effortlessly into a chair. I weigh six stone so it's no problem for them, but for me it is horribly disorienting. I feel instantly dizzy and nauseous; I think I am going to collapse. A whole new set of muscles I had forgotten about are brought into play and I am left, paradoxically, craving the safety of the bed I long to escape from. I feel vulnerable and out of breath but I gain a new perspective on the ward. I see the wall behind my bed and some of the monitors and sinks that until now I had only heard. And I become more aware of my fellow cot dwellers whom I can see through the window of my private room. There are both men and women in the unit. Nearest to the window is an elderly Asian man, on the other side a middle aged woman. There is a vague familiarity about them. Neither is conscious. I guess I'm lucky.

One morning as Kate and Tia are washing me, Kate says,

'And what about Josh? You're single aren't you, Josh?'

I tap once.

'There you go Tia, you could go out with Josh, you're always saying how handsome he is.' Kate cheekily raises her eyebrows at her colleague.

Tia tuts. 'You are so naughty. Actually I think Josh is the perfect man, aren't you, Josh?'

I tap once.

'Why? Because he never answers back?' Kate asks.

'No, because he just lies around naked in bed waiting for me.'

The two nurses burst into laughter. I want to laugh with them.

'What do you think, Josh? Is Tia your type?' Kate asks.

'Stop it, Kate,' Tia protests lamely.

I wink at Tia, it's the only thing I can do to participate in the banter.

'Ooh, he's got the hots for you,' Kate giggles.

'Be careful, Josh! Remember who feeds you,' Tia admonishes.

I wonder how many patients fall in love with their nurses

or indeed how many nurses fall in love with their patients. Not that Tia is remotely in love with me, but I am certainly growing fond of her. She is a bright, smiley redhead with a wicked sense of humour. Her words can be acerbic but her fingers speak of tenderness. More than any of the other nurses, she is gently intuitive to my needs.

At last Sheryl finds a moment to visit me when my mother is not present. She comes to the bed and takes my hand. I have mixed feelings about this. She told me she didn't want to see me again, so I can only assume that she feels sorry for me which annoys me, because the last thing I need is her pity.

'Oh Joshy, I feel awful.'

I bet you do.

'This is all my fault,' she says.

How can I tell her it has absolutely nothing to do with her? I got stuck in the cave, it's no one's fault.

'Nothing's gone right for me either since we broke up. The whole thing with Margaret was ridiculous. I was like a schoolgirl with a crush. I thought she would solve all my problems but once I moved in the reality was quite different. I found myself facing all the same anxieties. I can't keep blaming other people for my problems. This whole business with you really upset me, you know. I'm on my own again and I've started therapy. You are so much better off without me, believe me. I've been so down, Josh, so confused, but I never thought of taking my life. I don't know how you could do it. I can only imagine the terrible state you must have been in when you threw yourself in front of that bus. Will you ever forgive me?'

My heart jumps. What did she just say? WHAT DID SHE JUST SAY? I raise my hand and shake it feverishly as if to say stop right there and explain what you just said. She thinks this means that I won't forgive her. My mind does a somersault, it starts running backwards at a terrifying speed. Now nothing is real any more. I threw myself in front of a bus? What is she talking about? I don't remember any of this. My brain feels like it's melting as I race to and fro questioning every memory I ever had, every conversation, every person I ever met. I'm in the same bed as Angela. The same hospital. My leg is in plaster. Everyone is saying I tried to kill myself. We were both in a coma. My mother doesn't remember telling me her special news. I am tumbling into a world of impossibility, a world of mirrors and artifice.

'Do you remember what happened on that day, Josh?'

I tap twice.

'The bailiffs had just repossessed the flat. I had no idea you were defaulting on payments. Why didn't you tell me what was going on? You were in Lorenzo's round the corner, I guess you must have been very depressed. People said you were acting strangely. You ordered a doughnut and ate it very quickly. They said you were talking to yourself. Everyone was staring at you but you didn't seem to care. Then, all of a sudden, you just got up, walked out of the café and threw yourself in front of a bus.'

What does she mean, I was 'talking to myself'? What about Angela? What happened to Angela? My heart rate monitor is accelerating to dangerous levels. Alarms begin to sound around me. I feel something alien churning in my stomach. I have a violent urge to go to the toilet. There is nothing I can do to prevent it. My colon bulges painfully, my anal sphincter bursts open and, accompanied by an almighty fart, I shit in my bed with such force that it spurts out the sides and splatters the sheets. Nurses come running. The curtain is yanked closed. Sheryl is on the other side. I can hear her crying.

'What did I say? I'm sorry, Josh. I didn't mean to upset you.'

I feel a needle in my arm, my muscles turn to sponge, thoughts dissolve in billowing mist, agitation is replaced by syrupy serenity. I sleep.

I wake up in a state of blind fear. My life is like an iceberg collapsing into the sea. Old certainties are crumbling away. Where did the reality stop and the fantasy begin? I can't distinguish between my dreams, my imagination and my memories; there is no edge, no point where I could say this is real and this is false, this happened and this did not. Until now I had always thought that memories were grounded in reality, that even though they can be vague and inaccurate, they always flow from something that actually took place. They are the product of the conscious mind just as dreams are the product of the unconscious or sleeping mind. But what happened in my coma was neither fragmented nor ephemeral. It did not dribble away on waking like the nectar of dreams but was as genuine as any real life event. My coma was a fully clothed parallel reality in which I operated consciously. It was the stuff of memory, not dream.

If I had died in the hospital, would this parallel reality have continued or would it have come to an abrupt end? I am convinced that it would have continued, with the only difference being that the window of return would have closed.

And another baffling thought: when I came round in the hospital and found myself so utterly incapacitated, my first impression was that I was having a nightmare, as if real life was a dream from which I would soon wake. Now, as I look around the ward, it is not difficult to imagine that everything I see is an illusion.

I am frightened of sleeping lest I should wake up and find everything changed again. Instead I scroll through every encounter and wonder what it meant, but most of all I wonder about the arrival of Angela and what really happened to my mind during those endless seven weeks of solitude after Sheryl left me.

For a few days I refuse all visitors. I do this by pointing to the relevant picture on the card and closing my eyes when they come to see me. A parade of old friends, work colleagues and relatives come to my bedside, none of whom I have the energy to engage with. I can't handle any more revelations. In vain I try to hibernate from the truth, but the truth will not be silenced. Over and over I revisit those final moments: the eviction, Angela, the cafe and the bus. With each visit comes a new realisation. Angela had spoken the words I wished I had spoken, she had resisted in the way I wished I had resisted. She had embraced death in the way I felt I ought to have done.

Suddenly I remember stepping off the kerb. I am seeing through the eyes of Angela. I see the bus thundering towards me. With that single step I had busted through all the mental and physical boundaries that held me in place. I had done something so extreme that I was beside myself – literally outside myself. There was the me in the road, the me watching it all happen, the me that was my entire life until that moment, the me that refused to accept that I was capable of doing such a thing, the me that was floating away into uncharted waters. I had fragmented into a hundred shards of consciousness.

My father had been prepared to risk everything for a rush of adrenaline. He would launch himself off a cliff in a hang glider, climb a sheer rock face without ropes, disappear down a hole in the ground. He would flirt with death, challenge it, dare it to steal him away as if the proximity of death is what

271

gives life its meaning, as if you have to be within a millimetre of dying to fully appreciate its beauty. Was this how life should be lived, courageous to the last, risking everything for every moment? Do we owe it to life to take risks?

He had run the line between life and death without ever intending to cross it, whereas I, in a moment of desperation, had thrown myself over it without ever intending to return. In his case, Fortune had not favoured the brave. It had robbed him of a life and paradoxically returned it to me. I have done nothing to deserve it. But now that Fortune has given me a second chance I'm determined to prove I am worthy of it.

My mother fears that I am deteriorating, but I am in the final stages of an extraordinary transformation. Like a butterfly breaking out of its cocoon or a slave escaping his shackles, I need every sinew of my strength. I have killed Josh so Josh can live. The opportunity before me is glittering. I am reborn. Angela was the part of me that slept, the passion, the courage, the conviction. I brought her back to life.

CHAPTER 26

I can now sit for longer without feeling nauseous. The physiotherapy is slowly building my muscles. I have free movement of my arms, I can raise my left leg, the right leg is healing fast. Each day something is removed. I take less drugs and less of the secondary drugs intended to prevent the side effects from the first lot of drugs. The drips, the drains, the syringes, the taps and tubes are systematically disappearing from my life one by one, although a few stubbornly remain. The first time something is removed I am jolted by the realisation that the shooting pains I had felt in my neck and wrists when I fell down the stairs after being locked in the cinema were in exactly the same places that I had been punctured in the hospital, as if these drips and drains had penetrated my coma, and that the unnaturally hot mornings on Hampstead Heath and stifling nights in the storage facility equated with periods of fever when I had pneumonia. I notice that the selfsame photos I had put around my bed in the storage unit are now sitting on a table next to me. Over the coming weeks an unfolding symmetry slowly reveals itself to me.

Dr Knowles is optimistic I will make a full recovery; she hopes

I will be able to lead a normal life. But I don't want a normal life any more. Already the very fact of being alive feels extraordinary.

As my breathing improves, a new metal valve is put in my ventilator which allows me to breathe in through the tracheotomy in my neck but out through my mouth. And with the airflow over my voicebox comes the possibility of speech. My voice is husky, almost unrecognisable. I can hardly form my words without dribbling and I have to see a speech therapist to help me articulate again.

Tia takes me on a little tour of the ward in the wheelchair. Every day she seeks to expand my experiences and keep me stimulated. We pass between the beds of the Asian man and the middle aged woman who I had noticed the first time they sat me in a chair.

'Wha's his name?' I slur.

'This is Arjuna,' Tia says, 'he came a month after you. You were in the bed next to him until we moved you in there.' She pointed to the private room I had woken up in. 'And this is ... '

'Laura,' I blurt out.

Tia looks at me with amazement. 'Yes.'

'Pho ... to ... graph ... er?'

'Yes, I believe she is. Do you know her?'

I shake my head.

Tia smiles. 'You're a strange one, Josh.'

I begin a course of psychiatry; this is not my choice, but a policy of the hospital in the case of failed suicide victims. I am assigned the avuncular Jungian psychiatrist Dr William Gould, who is nearing retirement. Slowly and painfully, I am able to tell him everything. He is fascinated by my experience. He has a special interest in coma patients. He says no other state has the potential to reveal so much about the inner workings of the subconscious mind. I am part of a small minority of patients who wake up with a story to tell, as if they have been on a journey. It is Dr Gould's belief that all the characters I have met are either extensions of my personality or represent universal archetypes. And so begins a process of individuation and analysis in which I grow to see all the characters from my story in a very different light.

We discuss my childhood and he asks me if I can remember ever feeling passionate about anything. A little embarrassed, I tell him the only thing I can think of is my immature obsession with comic books and how I had been a prolific doodler into my late teens. He wants to know why I stopped.

'Because when I told my career advisor in sixth form that I wanted to work for Marvel Comics, she laughed and said, "Try and be more realistic."'

He suggests I rekindle my passion and make sketches of the coma.

'Be creative,' he says.

I am reluctant at first but slowly I warm to the task and with every drawing my pleasure grows. When I have finished, I amuse myself with a portrait of Dr Gould, which I intend to give him as a present when our sessions are over. It is a welcome diversion from the monotony of the hospital and the drawings trigger many interesting conversations with Dr Gould that open our minds to new interpretations.

He takes particular interest in the sketch of Angela's parents.

'What are the first words that come to mind when you think about them?'

'Repressed ... establishment ... old-fashioned values ... class-bound ... stuck ... loveless.'

Dr Gould pulls out a half-litre metal flask from his outside right jacket pocket and takes a long, slow mouthful. I see him do this many times during the course of our sessions but never find out what it contains.

'Angela was rebelling against her parents, against all those things you mention. Maybe she was fighting the battles you were frightened of.'

'Are you saying that the Mortons were a kind of grotesque embodiment of a society that has kept me back?'

'It's a suggestion. Does it ring true?'

'I'm not sure. Why would she be fighting my battles?'

'Because you described Angela as the part of you that slept ... as everything you were not. And didn't she say herself that the princess and the toad were the same person? That we all have a repressed part of our character that needs to be embraced before we can become one?'

'Yes, she did.'

He took a satisfied swig from his flask. 'Tell me, are you a conformist, Josh?'

'Yes, I suppose I am. I always tried to do what was expected of me.'

'And do you enjoy living like that?'

'I don't think I know how to live differently. But I've always admired people who break the rules and stand up for what they believe.'

'And what do *you* believe?'

I hesitate.

'I've never given myself the space to explore that properly.'

'Until now. Now you have time.'

I nod. Now I have time.

He looks down at his notes. 'Let's talk about your dream about Frank Godley. It was pretty extreme.'

'Yes, I really wanted to kill him but I couldn't.'

'You were very angry in your dream. Do you ever show that anger in real life?'

'No. And I don't want to.'

'But it's there. There is a fire inside you, Josh, that is trying to come out.'

Later, I sleep with this thought.

We start the next session discussing my various incarcerations in cinemas, basements, storage containers and caves. Was it a coincidence that I repeatedly found myself in dark holes or was this the darkness of the coma itself? Similarly, was the unnatural heat of the Heath correspondent to my fever in the real world? And as I sat by Angela's bed telling her stories, had I not heard the real voice of my mother at my bedside wishing me back home? And what of the symbolism of sleeping amongst the gravestones and Laura's two-headed photograph; or of Rabbi Feldenberg's story of the Great Plane tree closing its heart; or of removing my name from Arjuna's box of deceased patients; or of the death of Mikey – a character that Dr Gould believes was the 'personification of my self-hatred'. Were these not all clues about the state I was in?

'I'm sure new meanings will emerge over time,' he says, 'but we can't hope to solve every mystery from a fantasy world. The big challenge is how to live in the real world.'

Each day we pick at the carcass of my journey and chew over the details. Dr Gould highlights my choice to turn left instead of right when I arrived in the basement of the hospital. I had instinctively felt that opposing my normal choices might lead to a more exciting life, so could the breaking of old habits be the key to my future well-being? Gerry referred to intrepid cavers discovering 'a new system'. He also said the door to the cave could only be opened from the inside and not the outside. Perhaps the work I am doing with Dr Gould is opening doors to my heart from the inside.

Shortly after our fifth session, I am back in the ward when I see a man in a white coat glide through the door. I know this gently burdened man with the kindly face. As he passes my bed, distracted by some other business, a familiar acrid smell wafts over me. A horde of goosebumps march down my back. I watch him disappear behind a curtain at the end of the ward. Why has the spectre of the administrator followed me into the real world? I have to know who he is. I call Tia. She tells me that he is the consultant who stood over me and advised my mother to turn off the life support. Later he comes to visit me, looks at my notes and congratulates me for my 'miraculous survival against the odds'. I harbour an irrational residue of mistrust towards him. I should not judge him for a common turn of phrase but I am concerned that decisions to turn off life support machines are not made on certainties but statistics. I am offended by the word 'odds'. Who is to say that those odds are not skewed by the unknown potential outcomes of all those who were switched off too soon? The brain is so infinitely complex and neuroscience still so young that I am sure many others might have returned from their half lives given the chance. But the weary, sympathetic consultant no longer wields power over my fate. He is only a shadow of the man who pursued me through my coma, watching and waiting for me to give up.

This episode prompts a long discussion with Dr Gould about the administrator and the box. Like the angel of death, my life was in the administrator's hands. Some of the things he said about not letting the situation drag on for much longer were things that the consultant must have told my mother at my bedside.

'Why do you think he was in the photograph of my dad the night before he died?' I ask.

'Because Death had come for your father just as he was coming for you. What do you think would have happened if you'd given him the box?'

'I think … I think I wouldn't be here now.'

'Why did you give it to your father in the cave?'

'Because it felt right. I wasn't frightened of it any more and maybe … maybe because I knew only he could open it.'

'What came out?'

'Some kind of creature with enormous wings. It's strange because it came out of such a small box and it got inside me.'

'How did you feel once it had entered you?'

'Like a part of me had returned. Like I was inside myself and not outside myself … not detached. Do you know what I mean?'

Dr Gould nods. 'Tell me, Josh. What was written on the box?'

'Yoursoul.com.'

'And what happened when you visited the website?'

'It said, "Sorry, this site is currently under reconstruction."'

We both begin to laugh.

'I'm so glad I didn't give it away.'

'Do you believe in God, Josh?'

'I can't begin to answer that question.'

Dr Gould flicks through his notes until he finds a particular page. 'Ah, this is it. Arjuna said you were the God you didn't believe in. You said you didn't understand what he meant, but does that mean anything to you now?'

'No, does it to you?' I ask.

'Were you God in your coma?'

'No, I wasn't in control.'

'No, but everything that happened was a product of your subconscious. You created it, didn't you?'

'Yes, maybe that's what Arjuna meant. I was a god oblivious to my power.'

I wrestle with this idea and am overwhelmed by a mind-boggling thought:

'I created a new reality, a parallel universe with equal validity to this one. Everything in the coma was a manifestation of my mind. Does that mean that the reality we currently find ourselves in – you, me, the hospital – could just as easily be a virtual reality created by some greater being's consciousness?'

'Are you talking about God?'

'I think what I am saying is that I can no longer rule it out, but even if there is such a greater consciousness, it doesn't mean it is worthy of worship or necessarily a source of goodness. He or she could be struggling to make sense of everything, just as I am, which might explain why this world is so random, chaotic and unfair.'

Dr Gould nods sagely. 'Yes, and also full of miracles and love. I think we should stop there for this week. We both have a lot to reflect on.'

My sweet and lovely mum visits every day but it is at least a month before she breaks the news she has wanted to tell me all this time.

'I've met someone – I hope you won't be upset.'

I am genuinely delighted for her.

'That's good news, Mum. Who is he?' I slur.

'He's called Lenny, he has a hardware store on Edgware Road.'

'How did you meet?'

'Do you remember Janet from number 6?'

I nod.

'Well, it's her cousin. He's got a couple of grown-up kids. He divorced a few years ago. Janet thought we should meet and invited us both round for a drink. We got on so well and, you know how it is, one thing led to another and here we are. I swear if it hadn't been for Lenny's support I would never have got through this. He's the kindest person you could ever meet.'

'That's great, Mum. I want to meet him.'

'Oh do you? Well, that's … that's wonderful Josh, I'll bring him next time.'

My mum beams with delight and all the tension and anxiety of the last few months begin to ebb away.

'You know, Josh, in the first few months after Vince died, you kept coming up with crazy ideas of how you might see your dad again.'

I smile. It was rare to hear my mum talk about those days.

'One night … you must have been about seven … you hadn't been sleeping well and you called me to your room. Something was bothering you. I lay next to you in the bed and you asked me if I was going to die and I said, "Not for a long time, sweetie," and you asked me to promise that I wouldn't die before you. And, even though I shouldn't have, I promised I wouldn't die before you so that you would sleep. And then you asked, "What happens when you die?" and I said, "No one really knows". You were silent for a long time. You were thinking really hard. Eventually you said, "Dad knows," and I said, "Yes, Dad knows." I gave you a kiss and went back to bed, but five minutes later you called me back in and asked me if anyone had ever died and come back and I said, "No, darling, no one has ever died and come back." And then, quick as a flash, you said, "Jesus did." And I laughed and said, "Yes, Jesus did, but he was special." And then you looked me in the eye and said, "Am I special, mummy?"

'Josh, you were so sweet. I kissed you on the cheeks and I said, "Yes you are. You are the most special person in the world. Now go to sleep." And you did. You went to sleep. But I didn't, I stayed awake and I cried all night because I loved

Vince so much and I loved you so much that it actually hurt. Do you understand that, Josh? It actually hurts. And you really are special. You've proved it now. You came back to me. Lenny will never replace your dad, Josh. But he's a good man and it's a chance for me to be happy.'

I nod. It's all I can do as I thank all the gods, in whom I thought I had no faith, for delivering me back into the arms of my mother.

Three months later I am at home. I am thinking about Miranda Wilks, the woman I met on the train all those years ago and how I let the opportunity to ask her out slip between my fingers. I look at the photos of my dad on the mantelpiece and I am filled with courage. Risk everything for every moment. Turn left not right. I google Miranda's name and find nine in UK phone directories. One by one I call them. I ask the first if she remembers meeting a man on a train a decade ago, the 17.28 from Harlow Mill to Liverpool St to be specific. She hangs up. I change my tack for the next call and ask if I have the right number for Miranda Wilks, the research chemist. I draw three straight noes and one piss off from an unnecessarily rude man. Number six is a lingerie shop and number seven is an answer machine. I leave a long garbled message with my name and phone number. Number eight is Scottish and number nine rings out. No sooner have I put the phone down, it starts ringing. I stare at it and for some reason I know that it's number seven calling back. I take a deep breath and pick it up. Let there be no more regrets.

END

AUTHOR'S NOTE

A word of warning. If you are like me and read the acknowledgements and peripheral parts of a book before you have finished it, then I would urge you not to read the following until you have come to the end of the book as it will ruin your enjoyment of it. Otherwise please read on.

In researching this book I interviewed, read or heard about many people who had been on extraordinary adventures in their comas, although I am told that most people remember nothing.

A nurse told me the story of an elderly man who spent his coma re-fighting his enemies in the Second World War and woke up believing he had been captured and the nurses were his captors. I was told about a musician who had been recording an album at the time of his coma and wrote a new song in his coma. When he came round and the other band members played him the completed album, he couldn't understand why his new song wasn't on it.

There was the intriguing case of the patient who claimed to

have met the woman who had died in the bed next to her. She knew her name and many things about her, even though she had been in a coma the entire time the neighbour was there. This same patient awoke speaking fluent Persian, a language she had heard her mother speak in her youth, but which she had never spoken.

One man I was told about spent his entire coma believing he was in the TV show *The Sopranos*. Apparently it was the last thing he watched before falling ill.

Another came every day to the hospital to visit a friend, when in reality it was the friend who was visiting him.

But of all the stories I came across, it was the remarkable tale of Neil that really inspired me. Neil was in a coma for seven weeks more than 20 years ago. He told me that the memories of his coma journey were still fresh in his mind, in fact they were indistinguishable in quality from his childhood memories. He had been on, what felt like, a very real adventure. In his coma Neil spent several months in Africa (a continent he had never visited in real life) doing charity work. He was planting trees in poor communities and still remembers in great detail the work he did and the methods used to plant the trees. He lived with two women in a house built on stilts over a lake. One of the women was black and one was white. The white one always wore a black bikini and the black one always wore a white bikini. He frequently had sex with these women and went scuba diving with them in the lake where they caught fish with vagina shaped tails, which they would eat on a regular basis. He remembers conversations and games, he remembers meeting Mick Jagger and travelling in Monument Valley with friends. At no point did he realise he was in a coma. As far as he was concerned it was all real. Then one day in the midst of this fabulous journey he woke up in a hospital, bedbound, unable to speak and in terrible pain. His body had wasted away. It was a terrible shock. Was he having a nightmare? Little by little he understood that he had been in a coma, but he still thought his journey was real. It was only after a couple of weeks, when his father came to visit, that he realised something was wrong. In his coma, his father had seriously injured his hand but when he looked at his father's hand in the hospital, there was no injury and he remembers wondering how it had healed so quickly. It was then that the fear set in. Where exactly was the boundary between what was real and what was imagined? Which was the dream and which was the reality? At times he longed to go back to the coma, back to Africa. Later as he healed, the fear subsided and he began to feel lucky to be alive. Now he credits his coma for having changed his life for the better. By his own admission his pre-coma life was shallow and narcissistic, but his coma taught him that deep down he hankered after a life of service and meaning. Now he works as a psychotherapist in London, helping his clients find their way back to healthy lives.

ACKNOWLEDGEMENTS

I have been overwhelmed by the incredible support I have received from the hundreds of subscribers who pledged to get this book funded so quickly. You took a chance – I don't know why. You didn't know if you would like the book, you had read no reviews, but you pledged anyway. You made something happen. You brought a book to life and got it published. I have felt your presence throughout the editing process and I have tried, with all my heart, to create something beautiful for you. I hope I do not disappoint you. 'Thank you' is too feeble an acknowledgement for what you have done.

I'm not very good at sitting alone in the library. Days go by without speaking to anyone, so when I have an excuse to go on an adventure and meet people I get very excited. On one such escape I visited the South Wales Caving Club. I am indebted to Fred Levett for inviting me to stay, and to Clark Friend and Tony Baker for actually taking me in to Ogof Ffynnon Ddu, one of Britain's biggest cave networks, allowing me to experience first hand the joys and terrors of potholing.

You can see a video about that experience on the Unbound website. Click on the 'shed' icon on my author page and you will find it amongst the many posts there.

My medical research took me to meet neurosurgeon Dr Colin Shieff and neuropsychologist Dr Neil Parrett who generously gave up their valuable time to answer my questions on coma states and hospital procedures. Nurses Pippa Hart and Trudie McGurran kindly showed me around a critical care unit at the Epsom and St Helier University hospital NHS trust. Julie Bridgwater, from the brain injury association Headway, invited me to meet people who had suffered brain injury. Many of their stories informed the book. Thank you.

I am particularly grateful to Neil Hudson for giving me a mind-blowing insight into what it actually feels like to be in a coma and wake up from one.

For those interested in alternative viewpoints, read *Coma* by Arnold Mindell.

Many of Rabbi Feldenberg stories are not my own; they are reworkings of traditional stories and I want to thank Robbie Gringras and Gregory Thompson for sharing their knowledge over the years.

I always test my early drafts on a few poor friends. Their contribution has been vital in shaping the book. I listen very carefully to everything they say and make many changes based on their feedback. They are the wonderful Jessica Gavron, my best man Olivier Lacheze-Beer, the wandering troubadour and puppet tamer Josh Elwell, my theatre and film buddy David Annen, the author of the wonderful novel *Ayah* Thushani Weerasekera, the champion of good punctuation and TV documentaries Caroline Roberts-Cherry, and Norwich City's biggest fan Julian Wells.

But there is one reader who is extra-special and that is my wife, Sarah, who sits at my side as I write this and instructs me to write that she is amazing, brilliant and the most fantastic person in the world. Aside from these self-proclaimed attributes, which, in truth, hardly scratch the surface of her extraordinary qualities (she didn't tell me to write that bit!), she also spent a huge amount of time working on the book, challenging, editing and guiding me.

Big kisses to Poppy, Sol and Saffi for three gorgeous reasons to come home every night and not work too hard, and to Mum and Dad for giving me the perfect blend of confidence, tenacity and stupidity required to write books.

Thank you to Liz Garner, my editor, for her incredibly thorough and well-structured notes which made the editing process so productive and rewarding; to Sophie Hicks, my agent, whose judgment, determination and friendship mean so much to me; to my brother David, who took the stunning cover photograph; to Jon Gray for his eye-catching cover design; and to Hannah Cutts in Australia whose terrific illustrations have added an extra layer of depth and beauty to Joshua Jones's character. If you like her stuff, let her know at www.cuttscreative.com.au

And finally thank you to John Mitchinson and everyone at Unbound. Your passion for what you do is rare and contagious. I'm glad the future of publishing is in your hands.

Give me feedback through my website
www.dannyscheinmann.com

SUPPORTERS

Unbound is a new kind of publishing house. Our books are funded directly by readers. This was a very popular idea during the late eighteenth and early nineteenth centuries. Now we have revived it for the internet age. It allows authors to write the books they really want to write and readers to support the writing they would most like to see published.

The names listed below are of readers who have pledged their support and made this book happen. If you'd like to join them, visit: www.unbound.co.uk.

Neyire Ashworth

Ian Atkinson

Harvey B-Brown

Ruth Bacigalupo

Emily Badger

Charlie Baker

Lynn Baker

Miranda Ballesteros

Jason Ballinger

Kate Bauss

Richard Beecham

Carolyn Belman

Jay Benedict

Mark Benson

Stuart Bentham

Susan Berger

Mark Bergrer

Fiona Bibby

Lisa Blankstone

William Boardman

Noa Bodner

Nickie Bonn

Alrik Boonstra

Estie Boshoff

Erika Botkai

Sophie Boyd

Tom Boydell

Sam Bramwell

Rachelle Gryn Brettler

Christopher Bristol

Lucy Brown

Tom & Kate Bulman

Pam Burke

Kath Burlinson

Alyssa Nicole Burns

Emma Burridge

Corinne Byron

Lianne Campbell

Jean Capstick

Mick Carter

Sarah Carver

Sylvia Chant

Don Chapman

Edward Chapman

Kate Chell

Natalie Chouraqui

Lana Citron

Russ Clapham

Ed Clarke

Gail Clarke

Jo Clayton

Ginny Clee

Caroline Margaret Clegg

Melissa Dopman Clingan

Lucy Coats

Maureen Coleman

Alexis Paul Collis

Philip Connor

Peter & Gill Cook

Sharon Cooke

John Cooper

Ruth Corney

Emily Cosgrove

Isabel Costello

Sally Cotterell

Chris Cox

Nicolette Craig

Maria Crawford

Becky Crichton-Miller

Andrew Croker

Tom Cummings

Becky Cutler-Methven

Kathrin Dahm

Marcella Dawson

Donna Day

Ann De Jaeger

Rob-Jan de Jong

Sara Deane

Michelle Delaney

Sally Dellow

Jennifer Derbyshire

Alice Desbouvrie

Lyndsey Devine

Cristiane Lima Dias

Spyros Dimou

Richard Donovan

Jenny Doughty

John Douglas

Michelle Dovey

James Duke

Vanessa Earl

Sarah Eaton

Mitza Edge

Julie Ellen

David Ellis

Dawn Ellis

Jo Eltringham

Josh Elwell

James Engel

Sebnem Eryigit

Genieve & Elie Ezer

Claire Fabre

Marc Falconer

David Farbey

Jill Farries

Jane Farrow

Peter Faulkner

Susan, Bob, Talia
      Feldberg-Berger

Isabelle Fernandez

Alice Fernbank

Amy Finegan

Tony Fisher

Varda Flacks

Ann and Bryan Foggin

Cathy Fox

Ian J France

Hannah Francis

Stephan Frettlöhr

Jane Frisby

Pete Furniss

Zahida Galia

Michele Gardner

Gabriel and Elissa Garfield

David G Garioch

Jess Gavron

Kate Gavron

Rosalind Gill

Jonathan Gold
Tae Gordon-Jackson
Lizie Gower
Paul Gowers
Voula Grand
Jean Grantham
Robert Grays
Tim Greenhalgh
Rachel Greenwood
James Gregory
Jane Gregory
Rebecca Gregory
Hilary Grey
Michelle Grogan
Cathie Gross
Amanda Grossman
Ludic Group LLP
Amy Fisher Haddad
Bibi Hahn
Susana Halperin
Sherief Hammady
Lubna Haq
Gareth Harding, Clear Europe
Jane Hardisty
Gay Harper
Mairead Hart
Pippa Hart
Caitlin Harvey
Jennifer Harvey
Gillian Harwood
Andy Hayes
Andrew Hearse

Lani Henrico
Rachel Hermer
Melanie Heslop
Sophie Hicks
Amy Leanne Hill
Fiona Hinton
Jo Hislop
Caroline Hoffbrand
HoofSmith
Danny Hopkins
Johanna Hosking
TC Howard
Ben Hubbard
Neil Hudson
Sarah Hudson
Ann Hughes
Claire Hugman
Colleen Hunt
Toska Husted
Valerie Hynd
Dan Isaacs
Jeff Isaacs
Lilian and Robert Isaacs
Mandy Isaacs
Laura Ivanetic
Gerald Jacobs
Richard Jacobs
Saul Jaffe
Sybil Jaffe
Babar Javed
Cedric Jeffay
Dan Johnson

Mairi Johnson
Marion Kenyon Jones
Paul Kafno
Sam Kenyon
Miss Holly Kernot
Lynne Kersh
Verena Khan
Dan Kieran
Hilary King
Natalie King
Rebecca King
Simon King
Jo Kirrane
Ed Krancher
Claudia Kretzschmar
Paul Kuenstler
Olivier Lacheze-Beer
Bryan Lask
Rachel Lasserson
Ilona Lazar
Jimmy Leach
Mark Leadbetter
Linda Lefevre
Russel Levi
Naomi Levine
Clare Lewis
Crispin Leyser
Mrs Samantha Lighten
Diana Lilley
Alexandre Linden
Nigel Lindsay
Grace Livingstone

Jonathan Lloyd
Anna Longmuir
Vivien Longstaff
Tor Lorkin-Lange
Kate Lynn-Evans
Neil Macehiter
Eric MacLennan
Zhanna Macmillen
Mateaki Mafi
Yvette Mahon
Yulia Mahr
Tina Maloney
Chibane Manuèla
Annie Marcuson
Scott Marlowe
Laura Marriner
Angela Marshall
Lucy Matthew
Nadia Mazzucco
Sue McCullough
Martine McDonagh
Shaun McKenna
Gillian McMullan
Innes Meek
Liam Meekins
Harry Meintassis
Pauline Melhuish
Paul Miller
Minnie & Herbie
Nina Miranda
Diane Mitchell
Emma Mitchelson

John Mitchinson
Chris Mogridge
Rebecca Mondadori
Grace Moody-Stuart
Megan Morby
Martin Morgan
Lin Morris
Jacky Mummery
Penny Nagle
Araz Najarian
Stu Nathan
Fiona Neill
Jacqueline Saysell Nogueira
Brendan O'Brien
Maeve O'Sullivan
Georgia Odd
Lukasz Ostrowski
Andy Pandini
Carole Partridge
Matched Patched
Susan Paterson
Helle Patterson
David Pearl
Alison McGrath Peirce
Monica Pellegrini
Bella Pender
Filipa Pereira-Stubbs
Jonny Persey
Lou Petho
Oonagh Phelan
Joan S. Pine
Jack Pinter

Christopher Pizzey
Erik Poitrenaud
Sandra Pokrant
Justin Pollard
Dan Powell
Rhian Heulwen Price
Marie-Agnès Pierre Puysegur
Mia Quayle
Jess Quinton
Lena Rae
Martin Raiser
Modasar Rasul
Julia Rayner
Pamela Reilly
Robert Reti
Phyllis Richardson
Max Richter
Lisa, Elodie
          and Annika Rivers
Louise Rixon
Philippa Roberts
Caroline Roberts-Cherry
Jenni Roditi
Elizabeth Rogers
Helena Rohner
Maria Rooney
Jeryl Rothschild
David Rowe
Bee Rowlatt
Andrew Roxburgh
Deborah Russell
Theresa Sainsbury

Mussarat Saleem

Tracy Savill

Mark Scantlebury

Donna Scattini

David Scheinmann

Ella, Ruby

    & Willow Scheinmann

Feodor Scheinmann

Katalin Scheinmann

Phoebe Scholfield

Thecla Schreuders

Andie Scott

Bruno Selun

Augustina Seymour

Rachel Rose Shalev

Jo Shan

Shelley Shieff

Sara Shorten

Richard Shotton

Rebecca Sickinger

Adam Signy

Ruth Silman

Kim Slater

Tania Sless

Monique Sliekers

Ann Smith

Jennie Smith

Sophie Smith

Mari Solymar

Julie Soos

Samantha Spiro

Michele Stasi

Sarah Steed

Sue Steele

Caroline Steiner

Steve & Honey

Jason Stevens

Jane Stewart

Julia Stone

Shirley Stone

Rebecca Strickland

Mark Stubbings

Mauricio Suárez

Sue Sue

Diana Sutcliffe

Elisabeth and David Sutcliffe

Michael and Kay Sutcliffe

Stefania Swiatek

Jonathan Syer

Anna Szelest

Gabriel & Susan Tannenbaum

Rick & Alison Tannenbaum

Ron & Michal Tannenbaum

David S. Taylor

Jane Temple

Chris Tennant

Gregory Thompson

Lisa Thompson

Marylee Tinsley

Asher Tlalim

Gokhan Togrul

Cinzia Tommasi

Paul Tompsett

Alys Torrance

Alexia Traverse-Healy
Rosa Treibach
Jennie Treleaven
Ram Krishna Tripathi
Alison Turner
Jeroen van Duijvenbode
Marianne Velmans
Mark Vent
Tille Verhaeghe
Nicole Verity
Lynne Verrall
Georg Vielmetter
Kathleen Walker
Terri Wallington & Stuart Ball
Stan C Waterman
Gayle Waxenberg
Thushani Weerasekera
Emma Wells
Julian Wells
Ruth Wetters
Lily Whitcombe
Sarah Whittley
David Whitty
Eleni Whitty
Michelle Whitty
Gaynor Wilkinson
Dean Willars
Katharine Wood
Lucy Wood
Richard Wood
Simon Wood
Patricia Woodburn

Sheelagh Woodcock
Kirsty Woods
   "Happy 40th Birthday"
Martin Worley
Jo Worstencroft
Nina Young